REBECCA TOPE is the author of three bestselling crime series, set in the stunning Cotswolds, Lake District and West Country. She lives on a smallholding in rural Herefordshire, where she enjoys the silence and plants a lot of trees, but also manages to travel the world and enjoy civilisation from time to time. Most of her varied experiences and activities find their way into her books, sooner or later.

rebeccatope.com

The Troutbeck Testimony

REBECCA TOPE

Allison & Busby Limited
12 Fitzroy Mews
London W1T 6DW
allisonandbusby.com

First published in Great Britain by Allison & Busby in 2015.
First published in paperback by Allison & Busby in 2016.
This paperback edition published by Allison & Busby in 2017.

A CIP catalogue record for this book is available from
the British Library.

10 9 8 7 6 5 4 3 2

ISBN 978-0-7490-2270-9

Typeset in 10.5/15.5 pt Sabon by
Allison & Busby Ltd.

The paper used for this Allison & Busby publication
has been produced from trees that have been legally sourced
from well-managed and credibly certified forests.

Printed and bound by
CPI Group (UK) Ltd, Croydon, CR0 4YY

For Esther and her gang of devoted friends
Izzy, Bev, Karen, Hannah, Gemma, Red, Debbie, Evie and
all their babies

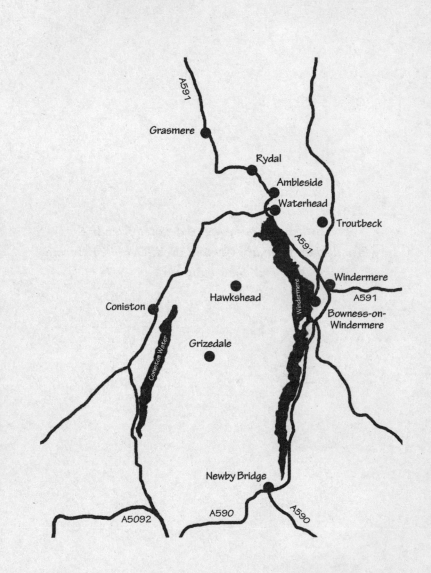

Author's Note

As with other titles in the series, the villages and public buildings in this story are all real. But Simmy's shop and the B&B are invented.

Chapter One

The first anniversary of Persimmon Brown's opening of her florist shop in the Lake District had almost coincided with Easter and an explosion of spring flowers and blossom. Wordsworth's daffodils performed to their greatest strength and pussy willow attracted hosts of honey bees who had failed to notice that they were meant to be in terminal decline. A month later, on the first long weekend in May, walking along a sheltered footpath to the west of Troutbeck, Simmy – officially Ms Persimmon Brown – could hear an energetic buzzing and murmured 'something something something in the bee-loud glade' to herself. Not Wordsworth, she was sure, but somebody like Yeats or Hardy. She would ask her young friend Ben, who knew everything.

The sun was warm on her shoulders; the light so clear that she could pick out numerous fast-growing lambs on the fells far above the village. Every weekend throughout the coming summer, she promised herself, she would get up at first light and go for an early walk. The anniversary had been a time for resolutions and one of them was to make much better use of the natural delights that surrounded her.

She felt an almost pagan euphoria at the burgeoning landscape, vibrant with flora and fauna at the start of another cycle of life. Her mother would say it was a mark in Christianity's favour that it had been clever enough to superimpose all its biggest rituals onto far more ancient moments in the natural year, with Easter an obvious example.

There was now a bonus Spring Bank Holiday that Simmy was savouring with complete abandonment. The late morning, with a sunny afternoon still ahead of her, brought feelings of richness and privilege that were almost shameful. But she had earned it, she reminded herself. The winter had been grey and protracted, interspersed with a number of unpleasant adventures. She had been repeatedly drawn into events that demonstrated the darker side of human behaviour, forced to confront far too much reality.

Now that spring had arrived with such a colourful crash, she was determined to shake all that off and concentrate on her flowers.

The plan for the day was to meet her father, Russell Straw, for a long-promised fellside walk after a modest lunch at the Mortal Man. The full walk, along Nanny Lane and up to the summit of Wansfell Pike – and back – was easily four miles in total, with some steep sections of stony path. 'By rights, we should go across to the Troutbeck Tongue at the same time, but that's rather ambitious,' Russell conceded.

'I shall want some fortification first,' Simmy had warned him. 'And if there's the slightest risk of rain, I'm cancelling the whole idea. Neither of us is fit enough to do anything rash.'

There was no suggestion of rain, the sky a uniform blue in every direction. It was, in fact, the most perfect day for very many months and Simmy was duly thankful for it. Her father would bring water, map, and dog. She would provide a camera, mobile phone and two slabs of Kendal mint cake.

The fells above Troutbeck were stark, dramatic and uncaring. There were barely any flowers or trees adorning them, other than the tiny resilient blooms that crouched underfoot. More than happy to accommodate her father's wishes, Simmy nonetheless preferred the softer and more moderated lower levels. This explained her morning stroll, taking a zigzag route from her house to the hostelry along lanes that had been colonised by humanity, with gardens and houses taking their place in the picture. The bees at least agreed with her. Azaleas and rhododendrons were in bud, reminding her of her startled surprise at the vibrant colours, the year before. Not just the natural purples and pinks, but brilliant orange, deepest crimson and a wide array of other hues shouted from gardens all over the relatively balmy area around Windermere and Ambleside. Even the wilder reaches of Coniston boasted spectacular displays. Aware that it might be foolish to expend energy on this pre-walk stroll, she nonetheless felt the need to exploit the sunshine and the flamboyant floral displays. It was semi-professional, too – she ought to be apprised of the full range of seasonal blossoms in gardens, in order to echo and embellish them in the offerings she stocked at the shop. Flowers were her business, and any lateral information she could acquire would always come in useful.

* * *

Her father was waiting for her at the pub, sitting at an outside table on a lower level, with his dog. She kissed the man and patted the animal. 'Is he going to cope with such a long walk?' she wondered. It was a rather ancient Lakeland terrier, officially named Bertie, but mostly just called 'the dog'. His forebears had failed a purity test, it seemed, and poor Bertie had found himself rejected as breeding stock and consigned to a rescue centre until eventually rescued by kindly Russell Straw.

'Oh yes. And if he doesn't we'll have to carry him.'

'When did you last take him on a jaunt like this?'

'About eighteen months ago. We've been waiting all this time for you.'

'Dad! That's ridiculous.' In spite of herself, she laughed. 'Poor old chap. He won't know what's hit him. His feet will be sore for weeks.'

'Not a bit of it. He spends all his time digging up stones. His feet are as tough as iron. He could easily outwalk both of us. Now let's get on with it. I want to set off by one at the latest.'

That gave them forty-five minutes to eat a hearty pub lunch with beer to wash it down. 'We shouldn't walk on full stomachs,' Simmy remarked. 'We'll get a stitch.'

'Better than trying to do it empty. We need the food to give us stamina.'

'At least we've got the weather for it. And listen to those birds!' A pair of collared doves cooed at them from an overhead wire, the gentle three-note song a backdrop that Simmy always loved, despite the blatant lack of musical variety. Her habit of feeding garden birds had attracted another pair of doves to her own little patch, a few hundred yards from the pub, and she had grown used to waking to their call, imagining that they were deliberately asking her for some breakfast.

Russell cocked his head. 'They're not native, you know. They're quite recent immigrants. I mean *recent*. I was about ten years old when the first ones settled here. The BBC put them in a medieval radio play by mistake not long ago. Lots of people wrote in about it.'

'Well, they're very welcome as far as I'm concerned.'

'I agree with you. I also like grey squirrels, even if I get lynched for saying so.'

She laughed again, after a wary glance around. In Troutbeck, the red squirrel was verging on the sacred and the grey accordingly considered devilish. Anyone overhearing Russell was liable to take exception to his views. But nobody at the neighbouring tables was reacting. Nothing could sully her delight at the carefree afternoon ahead with the best of all possible fathers. It took a lot to disturb Russell Straw – but then a lot had happened in recent times, and his daughter had certainly caused him some worry over the winter. His wife was the powerful half in the marriage, leaving him to contented pottering and sporadic researches into local history. They ran a somewhat eccentric bed-and-breakfast business in Windermere, in which Angie Straw broke a lot of rules and earned a lot of profound gratitude in the process. Her reviews on TripAdvisor veered from the horrified to the euphoric, depending on how much individuality her guests could stomach. She was a capricious mixture of old fashioned and hippy, refusing to use guests' first names unless they insisted, and cheerfully producing full breakfasts at ten-thirty, if that's what people wanted.

'Let me just pop to the lav and then we can be off,' Russell said. 'Mind the dog, will you?'

She took the lead attached to Bertie and nodded. The sun was as high as it was going to get, and the afternoon stretched ahead of them with no sense of urgency. The sky remained an unbroken blue. The views from the summit of Wansfell Pike would be spectacular. At least two lakes would be visible, and any number of fells on all sides. Russell knew the names of most of the main landmarks, and had a map with which to identify others. Simmy had only a rudimentary and theoretical knowledge of any of it.

Bertie whined and pulled annoyingly. 'He'll be back in a minute,' Simmy told him. 'Don't be silly.' Dogs were generally annoying, to her way of thinking. So dreadfully dependent and needy all the time. It had come as a surprise when her parents rescued this little specimen, and even more so when Russell developed such a fondness for it. To Simmy's eyes, the animal lacked character, which Russell insisted was a consequence of his harsh life, full of betrayal and confusion. 'He just wants everything nice and peaceful from here on,' he said.

Which was generally what he got, apart from a never-ending procession of B&B guests, who mostly patted his head and then left him alone.

'You were a long time,' she told him, when her father eventually returned.

'I know.' He was frowning distractedly. 'I overheard something, outside the gents, and I have no idea what to make of it. I kept out of sight for a minute, just in case they didn't like the idea of anyone hearing them.'

'Oh?'

'Two men talking. It sounds a bit wild, I know, but I think they were planning a burglary.'

Chapter Two

'What did they say, exactly?' Simmy's first reaction was impatience at the threat to interrupt their plans. 'Did you *see* them?'

'No, but one had a broad Cumbrian accent and the other sounded vaguely Scots.' He recited with concentrated deliberation: '"We should come back here this time tomorrow. The old man's always out on a Tuesday, so that's our chance." Then the other one said, "What about Tim?" And the first one said, "He can be the lookout. He'll be perfect for that." And then there was some more that I didn't hear properly. I wonder who the old man is?'

'Dad! They could have been talking about digging a ditch for him or cleaning his windows or delivering a surprise birthday present . . . or . . .' Her imagination ran dry at that point.

'What about the need for a lookout? That's nothing innocent, is it? And there was something about the tone. It was *furtive*. Why hide away behind a pub to discuss something harmless?' He rubbed his bushy hair. 'But I can't do anything, can I? You can't report people just for talking.'

'Actually, I expect you can, these days. But I wouldn't like to hear Mum on the subject, if you try it.'

Russell groaned. 'Arresting people before they commit the crime. Anticipating what they *might* do. In a way, it does make sense. Like preventive medicine. But in practice, of course, it's ludicrous.'

'Besides, you can't report them if you didn't see them. You don't know who they are.'

He was staring at a red car turning round in the parking area. 'That might be them, look. Two men in a car.'

Simmy looked. 'And there's a boy in the back. Looks about twelve. I suppose they had to make their evil plans at the back of the loos because they didn't want the kid to hear them?'

'Good thinking. I'm noting the registration.' He muttered the numbers to himself as he rummaged in his little rucksack for paper, but could only produce the Ordnance Survey map. 'Have you got a pencil?'

'I might have.' Simmy had thoughtlessly brought her shoulder bag with her, instead of a more suitable receptacle for carrying hiking necessities. 'Here's a biro,' she said after a short search.

'Thanks.' Russell took it and started writing on the edge of the map. 'Red Renault Laguna . . . now what was the number?'

Simmy blinked. 'I don't know. You're the one playing the detective.'

'Um . . . yes. VJ09 something, KB. I think it was CKB. There! That might come in handy, don't you think?'

'Description of the criminals,' she suggested, half joking. 'From what I could see, I'd say one man is about forty-five, very short dark hair, pale skin and fairly tall. The other – the one driving – is in his early thirties, thin and probably about five foot eight. You can't really tell when they're sitting down. He's got ordinary hair. Mousy.'

Russell kept writing, much to Simmy's surprise. 'How can you tell their ages?' he asked. 'I find that impossible, now I'm so old. Everybody looks twenty-five to me.'

'I don't know. I might be totally wrong. I couldn't see them very clearly. You shouldn't write that down as well. It's . . . I don't know . . . sneaky, I suppose.' The red car was disappearing in a northerly direction, where it would emerge onto Kirkstone Pass in less than a minute. 'Let's just get going, Dad, and forget all about it. Bertie's getting restless.' He wasn't, but it made a good argument.

'It's only a bit of fun, Sim,' he said. 'Like playing spies when I was a boy. A sort of *Just William* thing. I'll tear the page out when I get home, if you like.'

They gathered up their bags and walked out into the small road that ran through Troutbeck. A man with a beard and long untidy hair was standing by the entrance to the car park and nodded to them. Simmy had the impression that he had been watching the car as well. She even thought he might have given them a valedictory wave as they drove off. Bertie tried to go to him, wagging his short tail. Russell pulled him away and the man took no further notice of them.

'Hopeless judge of character, this dog,' he muttered, when they were out of earshot. 'He'd run away with the gypsies, given half a chance.'

The walk proved a ready distraction from boyish spy adventures, the uphill trajectory rendering conversation sporadic and limited to observations on the views and vegetation. Stone walls bordered the lane on each side, and trees had already become a rarity. On a welcome level stretch they paused and looked back.

'Wow!' breathed Simmy. 'We can't have come all this way already! You can see for *miles*.'

Russell pointed out various landmarks, with the aid of his map. Indicating a high ridge beyond the village, he drew her attention to a large quarry sitting in the middle of Sour Howes. 'Even up here, it's nowhere near being a natural landscape,' he said. 'Walls, roads, quarries, dykes – they've all changed it. There was probably a great forest covering all this, before mankind turned up and chopped down all the trees. And that caravan park's a bit of a blot, even if they have tried to keep it inconspicuous.'

'Like Dartmoor,' Simmy offered. It was a conversation they'd had more than once, with the usual inconclusive ending. Without the quarries there would be no buildings; without the stone walls all would be disorder. 'You can't really unwish the existence of human beings,' Russell often said. 'There's something impossibly illogical about that.'

The philosophy of this sort of remark could quickly make Simmy's head hurt, with its tendency to drift into Cartesian explorations as to the nature of reality and perception and whether the presence of *Homo sapiens* comprised an absolute necessity or an accidental aberration. 'It's a whole year since I moved here,' she said, mindful that the walk had been intended as a kind of celebration of this anniversary.

'Are you glad you did it?'

'Oh yes,' she began, automatically. 'Of course...Although it hasn't been quite as I expected,' she finished, more slowly. 'There've been a lot of surprises.'

Her father had urged her from the start to be cautious. 'It's going to be a big change,' he said when she proposed the move. 'New career, new people, new *everything*.'

'I'll have you, though, won't I?'

'That's what worries me,' he had replied. 'You're thirty-seven, Sim. That's too old to see yourself as a daughter. You need to be sure you can create a whole autonomous life for yourself that doesn't revolve around me and your mother.'

Now she was thirty-eight and Russell had not changed his mind on the subject of individualism and independence, despite several instances in which Simmy had needed direct and urgent help.

'Surprises?' he echoed.

'You know what I mean. I never dreamt that floristry would involve so much high emotion and extreme behaviour. It's been much more *eventful* than I thought.'

'Ah, yes. That *was* a surprise, I know. To me and your mother, as well. I'm not so much thinking about that side of things. I'm really wondering whether you feel we've got the balance right, between the three of us. I suppose it seems peculiar of me, but I worry about getting in your way. Sticking my oar in. Queering your pitch – if I'm allowed to say that.'

'Dad! There's nothing going on in my life that you could possibly disrupt. It *is* peculiar, you know, you talking like this. Other parents don't go in for so much agonising about being too interfering. And you're a million miles from anything like that – you always have been.'

'So then I worry I've gone too far the other way.'

'Stop it. I'm perfectly all right with things as they are. This past year has been exactly what I need to get over – you know – everything that happened. The business is working out nicely. I've got friends, interests . . .' she tailed off, painfully aware that when it came to friends and interests, her parents both felt things were somewhat thin. She had not made friends easily, and any incipient interests had been dashed by the succession of calamities that had befallen her since the autumn. Calamities which had come on top of the loss of her baby and collapse of her marriage. Regaining any sort of balance after these events had been slow and exhausting, and she was still unsure whether she had accomplished it.

'You were lucky to find Melanie,' he said. 'She's been a big help.'

'Yes, and she's leaving in a week or two. She's already doing way fewer hours, because she's job-hunting. I was a fool to think it was sensible to employ somebody on such a short-term basis. I was scared that a permanent person would end up wanting to become a partner in the business. I can't even remember now why that would have been such a bad thing.'

'She'll stay in touch. You've been very good for her, you know. She won't forget you.'

They were approaching the pinnacle of Wansfell Pike, the ground growing steeper again and the landscape more stark. The path divided, and they took the left-hand branch, which had no stone walls to mark it. Tufty grass and lichened rocks

21

were doing their best to create an appearance of green, but there remained a persistent greyish hue on all sides. The bright sky of the morning was hazing over as they climbed. 'At last we can truly call this spring,' said Russell. 'With summer only a few weeks away. You know – it doesn't matter how old you get, it still comes as a pleasant surprise every single time.'

The exposed fellside made Simmy think about guilty secrets and how hard it would be to hide anything out here. She had grown up in Worcestershire, where there were great trees and ancient verdant banks and concealed pathways in which all manner of illicit behaviours could be conducted out of sight. Up here, a human figure would be visible for miles, witnessed by walkers who came onto the fells during every season of the year. It made her feel oddly safe, and somehow cleansed. Admittedly, violent crimes had been perpetrated close by in recent times, but mostly amongst man-made settlements, not in the wide open pikes and fells.

'This is glorious,' she said, throwing her arms wide. 'How could you possibly think I could regret having come here?'

Then Bertie started yapping at something he'd found behind a large boulder and Simmy knew instantly that her sense of safety and cleanliness was about to be wrecked.

Chapter Three

'It's a dead dog, of all things,' said Russell. 'Poor creature! What can it have died of?'

'Exhaustion?' Simmy suggested.

'Its people wouldn't just leave it here, would they? They have *funerals* for dogs these days.'

'It doesn't look damaged.' She spoke optimistically, having avoided a prolonged inspection of the corpse. 'Does it?'

Her father was less squeamish and leant down for a closer look. 'It's stiff,' he pronounced. 'And I have an awful feeling it's been strangled. Or had its neck broken, more like. It's a terrier, some sort of Jack Russell. Male. Neutered.' He was getting into his stride, reminding Simmy of young Ben Harkness and his forensic tendencies.

'Leave it, Dad. There's nothing we can do, is there?'

'Seems a shame.' Of the three Straws, only Russell had any particular feeling for dogs. Simmy and her mother found them irritating, as a general rule. He straightened and sighed. 'But you're right, of course. We might watch out for any lost dog notices when we get back, though.'

'Right. We'll do that.' The outline of Wansfell Pike still lay ahead and above and Simmy was eager to achieve it. It was three o'clock and the afternoon would soon be waning. 'Come on, then.'

Bertie had been hovering a few yards away, evidently discomposed by the body of a fellow canine. His relief as the people began moving again was palpable. His little legs revealed unlimited energy as he trotted ahead, the dark-sand colour of his coat camouflaged against the bare rocks. 'Good boy,' Russell approved, for no apparent reason.

Simmy paused to examine a small beck trickling between rocks and creating a modest pool close to the path. 'Oh, look!' she exclaimed. 'Tadpoles!' There were numerous big-headed creatures with wriggling tails visible in the clear water. Russell turned back to see, and together they watched and reminisced about occasions where they'd made homes for just such as these, waiting for them to grow legs and miraculously turn into frogs. 'Pity we haven't got a jar to take them home in,' said Russell. 'They could live in my pond.'

It was windy on top of Wansfell. Simmy breathed the untainted air and turned in a slow circle. Windermere was spread out below them, to the south-west, its entire length plain to see. Rocky ridges were visible in a rippling pattern, rising and falling into the far distance. The one to the north had a stone wall running along its brow. Patches of surviving forest lined the edges of the lake. 'Wow!' she gasped. 'This is amazing!' She pulled her camera from the shoulder bag and spent ten minutes setting up her shots. Photography was something she had always taken seriously, but had given little time to in the past few years. Her husband had given her an expensive 'bridge' camera, during her pregnancy, saying she would have to capture every passing moment of their child's early life. Remembering those words had made using the camera impossible for at least a year after the baby was lost.

She set it to monochrome, on a whim, recalling early Lakeland pictures where the shapes and misty gradations had managed to reveal more than bright colours would have done.

Russell waited contentedly, the dog flopping down at his side. 'Did you bring the mint cake?' he asked.

'I most certainly did. A whole slab each.'

'We'll need it, if we're to take in Baystones. It's a bit windy, but I think you'll like it.'

'Um . . . ?'

'It's this ridge, look.' He pointed in a direction that Simmy guessed might be north. 'It's got that helpful stone wall to make sure we don't get lost.'

Simmy cocked an eyebrow at the dozen or more other walkers spread across the landscape. 'Not much risk of that,' she judged.

'All the same, the wall helps to keep us straight,' he persisted. Staying on the subject, he went on, 'Then we double back, meeting Nanny Lane again at the point where we branched off. All quite simple.'

'If we carried on from here, we'd come to Ambleside, right?' Simmy remembered an evening several months earlier, spent in a large house close to the spot where the path emerged onto an Ambleside street. She had been curious about how everything connected up ever since then.

'Right. But we don't wanna do that, do we? We'd end up without any transport.' He mimicked a TV quizmaster whose name Simmy had forgotten, and she laughed obligingly.

'Another time,' she agreed equably.

The sense of being on top of the world continued all along the ridge, following a path that was barely visible at times, and which at one point necessitated a slippery climb up and over a broken wall. Russell's pace was slowing, Simmy noticed. Eventually they came to a small cairn that Russell said marked the top of Baystones. 'Stones – geddit?' he smiled, still with the transatlantic accent. 'We're at the furthest point of the path here. We need to turn back towards the village and find this lane, look.' He prodded his map, which to Simmy's amateurish eye looked to be covered in confusing dotted lines that doubled back on themselves and traversed ominous scribbles that indicated rocky terrain.

'Lead the way,' she invited trustingly.

The way turned out to be less straightforward than anticipated, and despite being able to see Troutbeck below them, the actual detail of how to get there became unclear. When they found themselves in an oozing bog with thick, brown sludge covering their shoes, they both knew a moment of panic. 'Lucky it's not Dartmoor,' panted Russell. 'We'd be swallowed up, never to be seen again.'

A few determined strides saw them back on drier ground, and a more obvious path visible ahead. 'Must have lost the track for a minute,' said Russell apologetically. 'We'll be more careful from here on.' He looked pale,

Simmy noticed, and was moving more slowly. They had been out far longer than she had expected, and climbed more steeply. She couldn't remember a more demanding walk – and yet it was known to be one of the more gentle examples in the area.

Still, there was no choice but to carry on, and the ground sloped reassuringly downwards as they headed in the direction of the village, with the final section of Nanny Lane almost uncomfortably steep. Bertie gave himself up to the temptation to scamper down the hill, scenting the end of his marathon. 'The old chap's survived his long walk pretty well,' laughed Russell. 'Better than his aged master, anyway.'

'I still think he'll have sore feet tomorrow.'

'I doubt it. He's bred to this place, after all.'

'Unlike either of us. I have a feeling we've both overdone it.'

'Not at all. It's just what we needed,' he protested.

'What's in that bag, do you think?' She changed the subject abruptly as they rounded a bend in the track and found themselves following a man carrying a bulky black plastic sack. It was an incongruous sight, where walkers wore backpacks or canvas satchels.

'I have no idea,' said Russell quickly; but Simmy had already conceived a suspicion. Something about the obvious weight of the bag, the way it was held slightly away from the man's legs, and – most conclusively – the interest Bertie was showing in it, led to an inescapable conclusion.

'It's that dead dog, isn't it?' she muttered. 'He's been up and collected it.'

'Could be. What if it is?'

From the back, the man was unidentifiable. His clothes were unfamiliar, but Simmy was not generally very observant of people's garments. She thought she would recognise any permanent resident of Troutbeck, perhaps even from behind. But she was too tired to try to catch up and overtake the man, so as to see his face.

Then fate stepped in. The man was clearly irritated by Bertie's attentions, and moved sideways in an effort to avoid him. His foot landed on a patch of slippery mud, and slid from under him. In a second he was almost horizontal, one side of his body propped against the stone wall bordering the track, the black bag still held tightly. A wordless cry escaped him, and Bertie sidled away with a guilty expression.

'Uh-oh,' said Russell and went to assist. 'Bertie, that was all your fault.'

The man was up on his feet before Russell or Simmy could reach him. His right side was generously coated with dark-brown mud, which appeared to be the only damage. 'Are you okay?' asked Russell.

Simmy had a good look at his face, as it twisted in disgust and fury. It was the same man she had seen standing outside the pub, a few hours earlier. Weathered skin, beard and penetrating brown eyes. He had donned a greasy-looking hat for his fellside walk, and his clothes had apparently not been especially clean even before his fall into the unfortunate patch of mud. 'Bad luck,' she said to him. 'There must be a spring just here, making it so boggy. The rest of the track's almost dry.'

'Yeah, well,' he said. At least he wasn't going to make wild accusations against Bertie, she concluded.

'Have you got far to go?' asked Russell, sounding hopelessly patronising. 'Before you can get dry, I mean.'

Simmy hoped fervently that her father wouldn't invite the man to her cottage to get clean. It was definitely within the bounds of possibility that he would, giving no thought to the consequences. However protective he might wish to be of his daughter, his old-fashioned notions of trust and good fellowship could easily lead her into jeopardy. The man could make a mental note of her few valuable possessions and come back later to steal them. At the very least, he would learn more about her than she wanted him to.

But the danger passed. 'I'll be all right,' he said. 'Thanks.' And he loped off, still holding the sinister black bag.

Russell's car was waiting at the pub, and Simmy invited her father to tea and cake at her cottage. They would drive the few hundred yards, relieved at having no more need to walk. 'Call Mum and tell her we accomplished our mission,' she suggested.

'You think she'll be worrying? Which one of us is more likely to cause her anxiety, then?'

'Me, obviously.' But her father was over seventy and inclined to portliness. Despite all his brave talk, such walks were so infrequent as to present quite a significant physical challenge. Simmy herself had suffered broken bones shortly before Christmas, and still regarded herself as slightly fragile.

'We'll do it all again next weekend,' he said recklessly. 'I could get used to this.'

'No, we won't. I'm happy to explore with you now and then, but I'm not making four-mile hikes a weekly routine,' she protested.

'I thought you said you wanted to get outdoors more.'

'I do. But not a whole afternoon every weekend. I'd get jaded.'

'Jaded! With all this around us.' He waved an all-embracing arm at the pikes and fells and howes on every side. 'We'd never see a hundredth of it, if we went out every Sunday for the next ten years.'

'It's lovely, I know,' she conceded.

'But . . . ?' he prompted.

'But a little goes a long way.' She felt mean and obstructive. The walk had been a delight in every way, apart from the dead dog. Her father's company was undemanding in general and more than agreeable much of the time. It made no sense to live in Cumbria and fail to make full use of the opportunities it provided. Perhaps she was too influenced by Melanie who was twenty and regarded the open uplands surrounding her as nothing more than a draw for tourists and a pleasing backdrop to the more urban features of the region. Melanie never walked if she could avoid it, and valued human beings and all their works as the only really meaningful things in life.

Ben Harkness was more complicated. He had an adolescent passion for the vistas and planes of the natural world, eager to render the landscape into words and drawings. Ben was a lad of many skills, and felt constrained to exercise them all as far as was humanly possible. His mother had led family excursions onto the fells from his earliest days and he had no fear of the wilderness. Ben's problem was that there was never enough time for all the claims on his attention. A precocious student, he was deeply into sixth-form studies, competing as much with himself as with any fellow pupils. His ambition, conceived within days of first meeting Simmy and witnessing a murder, was to become a forensic anthropologist. A dedication to the TV series *Bones* had a great deal to answer for in this matter. Almost effortlessly, he had found himself a place on the most eminent university course for such studies, due to commence in a year's time when he would be almost nineteen. He had even landed a provisional agreement to accept him onto a postgraduate programme in America, several years down the line.

'At my age,' Russell began, rather ponderously, 'there is no sense in such a sentiment. There can never be too much of a good thing. Seize the day and all that. I could break my hip at any moment and be confined to the lowlands forever after.'

'You're not going to break your hip,' Simmy said, thinking she had come close to doing exactly that herself not so long ago. 'Take Mum instead of me sometimes. She'll be feeling left out if you're not careful.'

'Your mother – as you very well know – has little patience for this sort of thing. She regards walking as a bygone means of transport, to be used only in cases of dire necessity. And she's always too busy, anyway,' he complained.

'Cake,' said Simmy decisively. 'And stop trying to plan everything in advance. If we're seizing the day, then let's just be happy we had such a lovely afternoon.'

She let them into her cottage, eyeing Bertie's feet critically. Russell noticed and defended his pet. 'He's perfectly clean,' he said.

'Has that family with the twins gone now? And the other couples?' asked Simmy, when they were settled in her kitchen. She was referring to the bed-and-breakfast guests who had filled her parents' house in Windermere to bursting. Although busy throughout the year, the real season began at Easter, with a relentless stream of customers to be expected until October. Simmy made no attempt to follow the endlessly changing names and family compositions, but some stood out of the crowd and made themselves memorable.

'The twins left this morning, thank the Lord,' he nodded. 'The rest have another three days, and there's another lot due on Wednesday. I'm supposed to be helping with sheets when I get home. And tomorrow I'm destined for the cash and carry.'

'I'm not expecting many orders for flowers this week. I can do some work on the tax return. I like to get it done early.'

Russell shrugged. Tax was a topic he implacably refused to discuss. If pushed, he would laugh and claim that he and Angie just made up the numbers and hoped for the best. 'I don't think we're cheating anybody,' he would add.

'They'll put you in prison one of these days,' Simmy warned. 'And you won't like that.'

'It would be an interesting experience. Besides, I'd just put all the blame on your mother. She does the books.'

'I really did enjoy the walk, Dad.' She was feeling that perhaps he'd gained a different impression. 'It was all wonderful, apart from that poor dog. Do you think it belonged to that man? If so, how did he know where to find it? And why was it up on the fells in the first place?'

'I've been wondering the same thing. Could be somebody mentioned it to him, and he went off to find it. It did seem to be the sort of dog a man like him would have.'

'But you thought it had been deliberately killed. That might lead to a whole lot of trouble, if the man knows who did it. He looked as if he'd make a worrying enemy.' Again she winced at the thought of the bearded individual being invited into her house. 'I thought you might offer him my facilities to get himself cleaned up.'

'I nearly did,' Russell admitted. 'I didn't think there was anything objectionable about him.'

'I'm probably being prejudiced,' she said. 'But I thought he was actually rather unsavoury.'

'You could talk to your friendly local detective about him,' her father suggested. 'After all, it's illegal to go around murdering dogs. It might be a useful clue in something they're already working on.'

'I can think of at least five reasons for not doing that. First, I don't even know if he's back at work after what happened at Coniston. It's only about six weeks ago, after all. Second, he's much too senior to take an interest. And he's not *mine* in any sense at all. I don't think I like him much, as I keep telling you.'

'Like him or not, you're connected. And he likes *you*. You shouldn't upset him – he might come in useful one day.'

DI Moxon had not yet proved useful to Simmy in any way she could think of. He had drawn her into no fewer than three murder investigations since her arrival in Cumbria, and however irrational it might be, she blamed him for the resulting unpleasantness. Her involvement had arisen each time from an innocent flower delivery – deliveries that frequently turned out to be considerably less innocent than first assumed. All the detective inspector had done was follow up leads, request witness statements and do his best to provide protection. But still the associations persisted, and Simmy failed to discern within herself a responding affection to that which he plainly felt for her.

'He won't,' she told her father. 'However *could* he, anyway? All he does is upset me and get me into trouble.'

'Poor man,' sighed Russell. 'You're a cruel woman.'

'*You* could drop into the police station in Bowness on your way home, I suppose,' she continued, ignoring the jibe. 'You can describe the dog better than I can, anyway.'

'And while I'm at it, I could tell them about the suspicious men at the pub.'

She blinked. 'I'd completely forgotten about them. Don't, Dad. It probably wasn't anything at all sinister. Leave it. And don't forget to phone Mum.'

He smiled patiently at her and took the phone that Simmy produced from the pocket of her weatherproof jacket hanging on the back of a chair.

Chapter Four

Tuesday morning at Persimmon Petals in Windermere began as quietly as Simmy had expected it to. Melanie had important college assignments to finish and job applications to complete, which meant her attendance at the shop was more sporadic than usual. Simmy had little difficulty in coping unaided, with only one urgent order for flowers waiting on the computer when she opened the shop. A lady by the name of Cynthia Mossop living in Staveley was having a birthday the next day. It would be relatively simple to make up the bouquet last thing on Tuesday and deliver the flowers before work the next day. She had performed similar logistical miracles many times before. Other orders were for later in the week.

And then, to her surprise, Melanie came into the shop at ten o'clock. Behind her, like a shy little dog, came a fair-haired girl about half Melanie's size.

'Come on, she won't hurt you,' Mel urged impatiently. 'This is Bonnie,' she told Simmy without preamble. 'She wants my job after I leave.'

Simmy eyed the newcomer with her characteristic goodwill. 'Really?' she said. 'Pleased to meet you, Bonnie.'

'She's a friend of my sister's, actually. She was thinking of going into hairdressing, but she's allergic to the chemicals or something.'

'How old are you?' Simmy asked, thinking the girl couldn't possibly be over fifteen.

'Seventeen,' came a breathy reply. 'And a quarter.'

'Are you still at school?'

'Sort of. We finish this term. I'm not going in much at the moment. My aunt says I need to get a job for the summer.'

'Just for the summer? What's happening after that?'

Bonnie shrugged. 'Dunno, really. I might want to stay here – if you take me on, that is. I'm not good enough for college. Won't get many GCSEs. Just art and English if I'm lucky.' Her shoulders hunched again, in a forlorn demonstration of low self-esteem.

Simmy looked at Melanie and raised her eyebrows. 'What do you know about flowers?'

Melanie answered for her protégée. 'She knows more than I did when I started here. She's very artistic. She just needs . . . you know, a bit of encouragement. You'll get along fine together, trust me.'

Simmy's instincts were sending confusing messages. The girl was so small and colourless, so silent and somehow sad that any risk of hurting her feelings was terrifying. Such a little mouse would require constant care. But Melanie's people skills were not to be dismissed. Her burgeoning loyalty to Simmy was such that she had repeatedly expressed an intention to find a successor for when she left. And it was a relief to be handed someone on a plate, without a string of interviews and hard decisions.

'Bonnie's an unusual name,' she ventured. 'Is it short for something?'

The girl shook her head, with a very small sigh. 'No – it's from *Gone with the Wind*. You know – the little girl who dies. My mum and dad were mad about that film around the time I was born.'

'I see.' It struck Simmy as not a little macabre to choose the name of a dead child for their own baby. And lost babies were always going to be a very sensitive matter for Simmy, who had suffered a stillbirth herself and had no other offspring.

Melanie was closely monitoring every word and nuance. 'Give her a try, Sim. Why not? She can come in every day this week as a trial run, if you like.'

'You'll need to handle money and the computer, and write messages on the cards, and take orders,' Simmy rattled off briskly. 'Can you manage all that sort of thing?'

Bonnie met her gaze with a sudden directness. 'I can write, if that's what you mean. And count,' she added. 'I pick things up quickly.'

'She's not stupid,' Melanie summarised. 'It's just she's not too good at exams and pressure and that stuff.' She tilted her head and Simmy had the impression there was a lot more she needed to know, but that Melanie couldn't disclose it in Bonnie's presence.

'I had anorexia,' Bonnie supplied for herself. 'It got really bad last year. I missed a lot of school. That's why I'm older than the rest of Year Eleven. I'm all right now. It's not been decided about A-levels yet. I might go to a college to do them.'

The tiny figure suddenly made a lot more sense. She must weigh barely six stone, Simmy guessed. The translucent skin and wispy hair confirmed the story and compounded Simmy's urge to take this little thing to her bosom. 'Oh dear,' she said. 'That must have been grim.'

'She'll tell you all about it, I expect,' said Melanie, who seemed almost painfully robust in comparison to Bonnie. 'She's had loads of counselling and stuff, so she understands all about it now.'

'I'm not going to pry,' said Simmy, rather stiffly.

'So you'll take me, then?' Again, the girl met Simmy's eyes with none of the initial shyness. It was already becoming clear that there was more to Bonnie than might at first appear.

'If Melanie recommends you, I wouldn't dream of arguing.'

All three exhaled, as if an important and difficult problem had been finally resolved. Which it had, Simmy supposed.

'So, how was your Bank Holiday?' Melanie asked, with an alert look that suggested she had something of her own to impart on the subject.

'Restful, mostly,' said Simmy. 'I walked up to Wansfell Pike with my father. And then along a ridge to a pile of stones. We saw a dead dog,' she added, for no discernible reason. 'And my dad heard two men planning a crime.' She laughed at their expressions. 'Actually, I don't suppose it was anything suspicious, but he got quite excited about it.'

'Oh no! Had the dead dog been shot?' The question

came from Bonnie, whose blue eyes were wide with outrage. 'Those farmers are much too quick to use their guns, if they think their sheep are going to be chased.'

'No, no.' She could hardly add *strangled, actually*, for fear of further alarming the girl. 'There wasn't any blood on it. But it was quite a nasty surprise. As my dad said, people don't just abandon their dogs when they die. Some of them hold real funerals, apparently.'

'Course they don't,' scoffed Melanie. 'What a daft idea!'

'They do,' Bonnie assured her. Then she asked Simmy, 'What sort was it?'

'Some sort of terrier. Jack Russell, maybe.' Simmy was vague about dog breeds. 'White and brown, with shortish legs.'

'What did your dad hear, then?' asked Melanie. 'Were these men crouching behind a rock on Wansfell?'

'No, they were at the pub in Troutbeck, and then they drove away in a red car. There was a boy in the back, as well,' she added, on a sudden thought.

'What?'

'They said he could be the lookout. That's the bit that *does* sound rather suspicious.'

Bonnie was shifting restlessly from foot to foot. 'My aunt breeds dogs,' she said. 'Or she used to, until a little while ago. She absolutely adored them. But things have got difficult, lately. There's a gang of dognappers working in this area.' Her face tightened. 'Sounds as if you might have got them in Troutbeck now.'

'Lucky I haven't got a dog, then,' said Simmy lightly.

'I didn't know you weren't breeding any more,' Melanie

said to Bonnie. 'It was bringing in some useful cash, wasn't it?'

Simmy recalled hearing of a farmer near Coniston who was making thousands of pounds a year from Border terriers. 'I gather it can be lucrative,' she said.

'When it works,' Bonnie nodded. 'A lot can go wrong.'

'Like my father's Lakeland terrier. He ended up in a rescue because he wasn't right for breeding.'

'Too right,' Melanie said darkly. She was fighting a recurring battle with her mother over a rescue dog that had failed to come up to expectations. Mrs Todd wanted to send it back, and Melanie was trying to convince her that it was irresponsible to keep adopting dogs for a few months only to reject them in the end. It pained Melanie more every time it happened, but she was helpless to prevent it. 'As far as I can see, there are already way too many dogs in the world.'

'You can't generalise,' said Bonnie diffidently. 'Some are in huge demand and some end up in rescues. There's not much connection between the two.'

Simmy had nothing more to contribute to the conversation. She wished she'd had the sense to stay off the subject. 'What about you?' she asked Melanie. 'The Bank Holiday weekend, I mean.'

Her assistant gave a satisfied little smile before replying, 'I went out with Jasper, actually. On Saturday night. We had steak in a pub. It was great.'

'Hey – that's brilliant. He finally got his act together, then. After all these weeks.'

'Yeah. Well . . .' Melanie shrugged. 'We've both been busy. Lambing and all that. He's a vet, remember.'

'And . . .' Simmy prompted.

'That's it, really. He wants to do it again, so it must have been okay for him as well.'

Melanie's love life had provided Simmy with considerable interest in the time she'd known her. Jasper was the third man in her life during that period, and while it meant bad news for the besotted Wilf Harkness, brother of Ben, it was gratifying to have confirmation that the young vet was interested. Simmy had been there when the two first met, and noticed then that there had been sparks.

'Anyway, I should go,' the girl went on. 'I only came to introduce Bonnie. She can do every day this week, if you want her to. After that, you'll have to juggle with school for a bit. We can work it all out, next time I'm in. Tomorrow, with any luck.'

'There's the funeral on Friday,' Simmy said. 'I could do with your help for that. There were two more orders for it this morning when I got in. It's going to be huge at this rate.'

'Pays to be popular,' muttered Melanie. The deceased was a woman in her sixties, who had been a prominent member of the community, with an OBE to show for it. Her death had been prolonged and public, the struggle against cancer documented all too visibly as she went in and out of hospital. Simmy's mother, like almost everyone in the southern Lake District, knew her vaguely and fully intended to put in an appearance at the funeral. So far, there had been no fewer than fifteen orders for flowers received by Persimmon Petals of Windermere. The chief mourner was Valerie, a woman variously described as 'friend', 'lover', 'companion' and 'distant cousin'. She had come to Simmy for her own flowers, which had been flattering but scary.

'Valerie and Barbara were definitely not lovers,' said Angie Straw emphatically.

'How do *you* know?' asked Simmy.

'I just do. You get a sense for these things in my line of business.' Beck View Bed and Breakfast had undeniably seen more than its share of unorthodox relationships, Simmy supposed. But whatever the truth of it, the bereaved Valerie was very upset indeed at her loss.

'I'll never get all the flowers in the van at once,' said Simmy. 'Lucky it's the local undertaker, so it won't be too much of a pain to do two journeys.' The need to avoid the slightest hint of a mistake where funeral flowers were concerned was acute. 'It's going to occupy my every waking thought tomorrow,' she added.

'Good luck, then,' said Melanie. 'At least you'll have Bonnie to answer the phone for you.'

'What time can you manage tomorrow?'

'I'll try to make it by three or thereabouts. Don't bank on it, though.'

'That'd be a big help.' The unpredictable stop-start nature of the business made staffing tricky at any time. Aside from the obvious rush periods for Mother's Day and Valentine's, there was no knowing just when things would get busy. Mother's Day had been less of a trauma than they'd feared, but it had still entailed a week of late nights and total concentration. Easter, by comparison, had been a breeze.

Melanie was edging towards the door, apparently not eager to leave. 'Your dad was the only man you saw over the weekend then, was he?' she blurted. 'What about Ninian?'

'Ninian was his usual elusive self. It's like trying to communicate with somebody in the Dark Ages. I'm wondering whether carrier pigeons might work. He's given up using his phone since they put the costs up. And he still insists he doesn't want a car.'

'At least you've been to his cottage now. You can find him if you really want to.'

'True. Except he's often not there.'

Bonnie was showing signs of curiosity during this exchange, and Simmy explained, 'Ninian's a friend. He's a potter, living up on Brant Fell in an old stone cottage. We sell his stuff here, look.' She pointed to a row of stoneware vases, as well as one on the floor containing a collection of lilies.

'Oh yeah, I know who that is,' said Bonnie unconcernedly. 'Those lilies look a bit squashed like that, don't you think?'

'You're right – they do. I crammed them all in on Saturday, hoping somebody would buy the whole lot. They should have gone out to the back room, really. They won't last much longer.'

'There's a lot of waste in this business,' said Melanie regretfully.

'I liked the model you had in the window,' said Bonnie, as if trying to find something to admire. 'It was unusual. I saw it at Christmas, and wondered if somebody would buy it.'

'It wasn't for sale. Ben and I made it. It was always dreadfully fragile, though. I tried to move it last week and the whole thing fell to bits. I had to throw it away, which was an awful shame.'

The model had been a representation of a local landmark, which was itself a kind of model, being a small tower only fit for fairies or elves to inhabit. Simmy had fallen in love with it on her first day in Windermere, and when Ben described seeing clever constructions in America made of dried seedpods, sticks, nutshells and other natural materials, they had been inspired to try one of their own.

'Right. I gotta go,' said Melanie. 'Late already. See you.' And she made a determined exit, leaving the other two like abandoned children to make the best of it.

'Well . . .' began Simmy, unsure as to what came next. 'We'd better get cracking on those funeral orders, and see if we can work out a system for the week. I'll show you the back room first.'

But before she could act on her words, a customer appeared, wanting advice as to how to create an eye-catching centrepiece for her dining table. Whilst dealing with the questions, Simmy was half aware that Bonnie was talking into her mobile, near the front of the shop.

When the woman had gone, Simmy cocked a questioning eye at the phone still in the girl's hand. 'Sorry – don't you want me to make calls? It's just I'm supposed to say where I am.'

'No, that's okay.' It both was and wasn't, she realised. Reassuring that Bonnie had someone keeping tabs on her, and annoying that there were likely to be constant distracting conversations as a result.

Bonnie followed her into the back room and listened and asked a few questions and appeared to be coping with the new situation well enough. But Simmy found the need to go carefully something of a strain. Where Melanie had been big and capable and outspoken, she was almost afraid of breaking Bonnie if she accidentally trod on her.

'I won't be able to come on Monday,' the girl said, at one point. 'I've got a meeting with one of the teachers that day, and some sort of test to see what's best for me to do next year. At least, I could do the afternoon here, if you like.'

'No problem.' Simmy waved the subject away. Monday felt too far off to worry about. Anything might happen by then.

Chapter Five

The day ended with Bonnie promising to return next morning for further instruction.

'I should pay you,' Simmy realised. 'We haven't discussed that side of things at all. How very unbusinesslike of me.'

'Oh, just some pocket money will do for now. You don't have to get into all the paperwork and tax and stuff, as far as I'm concerned.'

A girl after Russell Straw's heart, Simmy thought, with a smile. 'Well, I suppose we'll have to eventually, but for a week or two I'm happy to keep it informal, if you like.'

'Thanks,' said Bonnie, as if relieved.

'How will you get home?'

'Walk. It's not far. I'm staying at a place in Heathwaite at the moment.'

This sounded odd to Simmy, and she tried to link it with the few facts that Melanie had conveyed that morning. 'With your family, you mean?'

'Sort of. I'm living with my aunt. It suits us both.

Don't worry about me,' she added urgently. 'I hate that.'

'I wasn't,' Simmy defended. 'You must be fairly near my parents, I presume. They're in Lake Road.'

Bonnie nodded carelessly. 'I'm in Oakthwaite.'

'Oh, I know,' said Simmy. 'There are all those tree-thwaite names. I think they're wonderful. Limethwaite. Thornthwaite. Like tongue-twisters. I even know what "thwaite" means,' she added proudly. 'And I've only been here a year.'

The girl looked at her warily. 'Oh?' she murmured.

'Yes. And I've been dreadfully slow in getting to know my way around. I'm determined to make up for it this summer.'

'Right. Well . . .'

'Sorry. You want to go. See you tomorrow, then.'

She drove back to Troutbeck wondering at her own sudden exuberance. It had begun the previous day, with the blue sky and the humming bees. There was so much to look forward to, with the lengthening days and the general lifting of pressure. Only with hindsight did she grasp how difficult the winter had been. Without Melanie and Ben, she couldn't see how she'd have got through it. But Melanie and Ben were temporary presences in her life. They were young and would move on. She had relied on them more than was wise.

So who *could* she rely on? Her parents inevitably came to mind, in spite of Russell's words on the subject. And Ninian Tripp, who was at least her own age and unlikely to move away. But Ninian was not a man to lean on. He was far too limp and fey for that.

The only person – and the realisation made her shiver – who was fully and persistently reliable was DI Nolan Moxon.

But there would be no necessity to make any further use of his trustworthiness, she assured herself. He had only crossed her path because horrible crimes had been committed. That wasn't going to happen any more. Even Ben Harkness would have to concede that.

She drove up the winding road from the lakeside into the village of Troutbeck, thinking of the weeks when an inconvenient rota had been established to drive her up and down to work, when she was still too convalescent to do it herself. Her father and Melanie had been the primary chauffeurs, but once or twice her friend Julie had been summoned into service, and there had even been mornings when the only choice was to call a taxi. As soon as she had been allowed to get behind the wheel again, Valentine's Day had demanded a dramatic return to driving, not least several challenging journeys to Coniston and back.

Her route took her through a tiny settlement named Thickholme, with a famous bridge over the Trout Beck. Woods and farms and unpredictable levels gave the little journey an ever-changing fascination, which Simmy fully acknowledged. The new sheen of green over the hedges proclaimed another miracle of revitalisation after the greys and browns of winter. Fields fell away to her right, edged by sturdy stone walls, and empty of animals. There was moss and dead wood and rutted tracks all adding to a sense of timelessness, where technology had made almost no impact. The imposing old farmhouse at Town End, with its mad collection of hand-carved furniture and weird cylindrical chimneys, reinforced the feeling that not much changed on these hillsides over a century or two.

But then she became aware that something was happening, in a farmyard close by. Two police cars were parked in such a way as to make it almost impossible to get past. A uniformed officer was talking into a phone. The sight brought memories and associations that thoroughly spoilt Simmy's mood. Hunching her shoulders and averting her gaze, she crawled past, with the side of her car almost scraping the wall bordering the little road. Nobody stopped her. Nobody took any notice of her.

With a sense of a lucky escape, she sped home to her cottage and thought no more about it.

Her garden was full of the westering sun and she sat outside on her tiny patio with a glass of juice and thought about Bonnie and Melanie and the necessity of change. In the past month or two she had acknowledged to herself that she was very nearly in a new relationship, with all the complex decisions and compromises that would be likely to accrue as it progressed. Melanie approved and Ben did not. The fact of a man in her life would force her to divide her attention; worse than that, it would invite the biggest decision of all – whether to risk another pregnancy. She had always been of the opinion that forty was the absolute upper limit for such a venture, which gave her alarmingly little time. It was also preferable to choose a father for the baby who would provide at least a degree of support and involvement. The way things stood with Ninian, it made her head hurt simply to try to imagine how he might fit himself into such a role.

The big funeral on Friday should by rights be filling her mind. The van could not contain all the tributes at once, which meant a very early start that morning and at least two journeys to deliver them all. There was the challenging central tribute from Valerie Rossiter, which would have to be constructed later the next day, then kept moist and fresh throughout Thursday. Other orders had come from an array of friends, colleagues and relatives spanning the globe. The dead woman had enjoyed a variety of roles locally, and had apparently been popular with everyone she encountered. The big church in Windermere was the venue both for the service and the subsequent interment. Traffic might find itself held up and media reporters were likely to put in an appearance. Florists from Ambleside, Bowness and beyond were sure to find themselves almost as overwhelmed as Simmy was. There would be friendly competition and a determination to avoid the slightest mistake.

But everything was under control, and further thinking about it threatened to prove both tedious and unproductive.

It dawned on her that there were rather too many subjects that she preferred not to think about. Her mind had grown accustomed to an automatic shying away from a long list of painful topics. Babies, boyfriends, any suggestion of crime, how she would manage without Melanie, what had happened to poor little Bonnie, and how her business and finances might work out in the coming years – not one of them brought anything but negative thoughts.

Crime was the worst. Since the autumn, she had ended up in the middle of some serious violence and personal damage. The sight of two police cars in a gateway half a mile from her home had sent shivers of dread through her. That specific glimpse was yet another avenue her thoughts struggled to avoid.

So she concentrated on Bonnie, as something new and intriguing. Then Ben, who despite his deplorable enthusiasm for the minutiae of murder, was endearing and amazing and highly entertaining. And finally, the sweeter points of Ninian, who, she supposed, was officially entitled to call himself her boyfriend after what had happened between them in February and a few times since then.

The landline phone was ringing, she noticed lazily. Probably one of her parents, since hardly anyone else ever used it these days. Tempted to leave them to the message-taking facility, she suddenly changed her mind and caught it on the last warble before it cut off.

'Mrs Brown?' came an unfamiliar male voice. 'It's the Windermere police here. We had a call from a Mr Russell Straw early today, about something he overheard yesterday. He said you could corroborate it if necessary.'

Her head swam in disbelief. Surely her father hadn't really reported a half-heard conversation that could be interpreted in a hundred different ways? Why hadn't her mother stopped him? 'I didn't hear anything,' she said.

'But you saw two men and a boy in a car.'

'Briefly. So what?'

'We've been working on a series of crimes in the area for the past several weeks, and there's a chance that you and your father stumbled on something relevant to our enquiries.'

'Series of crimes?' she repeated. 'What sort of crimes?'

'We call it dognapping. Stealing valuable animals for resale down south. Sometimes overseas as well.'

She almost laughed. 'And that's serious, is it?' she demanded. 'Something the police feel worth attending to?'

The man gave a very audible sniff. 'We do indeed,' he said. 'And I've been asked to inform you that a detective will be wishing to speak to you about it this evening.'

'Which detective?' she asked, with a sinking feeling.

'DI Moxon. I understand that you and he know each other.'

'I suppose we do,' she agreed.

'Then, if it's all right with you, he'll be over to see you in about half an hour's time.'

She could hardly demur, even though it was transparently obvious that Moxon simply wanted to see her again and was using the trivial little crime as a pretext. Since when did detective inspectors involve themselves in missing pets? And if they did, how normal was it to visit the vaguest of witnesses in her own home after working hours? She was definitely not deceived. But Moxon had won a reluctant little corner of her heart a few months earlier, and she found herself surprisingly willing to meet with him again.

Chapter Six

The fine evening persisted, and she left her front door slightly open, mainly to admit the scent of the lilac, which grew a few feet away. She made herself a hurried meal of scrambled eggs and bacon, having noticed that she was rumbling with hunger. If Moxon stayed for long, she'd end up pigging on biscuits, which was all she intended to offer him.

She heard his car coming up the road from the shop, and parking in the only available space for some distance. The village street was narrow for most of its length, in no way designed for cars. Small patches had been carved out here and there for residents' vehicles, while visitors had to take their chances.

The sight of him came as a small shock. He was thinner and looked much older than he had three months earlier. 'How long have you been back at work?' she asked him, almost before he was inside the house.

'Just over a week. I recovered pretty quickly, and it was no fun just kicking my heels at home. How've you been?'

'Me? I'm perfectly all right. I walked up to the top of

Wansfell with my dad yesterday. We were both very pleased with ourselves.'

He glanced towards the back of the house, where the designated fell stood, even though it was invisible through the walls. 'I'm impressed,' he said.

'I dare say Dad's knees will punish him for it, the rest of this week, but he'd insist it was worth it.'

'He tells us you and he saw some suspicious characters at the pub.'

'Two men and a boy in a car.' It was becoming a kind of mantra already, and she had a sneaking fear that she was going to have to say it quite a few more times yet. And she was still completely disoriented by the fact of her father having approached the police. It felt insanely out of character. 'And we found a dead dog,' she abruptly remembered. 'That might be more relevant. It looked as if somebody had strangled it.'

'Yes. He mentioned that. In fact, I had the impression he'd been thinking about that more than the conversation he overheard and decided that something ought to be done.'

Simmy frowned helplessly. 'You're saying he thinks those men at the pub killed the dog? And what about the man with the black bag? Did he tell you about him as well?'

'I'm not sure what he thinks, to be frank. And neither of you actually saw the contents of the bag, as I understand it. I don't think it counts as helpful. And no, we don't have any views as to how or why the dog died. Nothing as direct as that. Your father just passed over what he'd seen, thinking it might have some relevance. He said he kept on turning it over in his mind, and couldn't see any innocent explanation for what he'd overheard.'

Still none of this sounded convincing to Simmy. Hadn't she herself come up with a list of possible interpretations for the words Russell had heard – all of them harmless? Then dawn began to break over the obscurity. 'Did he phone you directly, or was it just a coincidence that he spoke to you?'

'He asked for me.' Moxon was shuffling on his kitchen chair. He rubbed his nose and avoided her gaze, confirming her suspicions.

'He wanted to talk about me, didn't he? All that stuff about the pub and the dog was just a pretext to get to speak to you.' She was still far from enlightened, but glimmers were detectable. 'Although I don't really see . . .'

'You've got it wrong.' He made a visible effort to relax. 'It's less about you than him, I think. And your mother. Although . . .' He rubbed his nose again and Simmy wondered whether he was suffering from the same spring allergy that seemed to be afflicting so many people. 'I oughtn't to speculate. I'll probably get into very deep water if I start trying to understand complicated family dynamics. The fact is, that whatever his motives, he *did* supply some rather useful information. The dead dog suggests a connection to the ongoing case we're investigating. And then there are the events of this afternoon,' he finished, with a look of real regret. 'Which we have an unhappy feeling is directly connected to everything we've just been saying.'

Simmy groaned. 'I saw the cars down near Town End. Don't tell me there's been some sort of break-in and those men are the ones who did it. I'm sorry, but I really wish my dad had kept quiet, in that case. Why the silly man should ever think it sensible to voluntarily get involved with the police defeats me. I mean' – she burst out with reckless anger – 'it's all so *trivial*. And you can't really think he's given you anything useful.'

Moxon adopted an expression she had seen before, in which he struggled not to display the hurt feelings she had caused. Throughout all her dealings with him, she had maintained an attitude that he found deplorable. Whilst acknowledging that murderers should be caught and wrongdoing punished, Simmy Brown remained her mother's daughter to the extent of wishing someone else would do the dirty work of apprehending and punishing. For her, the police carried an inexorable miasma of sleaze, combined with a jargon-ridden mindset that took little cognisance of the realities of human behaviour. She did not like them, and she was sure she never would.

'Sorry,' she muttered. 'But there it is.'

He sighed. 'There's more,' he said, almost reluctantly. 'I've been trying to lead up to it gently.'

She narrowed her eyes. 'What?'

'It wasn't just a break-in at Town End. A man has been killed. In a farmyard. It looks like foul play. And it turns out that the car you saw is registered to a man we believe to be the victim.'

Her hands curled into instinctive fists, while her stomach churned in terrified apprehension. 'Then why aren't you out there chasing the person who did it?' she blustered. 'Why are you *here*, for heaven's sake? Am I under suspicion? Are you hoping I'll magically name the culprit for you? What on earth are you *doing* here?' Her voice had become shrill and her heart was thumping.

He held her gaze. 'Your father heard two men talking as if they might be preparing to commit a crime. A crime has been committed. His testimony – and yours – are now possibly quite central to the investigation. Could you please try to describe those men you saw?'

She ground her teeth in futile fury, even as she wondered why she was so angry. He had wasted several minutes in convoluted preliminaries, when all the time he wanted something specific from her. She stared at his eyes, behind old-fashioned thick spectacles that implied poor sight. His dark lashes lowered, curtaining his thoughts. Her own thoughts were clashing painfully. She should do all she could to help, if something really serious had happened. But all she wanted was to go and watch the setting sun on her patio and remember the good feelings that had come from a strenuous walk with her father. 'It was only an hour or so ago,' she realised. 'I saw the police cars in that yard by Town End.' The speed with which Moxon had caught up with her seemed almost supernatural. 'What time did you find this dead man, then?'

'Middle of the afternoon,' he said briskly. 'About two hours after I spoke to your father.'

'And you've already checked out the red car, and got a name for the victim? That was quick!'

'We checked the car as soon as your father gave us the number, as a matter of routine. And the person who found the body knew who he was. The names matched.' He shook his head in wonderment. 'It doesn't often happen like that.'

'And now you've got the car?'

'Actually, no. There's no sign of it.'

Simmy sat back, reminding herself that she had no obligation to immerse herself in the details of a police investigation. But still her attention was irresistibly hooked. 'Dognapping,' she remembered, as she wrestled with the burgeoning strands of the story. 'Is it an old man who died?'

'Why?'

'Isn't that what the men at the pub said? Something about an old man?'

'Actually, he's in his thirties.'

'Oh.'

'And there weren't any dogs at the farm. In fact, nobody actually lives there. They just keep sheep on the land. The original house was sold decades ago and it's used as a holiday home now. It's not really a farm at all any more.'

'Oh.' She blinked a few times. 'Then why do you think it has anything to do with me and my father and what happened yesterday?'

'It's all in Troutbeck,' he said simply. 'And Troutbeck is a very small place.'

'Oh,' she said for the third time.

After that things seemed to drift. Moxon asked for descriptions of the men in the red car, which Simmy failed to provide in any detail. 'I've forgotten,' she said. 'It all felt like a game at the time. I guessed their ages, and Dad took me seriously. They were very ordinary. I'd say the boy was about twelve, maybe a bit more. Tim – I think he's called Tim.'

'Yes, he's the victim's son. Your father said he didn't

see the people in the car at all. That seems a bit strange.'

'It all happened very quickly. He was writing down the registration number, or sorting out his dog, or something. Look – why does what we saw yesterday matter now? You've got a name for the man who's died. You can find his son and ask him everything else you need to know. He can tell you who the other man was, and what they were planning to do.' She wanted to force him to agree with her, to admit he had only shown up because he liked her and hadn't seen her for ages. 'I'm definitely not going to be a witness or anything. I can't provide an alibi or give names of likely suspects. I refuse to get hurt again, either.' She lifted her chin defiantly. 'It feels as if you're *deliberately* trying to drag me into something, with no good reason. And it really isn't fair.'

'All right,' he nodded. 'If that's how you feel, I'll do what I can to leave you alone from now on. The trouble is . . .' he paused and took a deep breath, 'I can't make any promises. We have to follow the evidence wherever it leads us. And just at the moment, it's leading very directly to the conversation your father heard yesterday. I know you don't like people worrying about you, but there are inevitably some concerns . . .' He gave a weak smile, as if expecting a rebuff.

'But the boy? Why can't you just ask him?'

'We will. But he's just lost his father, and his mother lives in Scotland. She'll be coming down tonight to collect him, but all that's still up in the air. We can't bombard him with questions until she's here to chaperone him. Surely you can see I had no choice but to come and ask how much you can contribute that might help us. I'm sure you're aware that the more quickly we can understand the story, the more likely we are to make an early arrest.'

'I know you mean well,' she said. 'I appreciate it. And it's not your fault. I just wish my dad hadn't contacted you. Neither of us can be of any more help, as far as I can see. It's just a waste of your time when you've got better things to do. I'm glad we gave you the link with the car, even if I'm not sure how relevant it'll be.'

'I hope you're right about that,' he said, with a sigh.

She closed the door behind him with some force, knowing that she was being unreasonable. He had been very forbearing, resisting an obvious temptation to remind her that she had a legal duty to cooperate with all police enquiries. The 'enquiry' such as she could understand it, was a peculiar tangle that she might have followed better if she'd allowed Moxon to explain. More pressing, she discovered, was her father's almost treacherous behaviour. If anybody had dragged her into this new police investigation, it was surely him.

She picked up the phone, determined to demand what on earth he'd been thinking of to do such a thing.

Her mother answered. 'Beck View,' she said with a carefully judged mixture of welcome and efficiency.

'Mum? It's me.'

'P'simmon.' Only Angie could pronounce the name in a way that made it sound a perfectly normal appellation for a daughter. 'What's up?'

'Ask Dad. Did you know he'd told the police about a silly little thing that happened yesterday?'

'That dead dog on the fellside? He didn't, did he? I never thought he would.'

'Not so much that, as two men he heard talking at the pub. Now there's been a murder practically next door and the police are trying to drag me into it. It's all Dad's fault. Whatever came over him?'

'He came home in a funny mood yesterday. Didn't say much, but I had the impression the walk wasn't as much of a success as he'd expected. And poor old Bertie just collapsed into a heap and has barely moved since. You didn't say "murder" just then, did you?'

'I did, actually. Although Moxon tried to shield me from it, I think. He didn't use the word, but it was clear enough what he meant. That's very odd about Dad, though. I thought we had a wonderful time. The views were breathtaking, and we both managed a lot of steep terrain without any mishaps. He talked a bit about his showing as a parent, which was a bit disconcerting.'

'Exactly! That's what I mean. He's gone very introspective, all of a sudden.'

'He's always been a bit like that. It still doesn't explain why he talked to the police. I wondered whether he just wanted to bring me and Moxon together again for some reason.'

'Matchmaking, you mean? Sounds unlikely. I think he's happy with Ninian in that role.'

'So . . . what?'

Angie was silent for a few seconds. 'He feels you need protection, perhaps. He's been a lot more careful about locking doors and keeping a closer eye on the guests, these past few weeks. He worries about them coming into our rooms – didn't we tell you he's had signs made, saying "Private" for the doors? Jim-the-handyman came yesterday to screw them on. And he checks the car's there two or three times a day.'

Simmy felt the cold hand of anxiety clutching at her breast. 'That's awful. He was never like that. I haven't seen any sign of it.' She thought again of her apprehension that her father might invite the muddy bearded man into her cottage. Caution and nervousness were not remotely part of his character.

'It *is* awful,' Angie agreed. 'And I think he knows it's not right. He's liable to be trying to hide it from you. But it's driving me mad, to be honest. I'm starting to wonder if he's getting that ACDC thing that little boys have.'

'I think you mean ADD. Attention deficit disorder. And that doesn't really cover what you're describing.' Simmy had a nasty suspicion that her father's new persona was a direct result of the traumatic series of events over the winter. 'I'll try and come over after work tomorrow and see for myself. At least it explains why he spoke to the police, I suppose. And he's going to feel completely vindicated when he finds out there's been a horrible crime up here, isn't he.'

'So who died?' Simmy could hear how reluctant her mother was to ask this central question.

'A man. That's all I know. Moxon didn't tell me his name, or what was done to him. It was in a farmyard, which isn't really a farmyard at all any more. I suppose it might have a barn or two for storing hay. I pass it nearly every day, but haven't ever properly looked. I've never seen sheep or anything in the fields. Moxon didn't tell me very much, but there's something about dognapping that they've been investigating. Don't tell Dad. He'll start trying to stop Bertie from ever going outside.'

Angie snorted. 'Nobody's going to steal that old mutt.'

'Lucky for him he's neutered, or they might. Lakeland terriers are pretty rare these days.'

'Not only neutered, but far from pure-blooded. I sometimes think there's a dash of beagle in his ancestry. Something about the head.'

Simmy declined to discuss dog heredity, and found herself yawning. 'I've got to go, Mum. I haven't eaten yet, and then I'll need to get an early night. I've got to go to Staveley before I open up tomorrow, then it's a full day making wreaths for the funeral on Friday. I shouldn't be thinking about anything other than that.'

'Off you go then, love. Call in tomorrow if you get a chance.'

'Bye, Mum.'

For supper, she opened a tin of soup, and drank it from a large mug. Followed by a carton of yoghurt, it hardly comprised a wholesome meal. Her weight was gently dropping, month by month, as she grew decreasingly interested in food. *I'll be as bad as Bonnie, if I don't watch out*, she thought, with no sense of alarm. People who manifested too serious a commitment to eating were obviously living idle and unfulfilled lives. Or so Angie would say. Simmy did not doubt that it was more complicated than that.

But she was aware of a certain emptiness in these routine

evenings spent alone. There was the pub only five minutes' walk away, where people would be chatting and laughing and generally being sociable. In the summer the garden would be full of tired and happy walkers with stories to tell. Simmy could go along and join in, making herself a part of the community, a familiar face which would be welcomed and included. Once in a while, the temptation was almost enough to persuade her to do just that. Melanie would approve, and Ninian might be nudged into a better level of involvement.

It was only half past seven. She had two hours with nothing to do. It was mild outside, with birds singing and blossom blooming. The phone had dragged her indoors when there was still every reason to be in the open air. And perhaps instead of sitting quietly on her patio at the back, she could do a bit of weeding at the front, in the little patch of garden that she tried to keep presentable. Grass was growing rapidly amongst the shrubs and perennials, with buttercups and dandelions rudely intruding where they weren't wanted.

The other reason, of course, was to put herself in the way of anyone passing on foot. They would glance over the low wall and see her at work. Then they would pause and say, 'Lovely evening,' and she would agree with them. There were perhaps three local residents who knew her well enough to stop for a longer chat. And then, maybe, they'd casually invite her along for a drink at the Mortal Man, and all her dreams would come true.

She smiled at her own imaginings, but was not deterred. She collected a trowel and positioned herself on the edge of the weediest area of the little garden. For ten minutes, she dug out the interlopers while nobody at all walked past.

She had become so intent on her work, with its rewarding results, that she jumped when a male voice spoke a few feet away. 'So this is where you live, then. I reckoned it was hereabouts.'

She looked up, and met the gaze of the man whose features had returned to her several times over the past twenty-four hours. 'Hello,' she said, warily.

'Aren't you going to ask me whether I got all that mud off?' he teased, making it plain that he understood her nervousness of him.

'I assume you did.' She wanted to ask – *What did you have in that bag? Are you in a gang of dognappers?*

And more alarmingly, the question formed itself – *And did you kill a man today in a yard near Town End?*

Chapter Seven

Of course, the idea was ridiculous. If this bearded and unsettling individual had in fact just committed murder, he would scarcely be hanging around half a mile from the scene of the crime. There was no reason whatever to think he had any connection with burglary or stealing dogs or whatever else had been going on. But associations were inescapably forming in her mind, enough to render her speechless. She got to her feet, weighing the little trowel in her hand as if wondering if it could possibly defend her.

The man seemed unsurprised by her silence. 'Nice evening,' he went on, in a parody of the fantasy she had just been entertaining. 'Pity there's been trouble down the way.'

'Oh?' she managed. Her thoughts were slowly unscrambling, enough for the idea to occur that her father might well have informed the police of this man's presence in Troutbeck the day before, along with a description of him. Hadn't Moxon said something about it not being helpful? That there might have been anything at all – and all of the possibilities innocent – inside the black bag.

'Don't tell me you haven't heard. It's all round the place by now. Poor ol' Travis McNaughton's bought it, apparently. Terrible thing.' He looked genuinely distressed, his eyes shrinking into his head, and his lips tight against the emotion. 'And the woman who found 'im – she knew him, as well. She's never going to be the same, after what she saw.'

'So you knew him, did you?'

'Sort of. Lived up Grasmere way until a little while ago. Did some work with his brother a few years back. Harmless as they come. No reason in the world for anyone to kill 'im.'

Why was he telling her this? Was he simply splurging his feelings to anyone who would listen? Was the shock of sudden violence so great that he couldn't keep it back? Or had he a cooler more malicious motive, specifically directed at her? She and her father had witnessed his presence in Troutbeck the day before, carrying a mysterious object having earlier been loitering outside the pub. All decidedly suspicious.

But why would he *continue* to behave suspiciously now? She met his eyes directly, searching for an explanation, striving to appear fearless and even sympathetic. It was possible, she realised, that he had seen and recognised DI Moxon, leaving her house. It was all too horribly possible that this was why he was now talking to her, in an attempt to discover what she knew and what she had told the police.

'Well, I . . .' She was going to say *can't stop*, but it sounded fatuous as well as blatantly untrue. 'I'm sorry about your friend. I expect it was an accident – they happen a lot on farms, don't they? I mean, I have no idea what happened, but I'm sure it'll all be sorted out.' She sighed. That really *had* sounded fatuous.

'No accident,' he glowered. 'How does a chap get his throat torn out by accident?'

'What?' Her head spun and she felt sick. 'How do you know that?'

'The woman who found him told about a dozen people at Town End. Blood everywhere, she said. She'd got it on her hands. They're all talking about it.' He waved a vague hand towards the upper end of the village. 'Especially at the pub.'

'I'd much rather not know,' she said. 'It's got nothing to do with me.'

'Nor me.' The words were uttered forcefully. 'Do you hear? It's nothing to do with me, either. So don't you go thinking it has.'

She nodded timidly. It sounded like a threat. She took it as a threat. And yet there was an appeal in his eyes that softened his expression and made her less afraid of him. She glimpsed a life spent under suspicion simply because of the way he looked. Scruffy, thin, sly – he was nobody's idea of trustworthy. Impatiently she thought: surely he could clean himself up without any great effort, if it mattered to him how people judged him. He didn't really strike her as a murderer. But then, she had actually met three murderers since coming to Cumbria, and not one of them had shown any outward sign of their capabilities.

The man walked away, uphill towards the Mortal Man. Simmy went into her house and tried not to think any more about him.

Wednesday was a lot cooler than previous days had been, with grey skies over the lakes and fells. Determined to avoid any risk of getting embroiled in police activity at Town End, she took the alternative road out of Troutbeck down towards the church, turning left at the chestnut tree, which had the first hints of pink flowers that would cover it in another week or two. Making deliveries before opening the shop was efficient, but it meant an uncomfortably early start at times.

She drove first to Staveley with the delivery of flowers, where Cynthia Mossop was in her dressing gown, bemused at the doorbell going before she was properly awake. The flowers were well received, and Simmy duly gratified. She sped back down to Windermere and her shop, catching glimpses of the lake where an early mist drifted above the water.

She found her thoughts full of her mother's account of her father's startling change of character. Had it been coming on gradually, or was it as sudden as it seemed to Simmy? Was it all because of her experiences over recent months, into which he had also been drawn? Did he understand what was happening to him, or was it all unconscious? Would it help if she deliberately avoided all mention of the events of the Bank Holiday Monday, or make him even more paranoid? Perhaps it wasn't paranoia anyway, but a purely rational response to situations that really were dangerous? People had died, after all, including a man in Troutbeck less than a day ago. DI Moxon had taken Russell's report seriously, and had manifested concern for Simmy's safety.

It was all happening again – she had to face it. There had been another murder, close to where she lived. Ben Harkness would be avidly excited about it, and Melanie would probably admit to an intimate knowledge of the dead man's family and all their doings. And it was not going to do Simmy or her father any good at all.

The shop had a handy paved area in front, where plants could be positioned in a display that mostly had to be taken in at closing time every day. 'Persimmon Petals' was painted in fancy lettering above the window. When the handmade model of the well-known Baddeley clock tower had finally been removed after five months *in situ*, Ninian had promised to construct a more permanent attraction to include his trademark ceramic tiles, but nothing had yet materialised. Simmy and Melanie had both been remiss in failing to create a proper display in the meantime.

Still thinking about her father, and wondering how worried or annoyed she should be, it took her a moment to register that another man was standing outside the shop, clearly waiting for her.

'You're early,' she said, feeling moithered, or mithered, according to which north country dialect one adopted. In either case, it was a word Simmy found herself using a lot, when people approached her at an unsuitable hour.

'I got up at sunrise, which was nearly three hours ago,' said Ninian Tripp. 'The best of the day is almost over.'

'That might be true on a sunny day. As it is, it hardly feels as if the sun's risen at all. What do you want?'

'You,' he said disarmingly.

'Nin – I've got a mass of work to do. If you really wanted me, you'd have shown up over the weekend. Two and a half days were completely free, and you didn't appear for any of it.'

'You were busy with your dad, or so you told me.'

'There was still Sunday, and quite a lot of Saturday.

70

Where were you? I tried phoning. I nearly came to see you.'

'Why didn't you? It's easier for you. I have to wait for a bus, or walk, if I'm to get all the way up to Troutbeck.'

She had unlocked the door, turning her back on him and trying to identify her emotions. Impatience, confusion, a niggle of apprehension were all on the list. 'I didn't know whether you'd be there. Whether you'd want me. I *never* know.'

'I'm here now,' he said, as if that solved everything.

She sighed. Somehow it was her failing, not his, that made things so difficult. If she had driven up to his tiny cottage on the edge of Brant Fell, he'd have welcomed her and probably even taken her to bed. She knew that. She knew he assumed an easy bohemian relationship that saw no need for plans or telephones or irritating reproaches. The problem was that she still needed a clear invitation before risking it. She needed to know he wasn't constructing a delicate piece of pottery, or sleeping off a heavy bout of drinking or smoking pot. Or even entertaining another woman. She had no real evidence that he was loyal to her alone. He made no promises. Against her will, she found herself comparing him with the ultra-responsible and painfully devoted DI Moxon. A devotion that made very few demands, and which endured rejection and indifference with a terrible stoicism.

'I'm busy,' she repeated. 'Sorry, but there's that enormous funeral on Friday, which is taking up all my time.'

'Ah yes. The sainted Barbara Hodge. Choirs of angels must be singing her to rest, at this very moment.'

'Did you ever meet her?'

'Once by accident. I had a stall at a craft fair and she came by, doing her grand lady act. Bought one of my pieces, as it happens. I was gobsmacked. I think it was the only thing I sold all day. Kept me in bread and milk for a fortnight.'

'So you'll go to the funeral, then?' she teased.

'In your dreams. A better idea would be to break into the house while everybody's at the church and take the pot back. It'll go to some undeserving nephew otherwise.'

'I didn't hear that,' said Simmy. 'Now, get out of my way. It's nearly nine already. I suppose Bonnie'll be here soon.'

'Who?' He frowned worriedly, as if the name should be familiar.

'The new girl. Melanie found her. She's here all week, learning the ropes.'

'What's she like?'

'Small. Fragile. Pale. But she seems bright enough and fairly interested in the business.'

'Can't wait to meet her,' he grinned. 'How old is she?'

'Young enough to be your daughter.'

'Come on!' he remonstrated. 'Don't give me that look. I might be feckless, but nobody's ever accused me of lusting after young girls. To be honest, I find them boring. Except your Melanie, of course.'

'Right. Now go.'

He went, humming a tune Simmy didn't recognise. She watched him cross the little street and disappear towards the northern end of town. If he had suddenly dematerialised in a puff of white mist, she would hardly have been surprised. Ninian was elusive, almost slippery in his unreliable availability. His body was narrow and pale and bony, although his potter's hands were strong. He was easy to love, but impossible to depend on. She sighed and went out to the back room where stacks of funeral flowers awaited her nimble fingers.

Bonnie arrived at precisely nine o'clock, standing hesitantly just inside the shop. Simmy peered around the door of the cool room and called a welcome.

'Should I turn the sign to "Open"?' asked the girl. 'You do open at nine, don't you?'

'Yes. Thanks. You're very punctual.'

'I wasn't sure what time you wanted me, actually. And I didn't know whether Melanie was coming in today, either. She didn't sound very sure, did she? You might not want both of us together.'

'She said she wouldn't be in until this afternoon, if at all. She's sent you instead. She's not going to be here much at all from now on, as far as I know.' The pang at the loss of her assistant was sharper than anticipated. 'I'm really going to miss her.'

'She is amazing,' Bonnie agreed. 'I wish I could be more like her.'

Simmy cocked her head and smiled. 'I think you *are* quite like her, actually. In some ways, at least.'

Bonnie flushed and turned away. 'Where should I put my coat?' she asked.

Simmy showed her, as well as pointing out the toilet and emergency fire exit at the back. 'That's the basics done,' she concluded.

'What about upstairs?'

'Pardon?'

'There's another floor.' The girl pointed a vertical finger as if thinking Simmy might never have noticed. 'Does somebody live there?'

'Oh! No. It's just storage space. The previous people kept loads of stock up there. Technically I can use it how I like, according to the lease. But I've not needed it so far. I don't have a lot of reserve stock. It sounds funny, but I'd almost forgotten about it. There's no direct access from inside the shop. You have to go out the back and up some metal stairs. Like a fire escape.'

'Hmm,' said Bonnie thoughtfully. 'Would a person be allowed to *live* there?'

'Um . . . I doubt it. There's no loo or kitchen, for a start.'

'But there's electric? And water?'

'I think so. It's in two rooms, back and front. Why? You don't want it, do you?'

Bonnie made a grimace, part embarrassment, part rueful amusement. 'I might,' she admitted. 'I could work in exchange for rent. I could just get a little gas ring and kettle, and maybe some sort of chemical toilet?'

'But *why*? What's wrong with where you are?'

Bonnie wriggled her shoulders. 'Nothing really. I just prefer being on my own.'

'I don't know. I'll have to think about it – and go up there for a proper look. That's not going to happen before next week, with things so busy. And quite honestly, I can't imagine my landlord would be very happy. Or the council. They'd want it all made official. In their eyes, you'd be a squatter.'

'Right,' said the girl, as if none of these arguments counted for much. 'Okay. It was just an idea.'

A customer interrupted them, and Bonnie watched closely as Simmy dealt with a request for a mixed bouquet. Afterwards, she asked questions that reassured Simmy that her new helper was going to prove rather an asset. The morning drifted along with no mishaps or irritations other than the gloomy weather outside.

Shortly after midday, a familiar figure appeared. Ben Harkness hefted a heavy schoolbag onto Simmy's little table and extracted a lunch box. He looked at the girl standing beside Simmy and nodded. 'Bonnie Lawson,' he said carelessly. 'Fancy meeting you here. Started your exams yet?'

'Ben,' she returned. 'First one's on Monday.'

'You know each other,' Simmy realised, with a sense of being slow-witted. 'Of course. Are you in the same class?'

Two identically patronising looks greeted this question. 'They call them tutor groups now,' Ben told her. 'And no, we're not. Never have been. But everybody knows Bonnie Lawson.'

'They don't!' the girl protested. 'Not like they know Ben Harkness, anyway.'

'We're both famous,' he shrugged. Then he looked from one to the other. 'You're not *working* here, are you?'

'That's the idea, yes. I'm training, at the moment. Melanie thought it would work out. She brought me yesterday.'

Ben had grown an inch since the start of the year, and was likely to add another by Christmas. He was knobbly and scrawny and often awkward. His complicated mixture of confidence bordering on arrogance at some times, and acute sensitivity to criticism at others had endeared him to Simmy from the start. Impressive brain power and highly focused ambition singled him out from his peers, and yet he never seemed lonely. He was unquestionably a geek, but the existence of a large family of siblings and well-disposed teachers all seemed to have kept him reasonably normal.

'Training, eh!' The dash of patronage for a girl his own age was not lost on Simmy, who made a noise of protest. 'What?' Ben challenged her.

'She *is* training. Don't be so . . .'

'What?' said Ben again. 'I wasn't being anything.'

Again there was a feeling that the two youngsters had an understanding between them that excluded Simmy. Bonnie hadn't blushed or giggled or tried to efface herself in Ben's presence. There appeared to be a natural ease between them which was both surprising and enviable. As Simmy remembered it, her own school years had involved considerable awkwardness between the sexes.

'Anyway, I'm busy,' she said crossly.

'That's good, isn't it?' said the boy with a grin.

She sighed, and then remembered something. 'Hey, while you're here, I've got a question for you. What's the poem that has the line about the "bee-loud glade"? Is it Thomas Hardy?'

'Yeats,' he said carelessly. *'The Lake Isle of Innisfree.* "And I will arise and go now, and go to Innisfree, And a small cabin build there, of clay and wattles made; Nine bean rows will I have there, a hive for the honeybee, And live alone in the bee-loud glade."' He rattled off the lines with little feeling. 'I learnt that when I was fifteen,' he added. 'Nice to know it's still in here, good as new.'

'Wow!' gasped Bonnie in wonderment. 'That's awesome.'

'I thought it was either Hardy or Yeats,' said Simmy, defensively.

'So what does it have to do with anything?' Ben asked.

'Nothing, really. Just that it came to me on Monday, and I thought you'd probably know. As you did. Thanks.'

'Um . . .' Ben was taking out his phone, which was also a dozen other useful things. 'There's a bit of news, I see. A man in Troutbeck? Come to an untimely end?' His hesitancy was uncharacteristic, but Simmy understood it only too well. 'Did you know about it?' the boy concluded.

'Yes, but I'm not thinking about it today. I've got far too much else to concentrate on. It's nothing to do with me.' The words echoed in her head, taunting her with their mendacity. 'At least . . .' She could see there was no immediate prospect of getting down to her funeral wreaths until Ben was satisfied.

He was onto her like a snake. 'At least –' he prompted. 'Do you know who he is? I mean *was*. Anything else you can tell me?'

'Stop it!' she shouted. 'Don't be so damned gleeful about it. A man died in a farmyard yesterday afternoon. That's all I know. That's all I *want* to know.'

He stared at her, searching for the truth. 'How do you even know that much? I bet you haven't seen any news today. What time did you get into the shop this morning?'

'Half past eight. I did an early delivery in Staveley. The woman wasn't even dressed.'

'Did you have the car radio on?'

'No. Stop it, Ben. I haven't got time to be interrogated by you. I've already had Ninian bothering me, before I even opened up.'

'Surely *he* wasn't talking about the dead man?'

'No, actually. I don't know what he was talking about. Nothing important. I told him about Bonnie.'

Ben looked at her. 'Do you know Ninian Tripp, on Brant Fell?'

Bonnie nodded as if the answer were obvious, and Simmy felt a familiar sense of being at a disadvantage amongst all these people who had known each other for ever.

'Well, he's her boyfriend,' said Ben. 'He makes these pots. He's okay.'

Bonnie looked from one to the other. 'There've been murders before, haven't there? You were hurt,' she addressed Simmy. 'It must have been horrible. Now Ben wants to talk about something that happened yesterday, but you don't. Right? And you know it, don't you?' she turned to the boy. 'You know she wants to stay out of it. Why don't you just respect that and leave her alone?'

If defending was going to be done, Simmy would never have dreamt that it would be Bonnie Lawson standing up for Simmy Brown against Ben Harkness. She laughed. 'Thanks,' she said. 'Maybe he'll listen to you.'

'I knew she'd try and stay clear of it, yeah,' Ben muttered. 'But I'm set for a career in forensic archaeology and if I can get some hands-on experience now, it'll be good. It all started last year in Bowness. Simmy was there. And the Ambleside thing at Christmas – I was really helpful to the police that time.' He was gaining in volume and assertiveness. 'I'm not just tormenting her for the hell of it. If this is another murder, I should try and get some inside information about it. See?'

'Not really,' said Bonnie. 'But I s'pose it'll come clear before long.'

Simmy felt a stab of conscience at concealing so much from Ben. He was so focused and determined in his choice of career that any impediment seemed more than unkind. 'Moxon came to see me last night,' she said tiredly. 'He was really sorry, but my father and I could probably be of help to them. Dad heard some men talking on Monday, outside the pub in Troutbeck. And we took the number of a car and described the men in it. It turns out the car belongs to the dead man, so I suppose I saw him, just a day before he died.' She shuddered. 'I hate it, Ben. I absolutely can't cope with another load of trouble.'

Ben eyed her uneasily, and took a large bite of a sandwich from his lunch box. 'Doesn't sound as if you've much to worry about,' he suggested. 'Probably there'll be other locals who can help as much as you.'

'Is it anything to do with the dead dog you found, do you think?' asked Bonnie. 'I keep worrying about that. I wonder if its people ever found it.' The faint air of reproach hinted that the girl thought Simmy and her father should have done more than they did to put things right. She also looked rather agitated, Simmy realised.

'Dead dog?' said Ben. 'Where?'

'Halfway up Wansfell Pike,' said Simmy. 'I can't imagine it's got anything to do with anything. But probably Dad

79

said something about it to Moxon. We saw a man later on carrying something we thought might be that dog. In a black bin liner sort of thing.' A new surge of irritation against her father gripped her. Any involvement with this case was definitely going to be all his fault. 'And then that same man—'

Ben cut her short. 'Your dad spoke to Moxon?' While still treading carefully, he was clearly not going to remain silent.

'He did. I still can't quite believe it, but my mother thinks it's all pointing to a change of character, probably due to what's happened over the past months. He's got a lot more anxious and thinks I need protecting. Although that doesn't really explain why he's suddenly turned into such a good citizen. There was never the slightest suggestion that anybody was planning to hurt me. He just heard two men talking and thought it sounded as if they might be planning to rob somebody. That's the whole thing. Nothing the least bit sinister.'

'Unless he didn't tell you the whole story,' said Ben. 'What about this man with a bag? He sounds a bit dodgy.'

'I saw him again last night,' Simmy picked up where she'd been interrupted, and briefly told them what had happened.

'What's his name? Where does he live? Didn't you ask him what he had in the bag?' Ben fired the questions at her with rising incredulity, as she shook her head after each one. 'Simmy! What's the matter with you? How could you not even find out his name?'

'I just wanted him to go. He made me feel . . . I hate to use the stupid word, but he really did make me feel uncomfortable. As if he knew he could do anything he liked to me, and I'd never be able to stop him.'

'I know what you mean,' said Bonnie, with feeling. 'So, what did this man look like?'

'Quite tall, with a beard. Probably about my age or a bit younger. Dark eyes.'

'And your father saw him too – on Monday?' Ben asked. 'Is that right?'

Simmy nodded. 'He fell over and got muddy. But I have no idea whether my father mentioned him to the police. I suppose he must have done.'

'And the beardy man knew the chap who's been killed? Told you his name?'

'Yes. He said it was all round the village because the woman who found the body knew him and made a big noise about it. It sounded as if she was hysterical, poor thing. Covered in blood.'

Ben's eyes narrowed. 'Really? How come?'

'I don't know, Ben. She probably tried to do first aid on him or something. The man said his throat was damaged.' She couldn't bring herself to repeat the actual words. Her own throat went tight at the image they conjured.

'Hmm.' Ben's eyes were shining in an unwholesome excitement at this latest crime. 'Doesn't sound as if there's much doubt it was murder, then.'

'My father's really going to wish he kept quiet.'

'Right,' said Bonnie. 'Especially when he realises he's landed you in the middle of it. If he was trying to protect you, he's made a poor job of it, hasn't he?'

'That's a horrid thing to say,' Simmy protested. 'He

must have thought he was doing the right thing.'

Bonnie raised her hands in surrender. 'Sorry. But facts are facts,' she added obscurely. 'I mean, there have been dognappings around here. You must have seen the notices everywhere. So if somebody's been killed close to where you saw a dead dog, and where other dogs have been stolen, that's probably what this is all about. And what you and your father saw will confirm that, in the minds of the police.' She closed her lips, as if feeling she might have said too much.

'I don't see it,' Simmy insisted. 'Why would dognappers kill a dog, for a start? Don't they want a ransom or something? Then they give the animal back, and things carry on as before.' The whole idea continued to strike her as unimportant, even mildly comic. Nobody answered and she went on, 'As far as I'm concerned, I just want to get on with my work.' As if to emphasise the point, a pair of young women came chattering into the shop, pausing to look around at the flowers and associated goods for sale, as everybody did. Simmy went to greet them, relief rendering her idiotically effusive.

Ben went away again for an afternoon of revision, and Simmy settled down to a careful review of all the wreaths and sprays yet to be created for Friday's funeral. Bonnie successfully sold a bunch of white roses and another of dried grasses. She had no difficulty with the till and began to experiment with the computer, drawing Simmy's attention to a new order just in.

The issue of food had already been flagged where Bonnie

was concerned. Ben had munched through his packed lunch in front of the others, not offering them anything. Neither Simmy nor Bonnie had eaten. 'I usually go out for a roll or something,' she told Bonnie now. 'What can I get you?'

'It's okay. I've got a pack of nuts and raisins in my pocket. That'll keep me going.'

'Are you sure? It doesn't sound much.' Simmy regarded herself as a light eater, but even she wanted bread and cheese, at the very least.

'You can get me a banana or something, if you like,' Bonnie conceded.

Simmy laughed. 'Where do you suggest I do that in Windermere?'

The girl grinned ruefully. 'Sorry – I suppose you'd have to go out to the supermarket for that. Corinne does all the shopping. Don't worry about it.'

There wasn't time to enquire about Corinne – who was presumably the aunt who Bonnie lived with – and the domestic arrangements in Heathwaite, but it did occur to Simmy that if she allowed Bonnie to move into the rooms over the shop, the girl would most probably starve as a result.

At half past one, while she was working in the back room, she heard the shop doorbell ping. A minute later, Bonnie came in and said, 'Lady wants to see you.'

Brushing herself down, Simmy went to see who it was, with her mother as the first on her list of guesses.

'Sorry to interrupt,' said Valerie Rossiter, 'but I wanted to ask you something.'

It was Barbara Hodge's friend/companion/cousin and perhaps lover. She was wearing tinted glasses and a dark-blue bandanna thing around her head. She was pale and spoke thickly. 'No problem,' said Simmy, feeling a profound sympathy for the obvious grief. 'What is it?'

'I wondered whether you could somehow incorporate this in the flowers? I know it's silly, but Barb would have liked it.' She produced something wrapped in white tissue paper from her bag and gave it to Simmy. When unwrapped, it turned out to be a small porcelain flower, somewhere between a tulip and a harebell. It was blue, and barely half an inch across, with a slender stem. It was almost as fragile as a real flower, and appeared to be a fragment of something larger.

'I don't know . . .' she began. 'It's so delicate. And what's going to happen to it afterwards?'

'That doesn't matter. It's not valuable at all. We had this Meissen ornament, you see, and Barb broke it by accident, a year or two ago. We kept all the pieces, thinking we might get it mended, but now . . . it doesn't matter any more. I just wanted to have it as part of the funeral, somehow. I can't explain, but it would mean a lot. It's like a sort of message, you see.' She grimaced helplessly. 'Just tuck it in among the other flowers, okay? It doesn't matter if nobody sees it.'

Valerie was a large woman, her bones well covered. In her late forties, Simmy guessed, with a life ahead of her that currently felt like an empty abyss. Nothing she had heard suggested a demanding career or fulfilling social life. It seemed that Valerie had existed solely as sidekick or foil for the renowned Barbara Hodge.

'Would you believe people are already asking me what I'm going to do?' she burst out. 'Before we've even had the funeral.'

Simmy pulled a sympathetic face, while thinking the question not so very outrageous. The death had been foreseen for months, and surely it was reasonable to assume that Valerie might have a few ideas about what came next. At the same time, she could imagine that any sense of being hurried into a decision would be annoying.

'I've got a brother in Lincoln and an old friend in Shrewsbury. They both say I can stay with them for a while. Isn't it strange the way people assume you want to get away? All I really want is to sit in a darkened room and think about Barb. All the people I know best are here. Why would I want to go somewhere else?'

Simmy understood that she was not expected to reply. It was a familiar situation, in which her very anonymity and lack of emotional connection made her a useful confidante.

'And you've got the dog,' came a modest little voice from further down the shop.

Valerie whirled around, and replied in a flash. 'Yes, I've got Barbara's dog, who is pining for her at least as much as I am. He's out in the car now, whimpering and whining I suppose. He's just making everything worse, poor old boy.' She paused, focusing on the girl. 'I know you, don't I? You weren't here last week when I came in.'

'I'm Bonnie Lawson. I live with Corinne. She knows you. She knew Miss Hodge. I'm very sorry she died.'

'Oh, *Corinne*,' said Valerie, her voice full of meaning. 'Yes, I know Corinne. Who doesn't?'

'Plenty of people, actually,' muttered Bonnie, turning away before Simmy could give her a warning look.

Having received assurances that the porcelain flower

would be included in the intricate cushion that was Valerie's tribute, the woman left without saying anything more. As she went, a phone warbled inside her bag, and she stood out on the pavement for a moment with it to her ear. Simmy saw her glance back into the shop, as if something in the conversation applied to her.

'Poor woman,' she sighed. 'It must be awful.'

'She's a funny one. Came from nowhere ten years ago and moved in with Miss Hodge, just like that.'

'Maybe they just kept the details private. Are you saying there was some sort of mystery about it?'

'Sort of. Corinne thinks she's foreign.'

'Her English seemed pretty normal to me.'

'It's not, though. She's always so careful to get it right. That's what Corinne says, anyway. I've only seen her a couple of times. I'm surprised she recognised me.'

'Oh, well. Back to work,' said Simmy. 'Have you got something to do?'

'I'll tidy up the window display, shall I? Put a few pots and dried flowers in it?'

'Fine,' Simmy agreed. 'Good idea.'

Three o'clock came and went, bringing thoughts of a tea break. 'Time for a drink,' she announced. 'And I've got some nice choccy biscuits that Melanie brought in. She always makes sure there's a good supply.'

'Will that be part of my job, then?' Bonnie's already pale skin seemed to grow even lighter at the prospect. 'I don't really eat biscuits.'

'No, no. It won't hurt me to do without. But you'll have

to explain to me where things stand with you and food. We can arrange a proper lunch routine if you like. My mother always insists that's the right way to do it. We both need to keep our strength up.'

'I've always got a muesli bar or something in my bag. I don't really do regular meals. It's been like that all my life, and I can't imagine it changing now. You don't have to worry that talking about food might upset me, if that's what you're thinking. I'm past all that now. I suppose you're wondering what Ben meant about me being famous at school.' She pressed on without waiting for a reply. 'I collapsed in the playground, over a year ago, and they had to rush me to hospital. That was when people finally grasped what was happening. They made quite a fuss about it, and called in some anorexia awareness people to speak to the whole school. When I got out of hospital, it was still going on. It's all rather stupid, really. I often wish I'd got hooked on heroin or something instead. That would have been more glamorous.'

Simmy forced a quick laugh. 'Would it, though? I was under the impression that heroin's a bit unfashionable these days.'

'Cocaine, then. Or crystal meth. That always sounds quite tempting, don't you think?'

'It all scares me,' Simmy admitted.

'Right. But the point is, they amount to the same thing in the end. Losing control. Depending on some sort of high to get through the day. Starving yourself gives you a huge buzz, you know. People don't seem to understand that. They were good at explaining it, when I was in the unit.

It was a relief to feel there were others around who knew what was going on. It's not easy, though,' she sighed. 'They tell me it's never going to be easy.'

She was speaking in light, detached sentences, with pauses between them, her gaze fixed on a shelf of Ninian's smaller pots to one side of the shop. Simmy's instincts wavered between wanting to give the girl a long tight hug, and wishing she could dodge the likely pain and complications that hung around Bonnie like a mist.

'So go and fetch that museli bar,' she said. 'And then hold the fort while I make the drinks and then tackle another wreath. How do you like your tea?'

'I *like* it black with no sugar, but I've persuaded myself I ought to have some of both. I mean, milk and sugar.' She gave Simmy a forlorn little glance. 'I don't deliberately mean to damage myself, you know. I'm doing all I can to stay alive.'

Simmy's heart thumped. Of course, self-starvation did suggest a tendency towards suicide. If you didn't eat or drink, you died. Simple as that. But the spark of life was strong in this girl, and she resolved to contribute anything she could to maintain and strengthen it.

'Right,' she said. 'I'll be three minutes.'

Bonnie drank the tea obediently.

Chapter Eight

A late order for another lot of flowers for the same woman in Staveley interrupted Simmy's handiwork at four o'clock. The prospect of repeating the exact same procedure the next morning as she had that day was irritating. Cynthia Mossop's birthday was evidently an occasion of some significance, whether it fell on the Wednesday or Thursday. Simmy wondered why the woman's friends couldn't agree between themselves and make simultaneous orders, involving only one visit. Apart from anything else, fuel costs reduced her profits. A combined trip would have been a lot more satisfactory.

She voiced most of these thoughts aloud to Bonnie, who listened carefully, and then said, 'Why not make up the bouquet now and deliver them on your way home?'

'Because it expressly says they're for tomorrow.'

'Does it matter so much? Can't you say you won't have time tomorrow?'

Simmy paused. She had always been scrupulous about delivering as close as possible to the requested day and time.

'It won't really save me anything,' she concluded. 'Staveley isn't exactly on the way home. It's a detour whenever I do it.' And yet the prospect of getting the order out of the way, leaving Thursday clear for constructing the final big funeral tributes, was enticing. She thought ahead to the rest of the week. 'Plus there's a wedding on Saturday,' she added. 'I'll have to spend most of Friday afternoon seeing to that.'

'Busy,' said Bonnie, admiringly. 'I don't know how you get it all done, especially when things come in at short notice, like this Staveley order. Does Melanie do deliveries for you sometimes? I should have told you I can't drive.'

'She only does the local Windermere ones, and Bowness at a push. She has to walk or use her own car because I haven't insured her for the van. It didn't seem worth it, when she was never going to be staying long. And her car's such an embarrassment she has to leave it somewhere out of sight. It'd be bad for business if anybody connected it with me.'

Bonnie grinned. 'I doubt if that would matter,' she said. 'People wouldn't remember what sort of car the flowers came in.'

'They might. Anyway, it's worked out all right, most of the time.' The long weeks in January when Simmy was banned from driving while her injured bones mended had been difficult. Everybody had piled in with help and somehow they had muddled through. Simmy's own car was sometimes used for deliveries, but officially she had a roomy van with her company name painted prominently on the sides.

'I might start taking some lessons later this year,' said Bonnie vaguely.

'Don't worry about it.' The girl seemed far too delicate and small to sit behind the wheel of a car. 'Lessons are awfully expensive, anyway.'

'Yeah.' The accompanying shrug hinted that money was not the issue. A closer inspection of her clothes revealed good shoes, and a well-made jersey top that cleverly concealed just how small and skeletal the body beneath it was. Her fair hair was well cut, too. It had a natural curl that framed her face perfectly. Little Bonnie Lawson was like a creature from a fairytale, Simmy decided whimsically.

'Whose wedding is it?'

'Um . . . the woman's called Jennings. It's the second time for both of them. It's in the registry office in Kendal, then down to Ulverston. They both actually live in Windermere. It's a fairly small event, luckily. I used to think I liked wedding flowers, but now I'm not so sure. Brides can be outrageously fussy. The whole business is a bit yukky, most of the time.'

'Too right.' Bonnie spoke with such heartfelt agreement that Simmy was alerted to a story as yet untold. Noticing the interest, she added, 'My family goes in for big weddings. I was a bridesmaid five times before I was twelve. I loathed it every time.'

'Lord! That sounds dreadful. A different dress each time, obviously.'

Bonnie nodded and rolled her eyes. 'Each one more ghastly than the last.'

Simmy revised her initial impression of the girl, yet again. Large family, not short of money, something murky implied but not stated. Why, she wondered, did girls become anorexic? Surely it must be more than just social pressure to be thin? There were endless theories about it, half grasped from magazines and items on the radio, none of which she could have attempted to expound. A logic to do with control, as Bonnie had already told her. Too much or too little control, in a topsy-turvy pattern where one could be mistaken for the other. A strong implication of poor parenting, which might sometimes, at least, be utterly mistaken. Bonnie's apparent wish to live alone with few facilities was alarming, even possibly ominous and probably to be resisted.

'I'm going to make more tea,' she said. 'I'll need it if I'm going to Staveley before I get home. I'll do some for you, to make it worth boiling the kettle.'

Simmy realised she hadn't yet decided when to take the Mossop woman her second lot of flowers. It was close to five, and she began to tidy up the area around the till and check that everything was ready for the next day. She emailed an order for more flowers, explaining the system to Bonnie as she went. Then she remembered she'd told her mother she'd call in after work.

'I'll have to do Staveley tomorrow,' she said. 'I'm seeing my parents this evening, and it might be too late by the time I leave there. I want to talk to my father without feeling I need to rush off.'

'I expect you do,' said Bonnie, so knowingly that Simmy was disconcerted. 'It sounds as if there's a lot to sort out with him.'

'What do you think of Ben?' Simmy changed the subject.

Bonnie adopted a cautious expression. 'Clever at some

things, not at others,' she summarised. 'Ask me again when I've seen more of him.'

They parted at five-fifteen, each occupied by events of the day. Simmy had made up the second tribute for Cynthia Mossop and took it with her for delivery next morning.

'Be careful up there in Troutbeck,' said Bonnie, finally. 'Seeing that there's a murderer about. It's lucky you haven't got a dog that might get stolen.'

Beck View was busy with B&B guests arriving, and Simmy lurked in the kitchen until it quietened down. Her father would normally hide with her, but his presence was required when two couples turned up simultaneously. The routine spiel about places to eat, preferences for breakfast, the management of keys and introduction to the upstairs arrangements all took time. Simmy heard snatches of it and marvelled at the patience shown by both her parents at the inexorable repetitions. Angie's character had always betrayed a distinct lack of patience, and yet she was smilingly dealing with an endless procession of people, many with unreasonable expectations. She saved her wrath for those who posted adverse comments on TripAdvisor, having told her to her face they were perfectly satisfied.

'It's impossible to please them all,' she would complain to Simmy. 'Some want it all as it was in 1950, and others expect it to be like a four-star hotel with homely trimmings. Surely they can see I'm doing my best?'

'You do a great job,' Simmy reassured her. 'And most people love the place. Why else would they keep coming back?'

The truth was, as Angie herself had come to recognise, that the era of the cheap and cheerful home-from-home establishment was over. It cost as much to stay in a bed and breakfast as it did in a hotel, with far fewer facilities. There was often no lounge to sit in during the evenings, and a host of obstructive rules and practices. Many refused single guests, or insisted on a minimum of two nights' stay. Parking could be impossible and children were expected to be quiet and self-amusing. On the other hand, hotels were extending their scope to make the experience both friendlier and more flexible. 'There's one in Evesham,' Simmy observed, 'which has everything a B&B always had, plus huge rooms, a gorgeous garden and real milk with the morning tea. I remember people raving about it when I was in Worcester.'

Angie's ears had pricked up. 'Really? I bet they're expensive.'

'I don't know, but I got the feeling it really wasn't that much. Don't worry about it, Mum. You've resisted the worst of the changes. Anybody coming here can really make themselves at home. That's your unique selling point, and you shouldn't listen to people who thought they were coming to some kind of boutique hotel.'

'Yeah, well – I could never manage to keep everything as immaculate as some of those places, even if I tried.'

Russell was the first to escape from the latest batch of guests, and came huffing into the kitchen where Simmy was talking to Bertie. The dog was in his usual basket, in defiance of health and safety regulations, cocking an encouraging ear at her muttered commentary on the running of a B&B. 'Nice people,' said Russell.

'That's good.'

'Are you eating with us?'

'If that's all right.'

'Cottage pie in the oven.'

'Lovely.' She took a breath. 'Dad? I don't really get why you went to the police about those men you heard on Monday. It's so out of character. Moxon came to see me about it last night.'

Russell came as close to looking furtive as his open face could manage. 'I thought that might happen. Sorry if it annoyed you. I lay awake for hours on Monday night debating with myself. In the end, I couldn't *not* do it, if you see what I mean.'

'Well now there's been a murder, so I suppose that justifies you.' Her words were only the faintest approximation to her own thoughts and feelings. Rather, they reflected what she assumed was Russell's view. 'You'll be able to provide supporting testimony or whatever they call it.'

'Yes,' said her father thickly. 'I was badly thrown when I heard about that. It never crossed my mind that somebody could be killed.'

'I don't suppose it did. What have they told you about it?'

'Nothing. I've got to go and talk to your friend again tomorrow. Apparently he's tied up all day today interviewing friends and relations of the dead man.'

'I saw a poster on a tree just up the road here – asking for help to find a lost dog. Apparently they're all over the place, and I never noticed. Moxon seemed to think there was a connection between the dead man and dognapping. What do you think?'

'I don't think anything. But Moxon might want us to go and show him where we saw the dead dog on Monday. It probably won't still be there, of course, if we're right about it being in that man's bag. Or if it *is* still there . . .' He shuddered and left the thought unfinished.

'It'll be very nasty. Birds and so forth.' Simmy mirrored his shiver at the image that came to mind. 'Do you think we could find it again, anyway?'

'Oh, yes. It was on that straight part, where we crossed a little beck and saw those tadpoles in a pool. Just a little way before that. Surely you remember?'

'Not as well as you,' she admitted. 'I was too taken up with the view.'

'Your mother thinks I'm losing my wits.'

'She might have a point.'

'Just because I check that we're properly locked up at bedtime, she's diagnosed some sort of syndrome. Pre-Alzheimer's, I imagine. She doesn't acknowledge that *she's* the one out of step with the world. Everybody but her thinks it's entirely reasonable to give some thought to security.'

'I suppose it's the sudden change of character that's disturbed her. You didn't used to worry about that sort of thing.'

'A year ago, I had no *need* to worry. Then you turn up, and suddenly we've got dead bodies all over the place, and hospitals and policemen and I don't know what.'

'So it's my fault.' A low-level irritation was rapidly turning into full-scale anger.

'In a way – yes it is.' Simmy was reminded that none of the usual knee-jerk ploys ever worked when arguing with her father. He was too well focused and too honest. Self-pity, avoidance, accusations all rolled off him as he stuck to his main point.

As usual, she was disarmed. 'I'm sorry,' she said more quietly. 'I know it's been traumatic for you at times. But we've always recovered and carried on as before. It's a shock to me to find how closely I've come to violence, simply by delivering flowers, but there it is. It's all *about* the flowers, really. They're an integral part of the big moments in people's lives. Moments of change and crisis. I can't do anything about that, apart from abandoning the whole business.'

'I know,' said Russell.

Angie joined them five minutes later, flopping down into a kitchen chair. 'You got the easy end of that,' she accused her husband. 'Mine are absolute pigs. I'm going to put rat poison in their scrambled eggs tomorrow.'

It was not a new threat, and it appeared to serve its purpose of making Angie feel better. Politeness was one thing – which she managed quite well – but subservience to demanding and arrogant guests was quite another.

'What did they do?' asked Russell recklessly.

A torrent of grievances followed. The couple had wanted blankets rather than a duvet, Sky channels on the TV, skimmed milk in their tea, two chairs in the room and a whole lot more. 'They don't know they're born,' she raged. 'Haven't they seen the measly facilities most places up here provide? I know plenty who don't give you even *one* chair in their tiny little rooms. Not to mention a whole room downstairs to do as they like, all day long.'

Simmy waited it out with dwindling patience. It was true that Beck View gave much better value than most local establishments. Angie was flexible and accommodating to a fault. She permitted smoking in two of her rooms, and was happy for people to bring their dogs. On balance these concessions attracted more guests than they repelled, but those unwary enough to enter the premises expecting neither cigarette nor dog would sometimes raise loud complaints.

'I gather I'm invited to supper,' she interrupted. 'That would be nice. I was talking to Dad about his report to the police, actually. I am getting it slightly more clear, but it still seems an odd thing to do.'

'Well, it's done now,' said Angie briskly. 'No sense in going on about it. I expect you'll be careful up there until the person who killed that man's caught. I for one am not going to worry about you. Your father doesn't think you're the next victim, or anything like that, but it's not exactly a comfortable situation, is it?'

Simmy felt besieged. 'I'm going to use Kirkstone Pass, to avoid Town End, until it's all been sorted out. I'm hoping I can just stay right out of the whole business. Now, let me tell you about my new assistant. She's a lot more interesting than men fighting in a farmyard.'

Two pairs of eyebrows rose encouragingly.

'She's called Bonnie and she's seventeen. She's leaving school any minute now, without doing A-levels. She's catching up with GCSEs, having missed a lot because she had anorexia. She's very small and thin and fair.'

'Where does she live?' asked Angie.

'Heathwaite. I think she said it's Oakthwaite

Road. Not far from here. There's some sort of family complication because she lives with her aunt. Melanie will tell me about it when I see her, I expect. She's sure to know the whole story.'

'What's the aunt called?'

'Corinne something.'

'Aha! I know who they are,' said Angie in triumph. 'I've seen that girl. She's not her aunt, though. She does fostering. So she's Bonnie's foster mother. She keeps about fifty dogs in cages behind the house. Little fluffy white things. People complain.'

'How do you know it's the same people?'

'I remember the woman saying she'd got a girl living with her, who helps with the work and has been in hospital with an eating disorder. She was obviously worried about it. I had the impression she thought the authorities might blame her for it.'

'But how did you meet her?'

'It's a long story. I had a guest who was looking for a puppy, ideally a Lakeland terrier. We told her there was a shortage of them and she'd have to wait years, but I knew of a dog breeder who always had things to sell. You know what dog people are like – they can never resist going to see puppies, given half a chance. We walked round there, back in February or March, and we all got chatting.'

'I'm not sure how you made the connection with Bonnie so quickly.'

'The anorexia, of course. She was there, looking like a child of about seven. Corinne introduced her and let her show us the dogs. And I remember the name Bonnie

Lawson. I'm very good with names,' she reminded Simmy. 'I have to be, in this job.'

'Did the woman buy a puppy?' asked Russell.

'She did, actually. It was all a bit of a scandal, to my mind. No questions asked, just bundled the poor little scrap into a cardboard box and let it go without a second glance. I'm sure there must be laws against such irresponsible behaviour.'

'Were they living in tiny squalid cages?' Russell looked all set to march out and tackle the disgraceful situation. 'Why didn't you tell me about this before?'

'No, they weren't. It was all quite clean and pleasant. At least as nice as that boarding kennel we used for Bertie. The animals get to run about in the garden, and some are allowed in the house.'

'There can't possibly have been fifty, either,' Simmy said.

'Maybe not quite. There were three litters of puppies, which came to twenty or so. And two or three pregnant bitches. It was really a farming operation. You wonder how they find buyers for so many.'

'They probably don't. I imagine a lot end up in rescues or drowned or abandoned on motorways,' said Russell crossly.

Angie had been laying the table as they talked, and now brought out a generous cottage pie, along with a dish of carrots and peas. 'This is why I didn't tell you about it,' she snapped. 'I knew you'd overreact.'

'Well, I'm fond of dogs,' he protested mildly. 'I don't like to think of them suffering.'

'Bonnie wants to move out, anyway,' said Simmy, to

divert the subject. 'She's talking about using the rooms above the shop. I'm not sure the council would stand for that, would they?'

Both parents fell silent as they absorbed this question. 'She'd be a squatter,' said Angie, after half a minute, with a nostalgic twinkle in her eye. 'Remember them?'

'They haven't gone away. In London, people live in dog kennels and coal sheds and lean-tos under basement steps,' her husband informed her. 'I heard a programme about it.'

'She wouldn't be squatting if I gave her permission, surely?'

'Technically, I think the term would still apply. Best to say nothing about it and tell her to be discreet,' said Angie. 'I promise not to tell anybody.'

Simmy was both amused and exasperated by her mother's automatic assumption that she would permit Bonnie to use the rooms. The idea was still not at all appealing to her, and the more she returned to it, the more objections presented themselves.

The meal was interspersed with reminiscences from Angie about the years she'd spent in London after graduating, and how she'd become friendly with a large group of squatters in Chalk Farm and sometimes stayed overnight in their house. Simmy listened in fascination as the details returned in considerable vividness. It felt like total recall, with the atmosphere of the late 1960s as alien and incomprehensible as the 1860s would have been. 'We were so *free*. Everything seemed possible. We had money, the pill, education. Even the weather seemed fabulous. I remember weekends on the Heath, wearing the tiniest imaginable bikini and having absolutely nothing to worry about. Except men, of course. There was always some trouble over a man. That's one thing that doesn't seem to have changed.'

'But no unwanted pregnancies,' put in Russell. 'At least that was the theory. There were posters in the Underground that said "Every baby a wanted baby" or words to that effect.'

'Very idealistic,' nodded Angie. 'I had two friends who went for abortions, and two more who got some rather nasty sexually transmitted diseases. I count myself lucky I avoided those particular hazards.'

The telephone interrupted them. 'Another couple eager to sample our services,' sighed Russell as Angie went to answer it.

But he was wrong. His wife came back, unsmiling, addressing a space between him and their daughter. 'It's that Moxon man. He wants to come and talk to you both. Now.'

Chapter Nine

A more buoyant man might have manifested satisfaction at finding both his quarries in one room, saving himself a drive out to Troutbeck. But Moxon did not rub his hands together or bounce on his toes or show any signs of enjoying the time and trouble saved. Instead, he sighed and yawned and seemed to have trouble ordering his thoughts.

'Sorry to bother you,' he began. 'I hoped this would wait until the morning, but we need to clear a few things up as quickly as we can.'

Russell was patently wary. He turned his head away and nibbled his lip. 'I was hoping we wouldn't have to involve my daughter,' he mumbled. 'I expected to see you tomorrow.'

'I know. And if she hadn't been here, I might have been persuaded that I only needed to speak to you. But I hadn't much choice in the timing. For a start, we won't need you to lead us up Wansfell Pike after all. Another walker reported that dead dog this afternoon and we've been to remove it. So your theory that it was inside the man's black sack was unfounded.'

'Was it strangled?'

'I'm afraid so. And that makes us think it very probably has something to do with what happened yesterday in Troutbeck.'

'I see,' said Russell with a frown. 'You mean dognapping, I suppose. Do you think something went wrong, and the man got killed while he was trying to steal a dog?'

Simmy had pushed her chair back and was fighting with a succession of clashing emotions. Resistance, resignation, bewilderment and irritation swirled together. The deduction she was reaching was that the bearded man was not a dog kidnapper, or murderer, at least of animals. There was nothing to incriminate him at all, except the fact that he was acquainted with the murdered man, and had seen him the day before he died. And that hardly seemed suspicious.

All she could think was that every conversation seemed to circle around dogs, and however hard she tried, this element reduced the importance of the case for her. Dogs were of secondary significance. Stealing them and even killing them was not so terribly wicked, to her mind. But then, there was also a dead man to factor in. An annoying dead man who must have somehow got in the way of dog abductors and been savagely attacked as a result, or possibly he had been an abductor himself, as her father had said.

'Who was he, then?' she asked, slightly too loudly. 'The man who was killed. I heard he was wounded in his throat.'

'Who told you that?'

'The man with the bag. He accosted me last night when I was in my garden.'

'Accosted?' All three people looked at her in alarm.

'Not physically. But he knew who I was, and deliberately set out to scare me, or so it seemed. I assume he recognised

104

me and Dad from Monday, when we saw him. And I thought perhaps he'd seen you leave my house. He turned up only a few minutes later. And he definitely knew the murdered man. He told me his name. I don't think he lives in Troutbeck, though. I've never seen him around.'

'Travis McNaughton,' said Moxon with a frown. 'What's the bearded man's name, then? We still haven't identified him.'

'Sorry.' Simmy felt foolish and incompetent. 'I didn't ask.'

'Well, he's obviously relevant.'

'Is it true?' asked Angie. 'About the man's throat?'

'His jugular was cut. He bled to death,' said Moxon tightly. 'A local woman found him, and regrettably made it considerably more public than we would have liked. Several local people saw her and the story had already spread before we arrived at the scene.'

'Was he a dognapper?' asked Simmy. 'Is that what it's all about?'

'As far as we can tell, not at all. He came from Glasgow originally, but had lived in Carlisle for most of his life. He drove a red Renault Laguna, with a registration plate matching the one your father gave me yesterday.'

Very little in this résumé of the facts came as a surprise.

'What about his little boy?' asked Simmy. 'Is he back with his mother now? Has she let you question him?'

'He's not so little,' Moxon corrected her. 'He's thirteen. But he's not helping much with the most important questions. All I know is his dad left him on his own in the car while he went for a chat with someone in the pub, on Monday. Then on Tuesday, Travis went off on his own, late morning, leaving the boy in the house by himself.'

'Did he go in the car?' asked Russell.

'Yes, but it's not anywhere in Troutbeck. We still haven't found it.'

'The other man,' said Simmy urgently. 'He must have been meeting the other man. And the boy must know who he is.'

'He says he's got no idea. Never seen him before. He said they dropped him off in a pub car park miles up on the fells. Probably the one at Broad Stone. But nobody up there saw anything, as far as we can discover.'

'You've been very diligent,' said Russell approvingly.

'It's a murder enquiry, Mr Straw. We're obliged to follow every lead, as quickly as we can. Now, I have to ask you, can we be absolutely sure the men you heard were the same men you saw driving away? I know it seems obvious, but as far as actual evidence is concerned, there does appear to be room for doubt.'

Simmy heard her friend Ben's disembodied voice in her ear, stressing the importance of unambiguous evidence in police prosecutions. 'That would mean there were *four* men,' she said, as if making an immense discovery.

'Was the pub busy? A Bank Holiday lunchtime, sunny and mild. I would imagine it might have been.'

'It was, quite,' she conceded.

'So four men either together or in two distinct pairs wouldn't be very surprising.'

Simmy turned to her father. 'This is your testimony, not mine. Why am I answering for you?'

'Why, indeed,' Russell agreed. 'Shall we let the inspector guide us as to just what he needs us to tell him?'

'Thank you,' said Moxon, looking as if he might well have abandoned all hope of retaining control of the conversation, without some help. 'There is clearly some scope for confusion over what you saw and heard. But the fact that you supplied – yesterday morning – the registration number of a car belonging to a man who was killed yesterday *afternoon* makes you of considerable significance. Is there any more you can tell me about what you heard – or saw?' The detective glanced at Simmy and she thought he might be wishing her elsewhere.

'I heard two men, on the other side of a wall, when I came out of the Gents. I remember the exact words. I repeated them to Simmy minutes after hearing them, and they've stayed in my mind. "The old man's always out on a Tuesday, so that's our chance. Tim can be the lookout." I've gone over it a thousand times, and can't make any other conclusion than that it was a plan for a crime.'

'And you're sure they didn't know you were listening?'

'There was a wall between us,' Russell repeated.

'And you never saw them – while they were talking, I mean?'

'I saw a shadow. I've just remembered that. You know how the garden's on a different level – lower than the pub itself?'

Moxon shook his head. 'Sorry – I haven't been there for years. I'll take your word for it, though.'

'Yes. Well, it is. There's a curved wall and some steps. As I went down to find Simmy, I caught part of a shadow that must have been cast by one of the men. I did try to get sight of them, but there were bushes in the way. It's difficult to describe,' he finished regretfully. 'I didn't want *them* to see *me*, you see. They might have realised I'd heard them.'

Moxon nodded patiently. 'Did the shadow show anything that might be useful?'

'A hat, with a peak. At least, that's what it looked like. I imagine a defence lawyer might cast doubt on that – saying it could have been his hair or an overhanging branch or something.'

'But you think it was a peaked cap?'

'I do, Inspector. Yes, I do.'

'The dead man was wearing a peaked cap,' said Moxon heavily.

Simmy's mind performed a dramatic volte-face. From one second to the next, she began to care and to care seriously. Until then she had told herself it was all imagination and whispers, coincidence and distraction. Now it became real and sharply focused. She also drew instant deductions.

'Only two men, then. The same two men each time. Except, the one I saw driving the car didn't have a hat on.'

'You're sure of that?'

'I think so. His hair was colourless, light brown. I wouldn't have seen that under a cap, would I?'

'He could have taken it off. The car would have been very warm inside.' Moxon was plainly sticking to the same track, dismissing awkward objections. 'Maybe he was wearing it as a sort of disguise, which he didn't need any more.'

'And he put it on again to go dognapping next day,' said Russell. 'Except you say he wasn't a dognapper, after all,' he remembered. 'That's a pity. How can you be sure?'

'And you might never find the other man.' asked Simmy. 'Except . . . my friend with the beard probably knows him. He saw them both. I think he was actually waving to them, at the pub.'

Moxon had been quick to observe the change in her. 'Excellent,' he applauded, ignoring Russell's query. 'We need as detailed a description of him as you can manage.' And this time, he very nearly did rub his hands together.

She managed rather poorly. Given that the man was quite possibly a murderer, her testimony was unnervingly important. 'He's about my age. Looks as if he works outdoors. Long, thin legs. The beard's quite long and unkempt. And he said he worked with Travis's brother!' She recalled this detail triumphantly. 'I think that might have been in Grasmere, but I'm not sure.'

'Very good. What else did he say?'

'That Travis was decent and harmless and nobody would ever have a reason to kill him.' She shook her head. 'He seemed really upset about it. I don't think he did it.'

Moxon pursed his lips. 'Maybe he knows who did, though.'

'I doubt it, somehow. He seemed bewildered by it. But he wasn't really a nice man,' she finished.

'Why? What do you mean?'

'He didn't like me and Dad having seen him, and then getting the police involved. I think there really might have been something sinister in that black bag. And I think he's worried he'll get caught, because of us.'

'We really need to find him.'

'Isn't there anyone at the Mortal Man who can help? Don't they all know each other?'

Moxon shook his head. 'If they were farmers, all getting together on market day, that would be one thing. But we're not aware of any sort of identifiable network that includes Mr McNaughton. Of course, it's early days.' He sighed wearily and Simmy was reminded that his health had not been especially good even before his troubles in Coniston. 'He was thirty-three, often out of work, lived in a small rented cottage near Grasmere, by himself. Has an ex-partner and son still in Scotland, as well as his mother. Usual story. The boy sees his dad twice a year, if he's lucky. Well, not so lucky for him that his dad's getting murdered coincided with him being here on a visit.'

'But he could afford to run a car,' said Russell.

Moxon nodded. 'And not the sort of car you'd expect, either. Blokes like him generally have a van, or a pickup.'

'For stealing things, you mean?' asked Simmy.

'He hasn't got a police record,' Moxon told her, with mild severity. 'The idea that he was a burglar doesn't have much traction. It doesn't have *any*, other than what you overheard,' he said to Russell.

'So what was he doing in that farmyard?'

'We're still trying to work that out. The forensic bods think he might have been having a pee. They found traces behind a wall.'

Russell grimaced. 'Do you think his killer saw him and drove in behind him, then cornered him, before slashing his throat? Where would the car – cars, probably – have been? Wouldn't somebody have noticed? And who drove the Renault away afterwards?'

'Dad!' protested Simmy faintly.

Moxon seemed to think he owed it to Russell to engage in the speculations, even if it went against his inclinations.

'It needn't have made too much of a commotion. There wouldn't have been many people about, anyway. Only one couple visited Town End yesterday afternoon, at the time we think it happened. The killer could quietly have driven away – but what happened to the Renault remains the big mystery. Poor Mrs Herbert, who found the body, chanced to coincide with a group of walkers who were meeting outside the house. She practically collapsed in their arms, and they took her into Town End as the closest place. That was at two o'clock. It made it worse that she knew McNaughton. He'd built a wall for her, apparently, only a few weeks ago.'

'What was *she* doing in the farmyard?' asked Russell.

'She was picking elderflowers for a cordial she makes every year. She likes to get it as soon as it appears, and this week's sunshine has got it going nicely. You have to pick the blossom the moment the buds open, before they go bitter.'

'She told you all that?'

'Couldn't stop her. Some people react like that – they obsess about something totally other than violent death, as a means of coping. She hadn't found much, mind you. Her basket was near the body, with three flower heads in it.'

Simmy groaned, thinking that the woman might never face another elderflower, because of the associations. Moxon turned his attention back to her. 'Would you recognise the other man in the car, if you saw him again?'

She tried to conjure the face in her mind's eye. 'I don't know. I probably could pick him out in an identity parade, but I don't think I'd know him if I met him in the street. Not unless I was actually looking for him, if you see what I mean.'

'Hmm,' said Moxon. 'That's what people usually say.'

111

'Perhaps I would know him in profile,' she said. 'He was rather pale and had a small chin.'

'Clothes?'

'No idea. I never notice people's clothes.'

'But tall, you think?'

'How tall was the other one? Travis McSomething?'

Moxon frowned and tapped a front tooth. 'I don't know exactly. I'd guess something like five eight or nine.'

'I thought he was the shorter one, at the time. But you can't really tell when a person's sitting down, can you?'

'It must be a strange business,' said Russell thoughtfully. 'The way you have to rely on something as precarious as human memory and observation. Even though Simmy and I made a little game of it, and even wrote things down, I'm not sure we'd give very dependable testimony in a court of law. The car number is the only hard fact.'

'The part about the cap has been helpful,' Moxon reminded him.

Russell smiled faintly. 'But not much else. If they *were* planning a burglary, that doesn't seem especially relevant. Either they were new at it, or they were highly successful at getting away with it, given that they didn't have a police record.'

'*He* didn't have one – McNaughton, I mean. The other chap could be different. That's why it would be useful if Mrs Brown could have a look at some mugshots for us, just in case he or the man with the beard are in our system.'

Simmy groaned again at the prospect. Time was going to be very short the next day as it was, without spending hours looking at photos of hardened criminals. 'The people at the pub will have got a much better look at both of them,' she argued. 'And they probably even know who they are. I only got a quick glimpse of them through a car window.'

'Nobody's got anything helpful to say,' he sighed. 'They can't even remember who we're talking about.'

'You showed them a picture of Travis?'

'Nobody recognises it. And they're all adamant that there has been no sign of any dogs being kidnapped in Troutbeck. It's a very dog-friendly pub, and they seemed to take exception to the very idea. Personally I'm starting to doubt that it's relevant – dognapping, I mean. The frustrating fact is, we were within an inch of making some arrests on that front, when all this blew up. Now we haven't got enough pairs of hands for both that and the homicide. If we could find some link between the two, that'd help, of course,' he added reflectively. 'Which your observations led me to hope for, briefly.'

'It really did look like a dead animal in that bag,' Simmy insisted. 'Heavy, lumpy. I was even sure I could see where stiff legs were making the whole thing awkward to carry.'

'There's nothing to say there couldn't have been *two* dead dogs,' said Moxon with a sigh. 'To my knowledge, at least five have going missing this year, just from our local area. But they all date back to March or earlier, and they were all returned safe and sound. All the same, their people were extremely upset about it.'

'It's a rotten thing to do,' said Russell feelingly. 'The dogs must be so bewildered and frightened. I don't imagine they look after them very well.'

'They seemed to survive pretty well, actually. It's the *people* who suffer lasting trauma.'

'And you haven't caught anybody?'

'Not yet, no.'

All three fell silent, as they contemplated the limitations of the police and the wickedness of humanity.

Simmy left her parents' house at eight-thirty and was home fifteen minutes later. It was dark, with rain predicted for the following day. The uncertainty of May evenings was all part of the Lakeland experience, she was discovering. One day it might be light until nine, and the next, it was dusky gloom at seven. It all depended on the degree of cloud cover. It comprised a substantial proportion of many a conversation in the village shop and other points of local contact. Nervous drivers would dither as to whether to venture out, not knowing what level of visibility they would meet on the way home.

She switched on the lights in both the downstairs rooms and pulled the curtains closed. This was not a regular routine, but she had found herself, in recent months, disliking the idea that persons outside might see into the house and track her movements. She could not rid herself of the image of the man in the passenger seat of the Renault as it left the pub on Monday. In his forties, with dark hair cut short and taller than his companion. She had lodged those few details by voicing them aloud to her father, and in so doing had irrevocably lost many others. She had admitted to Moxon that she was far from sure that she would know him again, which made her virtually useless as a witness.

It all went round and round in her head, the presence of the murder scene feeling a lot closer than the half-mile it actually was. Her mind dwelt obsessively on the mystery of violent death. Once before she had witnessed the death of a man she had known, albeit briefly. This time it was even more brief, but the impossible change from living to dead carried the same impact. Accepting Moxon's certainty that it was the same man she had seen, she kept recalling his hands and strong forearms on the steering wheel, swinging the car around the gravelled area and out into the little road. Muscle and blood and all five senses alive and fully functioning – and now not. Now he was inert and in all essentials gone forever. It happened every minute of every day, around the world and it remained as profoundly inexplicable as it always had. No wonder that nobody willingly dwelt on it, that the conspiracy to ignore and conceal it explained a great deal of human behaviour. It made one's head turn to jelly and one's flesh crawl with dread.

Out of a strong but opaque instinct, she phoned the one person who might have a reassuring approach to such musings. He answered promptly.

'Sorry to call so late,' she said. 'It's probably past your bedtime.'

Ben's snort of derision made her feel better already. 'What do you want?' he asked, not quite rudely.

'I saw Moxon a little while ago, at my parents' place. I thought you might be interested.'

'Yeah? Yeah! I am. Of course. What did he say?'

'The dead man is called Travis McGinty – something like that. He must be the man my father and I saw on Monday, driving away from the Mortal Man. So our descriptions are important to the investigation.'

'Okay. Didn't we know all that already? They put his

name on the news today anyway. It's McNaughton, not McGinty. Scottish not Irish. Why do you sound so excited all of a sudden?'

'I don't know. I guess it just took a while to realise that it matters. I mean – that if I can help catch a murderer I should do all I can. And it's very local, after all. It's making me nervous to think he's out there somewhere.'

'Presumably he has no idea you and your father saw him and can describe him. Make sure Moxon doesn't visit you in a cop car and make it obvious to the whole of Troutbeck.'

'Too late. And there are *two* men to worry about. Not only did I see one of them very clearly, I actually talked to him last night. And he might easily have seen Moxon coming here. The other one probably didn't notice me, thank goodness.'

'Well, I expect you're safe enough. They'll be off and away, miles from here by now.'

'You don't sound very surprised.' She wasn't sure whether to sulk or be glad about that.

'I already worked out that the men you and your dad saw must be right in the middle of it all. Otherwise, why would Moxon take any notice of what you told him? You're telling me now that the victim was one of them? So the other one has to be the prime suspect. Doesn't sound very complicated.' His disappointment was palpable.

'There's a lot they don't know yet. In fact, I keep reminding myself that the only actual *fact* is the car. If Dad and I hadn't mucked about taking its number, there'd be no proof at all.'

'They'll find plenty, don't worry. There's sure to be lots

116

more stuff going on that we haven't caught up with yet.'

The *yet* and the *we* both reverberated. Again she had difficulty in reading her own reactions. The prospect of Ben conducting his own amateur investigation with every expectation that she would share each step of his reasoning was wearying. Ben knew a lot about the law and obscure police practices, but he could not claim to have ever actually *solved* anything. He made suggestions and drew diagrams and hovered as close as possible to the action, but seldom anything more. Moxon tolerated him far more patiently than any other senior detective would, probably because Ben was, in the final analysis, extremely serious. He wasn't getting involved for thrills or mischief, but because he wanted to learn as much as possible before embarking on his degree course. 'Think of it as work experience,' he had invited Moxon, more than once.

'I'm going to be horribly busy over the next two days,' Simmy told him. 'So don't expect much backup from me.'

'Backup? In what sense do you mean that?'

'Oh, I don't know. I won't even manage to *listen* to you, and certainly won't be able to take you anywhere.'

'So why did you phone me?' He seemed genuinely mystified.

'I'm not sure, really. I got myself in a bit of a state, I suppose, and wanted to hear your sensible voice.' The anomaly of a mature woman seeking solace from a teenage boy was impossible to ignore. But there had been other occasions when Ben's friendship had proved therapeutic, however strange that might seem to other people.

'So what's with Bonnie Lawson?' He suddenly changed

the subject. 'Have you any idea what you've taken on?'

'Probably not, but if Melanie vouches for her, it's got to be all right. Don't you think?'

'Melanie's sister was Bonnie's best friend, a bit ago. There's sure to be an agenda, and I'm not sure your interests are on it.'

'Don't say that. She asked if she could use the rooms over the shop.' This was a continuing niggle that Simmy couldn't shift.

'What for? To *live*?'

'Yes.'

'What about the dog?'

'What dog?'

'She's got her own dog. A fluffy thing that goes everywhere with her. They had to let her have it with her in hospital. Surely you heard about that? The paper did a story about it, because she says it saved her life.'

'She hasn't mentioned a dog,' said Simmy faintly. 'She didn't bring it to work with her.'

'She will,' said Ben. A voice could be heard in the background as one of his relatives shouted for him. 'Look – I've got to go. See you Friday or Saturday, maybe. I'll call in and chat, if you've stopped being busy by then.'

'Bye, then. And thanks.'

Because it was definitely the case that she now had a whole new set of things to think about, and for that she ought probably to be grateful.

Chapter Ten

Cynthia Mossop was dressed when Simmy delivered the second lot of flowers in two days marking her birthday. 'Oh, you poor thing!' she cried. 'Coming all this way twice, just because my friends can't get their act together.'

'All part of the job,' said Simmy. 'Although the weather could be better.'

The weather was in fact atrocious. Rain sheeted down, rendering the outlines of the fells and lakes fuzzy. The roads were splashy and the sky almost low enough to touch. Above Staveley the slopes of Hugill Fell were running with rivulets intent on joining the River Kent, which was the main feature of the valley. At least Ninian wouldn't be waiting for her again this morning, she thought. While in no way unhappy to see him as a general rule, she was much too busy for him today.

The car had no allotted space behind the shop, which meant finding somewhere on the street that permitted unrestricted parking. As a general habit, she left it in Lake Road, close to her parents' house, but sometimes she was forced to use one that turned off the larger road. It was less than five minutes' walk to the shop, whatever happened. This morning, the rain meant more people had travelled by car than usual, whatever their reason for coming to Windermere. She parked in a handy space in a side road, grabbing an umbrella from the back seat and trotting quickly into the town centre.

Once in the shop, she judged she had fifteen minutes to herself before Bonnie arrived, and she made good use of the time by checking and noting every order for the next day's funeral. In total, there were fifteen tributes, eight of which had yet to be constructed. Everything had to be meticulously controlled on this momentous occasion. While weddings might require a larger quantity of flowers than this, the urgency associated with a funeral and the horrors that could result from a mistake made this her most demanding experience since opening the business. Nothing could be forgotten because there were no second chances with a funeral.

When Bonnie did arrive, she was soaking wet. Her skimpy hair was plastered to her head, making her look even smaller and younger than before. 'Haven't you got a hood?' Simmy demanded, sounding like her own mother. 'Look at you! Your *legs*.' The girl was wearing a short jacket that had obviously not been designed for real weather. It had to be peeled off like a banana skin. Bonnie held it out at arm's length.

'You're completely drenched,' said Simmy, still not quite able to believe the extent of the wetness. 'I've never seen such a wet person.'

'I'm okay. It's warm rain. I rather like it,' came the careless reply. 'I did have a nice big mac, but I couldn't find it this morning.'

'Well you'll have to handle the customers for me today, if you think you're up to it. Melanie did say she'd try and come in for a bit, later on, although she's very unreliable these days. She knows I'm going to be awfully busy, so I guess she will turn up at some point.'

'I'll do my best,' said Bonnie, squaring her wet shoulders. 'I can shout for you if I need help.'

'Let me go and find a towel.' She came back with an inadequate offering from the toilet at the back and briskly rubbed the girl's hair. 'My mum says she knows your aunt. Corinne – is that her name? She went to look at some puppies you were selling.'

'They're all gone now.' Bonnie pushed away the towel. Her voice echoed with melancholy. 'We were closed down just after Easter.'

'Closed down? Who by?'

'Local authority. The RSPCA had a complaint about us, and said we were overcrowded. There's an injunction. They only let us keep Spike and Millie, because they're both neutered. We're not allowed to breed again.'

'You've got a dog of your own, I hear. Ben said something about it.'

'That's Spike. They wouldn't dare take him away from me, after all the publicity.'

'What sort is he?' asked Simmy, not really interested in the reply.

'He's a funny mixture. His mother was a shih-tzu, and

121

his father was a cross between a poodle and a golden retriever. He's mostly white and fluffy, but quite big. We had his mum, Delilah. She died last year.'

'Well, you couldn't possibly have a dog with you in the rooms upstairs. It makes it even more impossible.'

'Why?'

'Well – it'd bark. And those metal stairs would be hopelessly tricky for a dog.'

'He'd be fine with them. He's very agile.'

'I'm not going to argue with you about it now. There's too much to do. You'll have to go home and get more clothes. I can't have you dripping all day. Look at the puddles you've made already. How long would it take you?'

'Probably about forty minutes, there and back. But I can't do that. It'll confuse Spike if I show up and then go again. He hates us being separated. I'll be all right. I'm not cold.'

'You will be.'

Bonnie simply stood where she was, fluffing out her hair and making soft squelching sounds with her sodden trainers. 'Oh, there's something I forgot to tell you. I'll be going to the funeral tomorrow. Miss Hodge was really nice to Corinne and me last year. I ought to go and pay my respects, because Corinne says she can't make it. I won't stay for the thing afterwards, though.'

Simmy digested this carefully. 'Am I missing something?' she wondered. 'You seem to know a lot of people. And they all know you.'

'Oh, I'm nobody special. In fact, that's my motto. Little Bonnie Lawson from a big untidy family, that's me. Nobody pays her any attention.'

Simmy felt a growing impatience. 'I'm not sure I believe that. It's not the impression I've been getting so far. Now, for heaven's sake, what are we going to do about your clothes? There's absolutely nothing here.' She entertained wild thoughts of going across the street to the large lingerie shop and trying to buy a warm vest as being better than nothing.

'I could try phoning Mel and see if she could bring me something when she comes in.'

'She's twice as big as you. Nothing would fit.' *Three times as big, more like it*, she thought.

'I mean, something of Chloe's. Mel's sister. She's my friend. We were best friends from Year Eight on. That's how Melanie knows me. Didn't she say that on Tuesday?'

'Possibly. Phone her, then, and see if she can help. And tell her to bring a brolly so you can get home again.'

'It'll have stopped raining by then. Sorry to be such a nuisance, Simmy. I didn't think, did I? I just set out, and sloshed through the puddles, thinking how lovely it all was. I never dreamt anybody would mind.'

'Your aunt won't be too happy if you get pneumonia.' Simmy vaguely suspected that someone so malnourished might well be unusually vulnerable to all sorts of infections and problems.

'She's not actually my aunt. She's just Corinne, okay. I'll explain it all to you sometime.'

Simmy refrained from admitting that she knew this already, and more besides. She almost ran through to the back room, acutely aware of having lost a precious half-hour and throwing her schedule as a result. There'd be no time to stop for lunch, at this rate. And that brought to mind the other problem surrounding Bonnie. The girl was supposed to eat. Simmy had made that assumption the day before, and now felt obliged to ensure that she did so. Irritation blossomed as the numerous responsibilities associated with her new assistant weighed her down. It felt like a real imposition, that she had not invited. It was all Melanie's fault, she decided. If and when she showed up, Simmy would have a word with her. If she had time.

The two main floral tributes for the funeral were going to require considerable care. A wire frame had to be constructed for a cushion of blooms intended to sit on the middle of the coffin's lid. It would be the focal point of the procession from Barbara Hodge's house to the church, and then out to the graveyard. Every flower had to be precisely positioned and anchored, and a place found for the little ceramic addition that Valerie had supplied. It would take well over an hour to make.

There were voices out in the shop, as far as Simmy could tell discussing something quite calmly. She resisted the temptation to have a look, and pushed away a mental picture of Bonnie as a dripping object of surprised concern to any customer. There was every chance that the girl would overcome any awkwardness with her blithe manner, but it was still potentially embarrassing. For the first time, Simmy saw personal implications in the fact that Bonnie seemed well known throughout the town. Word would already be spreading that she had found a position in Persimmon Petals and now there would be additional spice to the story. *That Bonnie Lawson was soaking wet in the flower shop*

this morning. Like a drowned rat she was. And her such a
fragile little thing – you'd think she would be better looked
after, wouldn't you? And Simmy would look bad, as a
neglectful mother figure.

She quashed these thoughts down and carried on with
the floral cushion. The problem was that while it presented
a technical challenge, it did not occupy her whole mind.
After the first dozen flower heads had been put into position,
the rest fell into place almost automatically. Nimble fingers
pressed them into the mesh and checked they were properly
anchored. Every few minutes she stood back to examine the
effect. It was destined to be an impressive piece of work. A
shame, she thought, that the dead woman wouldn't see it.
Funeral flowers served many purposes, their quantity and
quality dictated mostly by the preferences of the deceased.
Ironic, Simmy always thought. And really rather wasteful.
There was still a slight awkwardness as to the subsequent
fate of tributes, when the cremation or burial was over.
Relatives took them home reluctantly, and old people's
residences would often plead for respite as yet another batch
of flowers was deposited on them. In a busy season they
could find themselves inundated. Undertakers factored in
post-funeral flower deliveries as part of the overall service.

And still, waiting sneakily behind these trains of thought,
was the fact of a murder in Troutbeck. Ben would probably
be industriously seeking out further information from his
network of contacts. His brother's friend worked in the
mortuary where post-mortems were carried out. Melanie
maintained a lopsided relationship with a police constable
and passed any snippets directly to Ben. The boy was adept

at tracking online news reports and gossip. Before long he would be apprised of a great many details. And there would be no chance of preventing him from sharing them with her. She had, after all, rashly invited him to do exactly that.

Her own shaky analysis of what had happened was along the lines of a dognapping episode gone wrong, in spite of Moxon's doubts about that. Either that or a burglary. She visualised a scenario where the criminals had been discovered and chased by an irate householder into the empty farmyard. But there her imagination failed. Surely nobody could be so irate as to slash a man's throat with a sharp implement? And where had the second felon been throughout the chase? He, then, had taken against his companion for some reason, and attacked him in a murderous frenzy.

She tried to force her thoughts on to another track. Whatever had happened, the police would surely have little difficulty in resolving the matter. Issues of forensic evidence; finding witnesses to who was where when; examining decomposing canine bodies and an investigation into the wider world of animal theft would all eventually receive their due attention, and order would be restored. None of it would require any further assistance from Simmy or her father, or so she hoped. There was every prospect of an arrest and charge that very day, she told herself, with outrageous optimism.

It was quiet again in the shop, and Simmy was thirsty. Breakfast had been several hours ago, after all. Again she felt burdened by the apparent requirements of her new assistant. She ought to force Bonnie to eat a biscuit or something. She ought to have done much more than that, at the outset – such as contacting the girl's legal guardian and checking that it was all right with them for her to be working in the shop. The casual arrangement had seemed entirely unremarkable at first, but by this, the third day, a whole lot of complications were starting to dawn. Bonnie's imperviousness to heavy rain was alarming, for one thing. And Simmy had been lax in failing to get her dry. Now the cushion was finished, she could breathe more easily. None of the other orders was for anything so demanding. She filled the kettle and set it boiling, and went out to the shop.

'Tea or coffee?' she asked.

'Oh – neither, thanks. I mainly just drink water, or juice.'

'You had tea yesterday.'

'I mean, in the mornings. Sorry – you'll get used to my silly ways. Don't worry about it.'

'Did you get Melanie? Is she bringing clothes?' The girl looked no less wet after an hour or more. 'Who was that in the shop just now?'

'Oh, just somebody buying a mixed bunch. It was easy so I didn't bother you. She paid with cash.'

'Was she surprised at how wet you are?'

'I made a joke about it. She said she remembered walking through a downpour in London years ago, and what fun it had been.'

'Hmmm.' Simmy felt middle-aged and dour. She had never willingly walked through a downpour in London or anywhere else. Getting wet had always struck her as a highly undesirable experience, especially when wearing normal clothes. Even swimming wasn't her favourite activity.

'Melanie said she'd be here about eleven for a couple of hours. She sounded a bit stressed out, actually. Something to do with the car, I think.'

'She's always stressed about that car. I'll leave all the computer stuff for her, then. She can check for new orders and sort out tomorrow's deliveries for me. I need to get back to making the next funeral wreath.'

'Can I see what you've done so far?'

'If you want.'

Simmy stood back diffidently as Bonnie admired the cushion. 'It's fabulous!' she squealed. 'I could never manage anything like that. Where did you learn to do it?'

'I took a course, before moving up here, but mainly it's trial and error, and practice. I had to look through my notes to see exactly how to get started, I must admit. This is only the third one of this style I've ever done.'

Bonnie leant close to the massed white chrysanthemums with a tasteful spray of rosebuds and freesias in one corner. 'It smells gorgeous, as well. What a lovely thing. How much did the person have to pay for this?'

It was a fair question, for someone intending to work for her, but Simmy winced at the directness. 'A hundred pounds,' she said. 'You have to factor in the time it takes.'

'Oh, yes! That's obvious. Valerie's going to love it – and how clever you've been with her little blue flower!'

Simmy was rather proud of the way she'd added the porcelain fragment to the rosebuds and freesias. 'It looks okay, doesn't it?'

'More than okay. Absolutely brilliant.'

Too late, Simmy remembered that Bonnie had known

Barbara Hodge, as had probably her closest friends and relations. 'You know Valerie, do you?'

'Not really. I've heard a bit of the gossip about her, same as everybody else. Corinne says—' she was interrupted by the telephone, and cocked an eyebrow at Simmy to check whether she should answer it.

'No, let me,' said Simmy.

It was the woman who was getting married that weekend, efficiently running through everything she was expecting the florist to provide, and when. Simmy rummaged for the checklist she had already made, and compared it with the bride's requirements. All was in order, none of it unduly demanding.

'Wow!' Bonnie said, when she'd finished. 'You really see life in this job, don't you. I never dreamt you got so much of the emotional stuff, right in your face.'

'It came as rather a surprise to me, at first,' Simmy admitted. 'What were we talking about?'

'Valerie Rossiter. She'll be lonely without Miss Hodge. Corinne says they were joined at the hip. It's sad that one of them had to die so young.'

Simmy's eyebrows lifted. It was unusual for a teenager to regard a person in her sixties as 'young'. 'She was sixty-four,' she pointed out.

'Oh, yes, but she always seemed much less than that. And most people live to be ninety now, don't they. So really it *is* young. And Valerie's barely fifty. What's she going to do now?'

Simmy shook her head. She wasn't sure what she made of Valerie Rossiter. She had seemed pleasant enough, and was obviously suffering. But the death had after all come as no great surprise, with ample time for preparations and farewells. 'She's young enough to start again in a new life,' she said. 'Which I gather is what she did ten years ago. She seems a pretty capable person to me.'

'Capable doesn't come into it,' said Bonnie, making Simmy feel oddly heartless and insensitive. But she was proud of the floral cushion.

'We'll need to keep this cool in here until tomorrow. Don't touch it, will you?'

Bonnie moved back. Her trainers squelched at every step. 'Okay,' she snapped defensively. 'I wasn't going to hurt it.'

'I didn't mean . . .' Irritation rose to the surface again. 'Have a drink, will you, and go and wait for Melanie. She won't be long now.'

The small room was always crowded if two people occupied it at once. With the mass of funeral flowers taking up every surface, and overhanging in places, it was almost impossible to move without knocking into something. Even with Bonnie's small stature, it felt dangerous. 'Sorry,' Simmy said. 'I'm just so scared we'll send it all crashing to the floor. I've got everything precisely organised, you see.' She edged over to the tiny kitchen corner. 'Let me get you some water and a biscuit, okay?'

Bonnie removed herself and Simmy followed quickly with a tray. 'I don't want you worrying about my food intake,' Bonnie said firmly. 'It doesn't help. I know what I'm doing.'

'Sorry,' said Simmy again. 'I really ought to speak to

someone about it, I suppose. I mean – you're under eighteen, which probably makes for a whole lot of employment complications. I'll need to check the paperwork when I get a minute.'

'Sounds like a hassle.' Bonnie looked forlorn and pale, with her hair in lank tails and her clothes all stuck to her. She was shivering, too, Simmy noticed with alarm.

'Not really. I just need to find a bit of time. Oh, Lord, you've really got to change those clothes. It's not at all warm in here. You're bound to catch a chill. I should have sent you home. I should have *taken* you home.' Her shortcomings crowded in on her, and a feeling of harassment and frustration flowed through her.

'No, you shouldn't. It's my own fault. I'll be fine as soon as Mel gets here.' They both looked at the door as if they might conjure Melanie into existence.

Instead, causing Simmy a surge of panic, Detective Inspector Moxon came in.

'I'm dreadfully busy this morning,' she blurted before he'd closed the door. 'Whatever you want will have to wait.' She remembered his request that she examine pictures of known burglars. 'Sorry,' she grimaced. 'You want me to go to the police station, I suppose.'

Moxon merely gave her a forbearing smile. 'I haven't come to see you. It's Miss Lawson I need to talk to,' he said.

Chapter Eleven

'Me?' Bonnie showed no sign of being worried by the attentions of a police detective. 'But why?'

'If you could come with me, I'll try to explain.' Then he noticed the state she was in. 'Why are you so wet?'

'It's raining,' Bonnie pointed out, without a hint of sarcasm. 'Do I really have to go with you? Am I allowed to without a responsible adult? I'm only seventeen, you know.'

Simmy hovered helplessly. A vague association came to mind, from TV dramas involving young prostitutes. Horrified at her own thought processes, she tried to push the idea away. But something about Bonnie's confident defiance suggested a ready familiarity with the limitations of police powers. But then, Melanie would probably behave in the same way, and Ben certainly would. Perhaps their entire generation had grown up with an acute awareness of their rights and a refusal to be intimidated.

Moxon sighed. 'Your foster mother will be there as chaperone. Everything's been arranged. It's nothing to worry about.'

'I prefer to call her my aunt,' said Bonnie stiffly.

Simmy found herself thinking, rather wildly, *At least he can't be intending to charge her with the murder of a burglar.* In the circumstances, that appeared to be the worst-case scenario.

'Whatever you call her, she's *in loco parentis.* That's good enough for us.'

'I promise you I haven't done anything. And I can't go like this, can I? We're waiting for Mel to bring me some dry clothes. Why can't you ask me whatever it is here? What's so important, anyway?'

Moxon glanced thoughtfully at Simmy. She did her best to look responsible and discreet. 'I can go into the other room, if it helps,' she offered.

He shook his head and addressed the girl. 'We want you to look at some pictures, that's all. They're on our computer. People we think you might recognise after that trouble you had with the dogs.'

'Oh . . . Right.' Bonnie, who had not seemed especially tense, now became positively buoyant. 'Sounds like fun.' She paused. 'But why is it suddenly so urgent? The thing with Spike happened months ago now.'

Moxon just sighed and said nothing.

Simmy clamped her lips together, to prevent herself from asking questions of her own. If Moxon himself had come for Bonnie, that made it obvious that he wanted her for something connected to the murder investigation – which he had strongly implied the previous evening bore no connection to the dognappings. Then she recalled his bemoaning the fact that there was no way they could conduct both investigations at once, and the idea occurred that he was contriving to combine them, in order to make best use of manpower. Was that ethical? Or even rational? Or had something just happened to suggest that there was, after all, a link?

'I can see your mind working,' he told her, with a little smile.

She took it as an invitation. 'Well, yes. Are you now thinking the murdered man *was* after dogs, after all?'

He smiled again, an annoying smile that told her nothing. 'I can't disclose what we're thinking,' he said.

'I see. Well, I don't know anything about the incident that Bonnie was involved in, do I? It doesn't sound very significant, from what you've said.' She was deliberately goading him, surprised to find herself so cross.

'I don't mind,' said Bonnie, in a squeaky voice. It sounded like a quote from somewhere, or a family catchphrase, which Simmy found even more irritating. The girl added, 'It was a horrible thing to do, trying to steal Spike and Millie. You should have taken more notice of me at the time. I *told* you I'd seen one of them. I would have absolutely *died* if Spike had been nabbed. And look at how frantic Barbara Hodge was when they took her gorgeous Roddy last year. It was so lucky they got him back.'

'Miss Hodge?' Moxon frowned. 'The one who—'

'Right. Whose funeral's tomorrow. I guess she never did report it to the police. The men told her not to, same as with everybody. They said they'd find ways to get revenge if anyone went to the cops. There are loads more of them than you know about.'

'But Miss Hodge was a pillar of the community,' said

Simmy. 'Surely she wouldn't have been scared of that sort of threat?'

'She was ill. She got a lot worse, because of the worry about Roddy. I s'pose she didn't see much point in reporting it.'

'How do you know all this?' Moxon demanded.

'Corinne gets to know most of the dog stories around here. She's still doing the classes and all that, even if they've stopped her breeding.'

'But she never saw the man who took your dogs?'

'No, it was all me,' said Bonnie proudly. 'I screamed the place down, and Spike and Millie howled and barked, and he just dropped them and ran. He must have been a complete idiot to go for those two in the first place.' She looked from Moxon to Simmy and back. 'But it's not him who was murdered, is it?'

'Not as far as we know. You can help us settle that for certain.'

Bonnie preened. 'Hey! That makes me feel important.'

Both the adults laughed at her.

Then Simmy remembered something else. 'I thought it was *me* who was meant to be looking at pictures of criminals. The man in the car and the one with the beard.'

He inclined his head and looked at her from under his brows. 'You only caught a glimpse. Miss Lawson got a much better look. We decided to start with her.'

'Are you thinking it's the same man?'

'There you go again. I can't make you privy to what we're thinking. For obvious reasons.'

'Sorry,' she said mulishly. 'But I'm busy, and this is all very confusing, and Bonnie's soaking wet.'

'Don't panic, Simmy,' said Bonnie, infuriatingly.

'I'm not *panicking*.' But she was. The funeral wreaths were calling to her from the back room and time was rushing by alarmingly. 'I just—'

Then Melanie walked in, her arms full of bags and a brolly and her head covered with a voluminous hood for good measure. When she'd discarded it all, she was perfectly dry underneath. The threesome watched her in relief. Even DI Moxon had always found Melanie Todd a reassuring presence. He understood her and her background and her place in the community, which was more than he could say about Ben or Simmy.

'Bloody hell, you're wet!' Mel said to Bonnie. 'What have you been *doing*?'

'Just take her somewhere and change her,' said Simmy, as if the girl were a small baby. Then she paused. 'But where? There's no space in the back room.'

Melanie made her own special face, which, thanks to an artificial eye, conveyed scorn better than anyone else could. When only one eye rolled up to the sky, the message was somehow twice as powerful. 'She can sort herself out in the loo,' she said, handing a bulky plastic bag to Bonnie. 'There's pants as well, but no bra.'

'I don't wear a bra. Why would I?'

All three females glanced at Moxon, who stared at a bunch of tulips and said nothing. Melanie snorted her amusement. 'Why are you here?' she asked him.

'He's taking Bonnie in for questioning,' Simmy answered for the detective, who gave a strangled sound of protest.

Bonnie trotted off to get herself dry, and a customer

interrupted any further conversation. 'Mel, can you deal with the shop?' Simmy muttered, before answering the call of the wreaths.

'Okay – but you were joking, right, when you said that about Bonnie? She's not wanted for questioning, is she? What do they think she's done?'

'They want her to look at pictures of known dognappers – that's right, isn't it?' She looked from Moxon to Melanie, and left them to work it out between them. Melanie might not even know there had been a murder, and the prospect of bringing her up to speed was too much to contemplate.

A second customer came in, glanced at the group, and began browsing contentedly amongst the displays. 'Sorry – I've got work to do. Can you see to these gentlemen?' she said to Melanie, indicating both the newly arrived customers, before firmly closing the door between herself and the shop.

Bonnie slipped past her a minute later, dressed in a pair of black leggings and a baggy blue sweatshirt. Her hair looked slightly less bedraggled. 'That's better,' Simmy approved. 'I assume they'll bring you back again when they've finished with you.'

'I doubt it,' said the girl. 'These things can take all day. And even if it doesn't, they'll probably leave me to walk back.' She disappeared and Simmy was left worrying about a repeat soaking and yet another set of dry clothes needing to be found.

An hour later, with the biggest wreath completed and another one started, she was feeling slightly less harassed.

Melanie had left her alone, and she ignored all sounds from the shop. She worked for another twenty minutes and then went to join her assistant. 'Time for a sandwich,' she said. 'I'll go and get some, shall I? And something for Bonnie. She ought to be back soon, don't you think? It can't really take very long, can it?'

'Don't ask me. I'm still wondering what she has to do with dognappers.'

'I thought you'd know. I have to say, I'm not entirely sure it was a good idea to drop her onto me the way you did. She's so young and fragile, and mysterious. I can't understand her family set-up, for a start. And how bad is the anorexia now? I feel I have to keep nagging her to eat something, but that's probably all wrong.'

'She's fine. All you have to do is show her how the business works, pay her the minimum wage and think yourself lucky.' Melanie was showing signs of impatience. 'You'd never have found anybody to replace me, otherwise. You hadn't even started advertising.'

'I know. It was very good of you. But you can see for yourself, she's a bit flaky. Getting so wet for no reason. Wanting to move in upstairs . . .'

'What?'

'Yes. She asked if she could have the rooms – not just for her, but her dog as well. She's obviously a very dog-centred person. Not to mention the non-aunt. Corinne something. My mother knows her slightly. They were selling puppies, but got closed down. I'm sure you know the whole story.'

'Corinne's done fostering for ages, but she likes the kids to call her Auntie. I don't know the whole story – it's better not to, probably. The family's in Workington. There are three other kids, one with special needs. Bonnie was taken into care when she was about twelve – something pretty nasty going on, I think. She's hinted to Chloe about it. But she had the sense to blow the whistle. There's a rich grandmother, who got some huge compensation payout when her husband was killed, and has paid for everything for years. Still buys fancy clothes and sends them to Bonnie. But that doesn't seem to have helped much. The opposite, if anything.'

'So the abuse sparked off the anorexia?' said Simmy.

Melanie gave her a patronising look. 'You're not listening. She's been with Corinne for three or four years, and the eating thing only got really bad last year. It's way more complicated than you seem to think.'

'Sorry,' Simmy snapped. 'All this is outside my experience.' She hesitated, hearing herself with shame. 'I'm being naive, aren't I,' she sighed.

'A bit, yeah. Anyway, my sister, Chloe, was great with Bonnie. She's really kept her going, just by being a good friend.'

'And Spike,' said Simmy. 'I gather he's famous in his own right.'

'He's just a dog,' said Melanie. 'But listen – you can't let her use the rooms. Not before she's eighteen, anyway.'

'I wasn't going to,' said Simmy. 'Although she seems very determined about it.'

'You mustn't let her,' said Melanie again. 'And I know it's a pain, but I can't stay much longer. I've got another interview this afternoon, and the car's making that noise again. I'll have to get the bus.'

'Where is it?'

'Grasmere. Not really where I was hoping for, but it's all good practice, even if I decide not to take the job.'

'Can you manage any time tomorrow?'

'Tomorrow's Friday,' said Melanie as if this was a detail Simmy had forgotten.

'I know. But the old routines don't seem to be working any more.'

'True, but I didn't think you'd need me once the funeral stuff's out of the way.'

'There's a wedding on Saturday, remember?'

Melanie's impatience increased. 'If I do come, it won't be till tomorrow afternoon. It's all going crazy, you don't understand. I need to *focus*. This is my *career* I have to think about.'

Simmy took a deep breath. They were both obviously feeling the strain of imminent separation and new arrangements. 'Okay. Thanks for coming in today. Have you had a look at the computer?'

Melanie pointed to a printout of the day's orders. 'Nothing until tomorrow afternoon, in Bowness. Shouldn't be a problem. The next one's Monday.'

Outside the rain had stopped, Simmy noticed. A trickle of customers arrived, representing the usual lunchtime increase, regardless of the weather. Simmy dealt with them, leaving Melanie to file orders for fresh flowers the next day. There were only five tributes still to prepare for the funeral, all of them sheafs or similar, and therefore quick and easy by comparison with the cushion and wreaths. If Bonnie came back, everything would run smoothly, she hoped.

'She'll be back soon,' said Melanie, as if reading her mind. 'She's really quite reliable. I wouldn't have dumped just any useless dropout on you.' The hint of reproach wasn't lost on Simmy. 'As far as I could see, it was the perfect answer for everyone, even if she is a bit . . . well, flaky's right, I guess. Does Ben know she's here?'

'He saw her yesterday. Seemed pretty surprised, actually.'

'He'll know quite a lot about her. Basically, you're the only person in town who doesn't. You need to follow the news more closely. It'll make you feel more connected.'

'I'm sure you're right.' Melanie's admonitions were regular and reasonable, but somehow Simmy mostly failed to follow them. 'But I can't see how I'd ever have got to grips with all that's happened this week.'

'It doesn't sound particularly weird to me.'

'It is,' Simmy assured her. 'And I blame Moxon for most of it,' she said. 'I never quite trust his motives for coming here all the time. More often than not, it's obvious some junior could do it instead. Whatever it is.'

'He fancies you, I keep telling you. Poor bloke.'

'I know. It's one of life's great tragedies.'

'Come to that, I'm still not sure you treat Ninian as nicely as you should.'

'Don't start. He's impossible at the moment. He says he's not going to the funeral tomorrow, incidentally, although I'm not sure he'll be able to resist, when it comes to the point. I must be the only person in Cumbria who didn't know and love Barbara Hodge.'

'No you're not. There's me as well. Although Chloe met her a few times. She volunteered to help with the school garden club, when Clo was doing it in Year Nine. A woman of the people, our Barb.'

'As everyone keeps saying,' Simmy agreed. 'I'm just relieved she didn't stipulate no flowers at her funeral.'

Melanie rolled her eye, while its artificial partner did its own special trick. The girl's lack of embarrassment at the strange effects her eyes could perform was one of many aspects of her personality that Simmy was going to miss.

'You and Ninian don't seem to be getting it together much these days,' said Melanie boldly. 'What's gone wrong?'

'Nothing, as far as I know. It's probably the usual business of getting the right balance and being scared of commitment. I don't like having to be the one to make all the moves. If I didn't do anything, he wouldn't either, and it would all just fizzle out.'

Melanie pondered this for a minute. 'That's no good,' she concluded. 'You want somebody with a lot more backbone. You can't leave it forever to get a baby or two. I mean—'

'I know. Body clocks wait for no woman and all that. Don't remind me. Most of the time, I think it's already too late.'

'But it's not. There's a woman in Ambleside who had three after she married at forty-four.'

'Triplets?'

'No, no. One a year. All big bonny babies, too. Her husband's a bit younger. He knows my dad.'

'Ninian wouldn't want babies.' The certainty of this flooded through her for the first time. 'He's too . . . I don't know.'

142

'Limp,' said Melanie brutally. 'And they'd break his pots.'

Simmy sighed and changed the subject. 'I'll be glad when this week's over. It's always the same after a Bank Holiday. Nobody knows what day it is, and you never feel you've caught up properly.'

'Go and do the funeral stuff and let me get the computer up to date for you. Then I'm off, right?'

'Thanks.'

The appearance of another customer sent Simmy into the back room again for ten more minutes. Space was going to be reduced to a few square inches by the time the last tribute was done and laid out carefully on the remaining gap on the shelving. Her thoughts centred on the next morning and the timing of her trips to the undertaker's. There would be a buzz amongst the people there, preparing for the biggest funeral of the year. She had come to know Bruce, the conductor at most of the funerals, as well as Mr Manning, the boss of the whole establishment. Bruce was handsome, with a shock of dark, wavy hair and a charming smile. The rear of the building was a complex of mortuary, viewing chapel, flower bay, coffin workshop and a changing room for the men. She had dimly worked out that they were perpetually changing their clothes, according to the task ahead of them. Smart suits for funerals, smart-but-casual for collecting bodies, overalls for the coffin-making. Simmy could not imagine a working day in which dead bodies came and went all the time. She seldom saw one herself, despite coinciding with the vehicle they used for collection a few times, and witnessing the removal of an obvious receptacle containing one of their customers. She also saw coffins on wheeled gurneys, going in and out of the chapel.

Florists were privileged members of the whole team, permitted around the back when almost no one else was. They were expected to take the business of death in their stride. Simmy had been slow to understand this and had made a few blunders in the early months. The worst was when she caught sight of a small child's coffin and had started crying helplessly. She had also parked in the wrong place, impeding the manoeuvring of one of the limousines and earning herself a sarcastic reproach from one of the men. Bruce had rescued her, and explained how vital it was that all their vehicles had ready access to the road outside.

All of which meant she had to take care, not only to deliver all the flowers on time, placing them in the right section of the bay, but also to remain inconspicuous on a day which was sure to be stressful.

Female voices floated through from the shop, one of them rather shrill. Simmy went to see who it was.

A woman was standing much too close to a display of ornamental grasses, waving her arms. 'They made her look at about a thousand pictures before letting us go. It's so *typical*.'

She had dyed purple hair, with pink streaks. At a glance, Simmy could see three studs in her eyebrows and lip. Bonnie stood passively at her shoulder.

'I'm back,' she said to Simmy. 'This is Corinne.'

Chapter Twelve

Simmy's first thought was that if this was the responsible non-aunt who was such an improvement on Bonnie's biological parent, then what in the world could *that* person be like?

'Pleased to meet you,' said the woman. 'Thanks for taking Bonnie under your wing. She really likes it here.' Her voice was rich and low, her accent neutral.

'That's okay,' said Simmy feebly. 'Are you here for the rest of the day now?' she asked the girl.

'Absolutely. Corinne drove me back. I've done my duty as a citizen.'

'Did you recognise anyone?' asked Melanie. 'In the mugshots, I mean. I still don't understand why they thought you would. You never had any dogs nicked, did you?'

'We had some trouble, before Easter,' said Corinne tightly. 'Bonnie caught a bloke in our backyard, where the dogs live. He'd grabbed one of them, but she scared him off. Screamed blue murder, she did.'

'You reported it?' Melanie sounded sceptical.

'There was someone else there at the time, and she told the cops. We wouldn't have bothered. They never did anything – obviously.'

'Seems a bit of a stretch to think that man had something to do with the murder in Troutbeck,' frowned Simmy. 'Doesn't it?'

Melanie's intake of breath reminded Simmy that they had said nothing about the violence in Troutbeck. 'What?' the girl demanded. 'What did you just say?'

'Didn't you hear about it? A man was killed there on Tuesday. I've had Moxon after me, because my father and I saw the man on Monday. It's all jumbled up with people stealing dogs – although I don't think there's any real evidence of a connection.' She looked at Bonnie. 'You didn't recognise anyone in the database, then?'

'No one,' said the girl. 'It was a right waste of time.'

Simmy could barely take her eyes off Corinne. Somewhere deep down she felt she should be wary of the woman, even apologetic for accepting Bonnie as an employee without due consultation.

'Much as I wish I could stay and catch up with the whole story, I need to get the car sorted,' said Melanie. 'I'll come in on Saturday, shall I? Then I can cover for you while you go and see to the stuff for the wedding. And I will make an effort to do a couple of hours tomorrow.' She looked around the shop, pausing at each face in turn. 'I'm going to miss all this,' she said. 'But funny as it might sound, I don't want to get involved in any more police business. I always was one step behind you and Ben, and now I seem to be about ten steps back. I'll just let you get on with it.' She smiled sweetly, and headed for the door.

Corinne was striding around the shop, peering at the cards, fingering the flowers and Ninian's pots. Her foot nudged a bucket of lilies on the floor, not quite tipping it over. Simmy watched anxiously, noting that the long skirt was not only wet at the hem but well coated with white hairs, presumably from a dog. The woman was dressed for an Edwardian spring day on the fells, not a wet visit to a contemporary flower shop.

'Yes, go,' said Simmy distractedly. 'Thanks, Mel. Good luck with the interview. Knock 'em dead.'

'I'm only going for the practice. I told you.'

'I know, but it wouldn't hurt to have an offer, even if you turn it down. Think what a boost it would be.'

'To my ego, you mean? Right.' Melanie rolled her eye again, and made her departure without a word to Bonnie or Corinne.

'I wanted to check with you,' Simmy blurted awkwardly, 'about Bonnie's eating. I wasn't sure how involved I should be.' She glanced at the girl, feeling increasingly apologetic. 'She says I don't have to worry, and she's—'

'Oh, no. Don't bother yourself about all that. She's fine now. It's better just to ignore the whole business. Isn't that right, Bon?'

Bonnie flashed a tiny smile of agreement that suggested to Simmy that she'd have done better not to broach the subject. Any temptation she might have had to go on to talk about the rooms upstairs was quickly quashed. 'I think there's a customer,' Bonnie said, tilting her head towards the door. A man was standing just outside, apparently uncertain as to whether to come in. He was rubbing the glass, which was smudged with rain, and peering into the shop. For a moment, Simmy thought it was Ninian until she looked closer and saw it was a younger shorter individual.

'What's he doing?' she wondered aloud.

Bonnie moved to the door and made a beckoning movement. 'Do you know him?' Simmy asked.

'It's Murray,' said Corinne, on a falling note. 'Bloody Murray. I bet he's been following me.'

'He hasn't, Con. Don't be daft. He'd have had to wait outside the cop shop for hours in the rain. Maybe he wants to buy you some flowers, and is shy, because you're here and you'll see him.'

'Fat chance. He must have come to get something for the funeral and he knows I'll have a go at him for leaving it so late.' She grinned at Simmy. 'Tell him he should have done it a week ago.'

The man finally came in, with a sheepish expression. 'Hi, Con. Bon. Never expected to see you two here.'

'Bonnie's working here now,' said Corinne. 'Has been since Tuesday.'

'Never.' There was a Welsh lilt to the word, although his previous remark had sounded more northern. He looked at Simmy, as if for rescue. 'Not too late to order flowers for Miss Hodge's funeral tomorrow, am I?'

Simmy squared her shoulders. 'Not quite,' she said. 'So long as it's nothing too complicated. I'm having to do a lot this afternoon.'

'Just something basic.' He gave Corinne a bolder look. 'I thought you'd do it from both of us,' he said accusingly.

'How d'you know I didn't?'

Good question, thought Simmy, finding herself more and more fascinated by these people.

'Lindy told me. Said she helped you do the order online and you just put from her, Bonnie and you.'

'Yeah, well, I didn't want people getting the wrong idea, did I?'

Murray made a brushing movement with his hand, and treated Simmy to an engaging smile. 'Something with lilies,' he said. 'And put "With sympathy from Murray Pickering", if that's okay.'

Simmy found her order pad and wrote on it. 'You can do the card yourself, as you're here,' she offered.

'No, that's okay. My writing's rubbish. You do it for me. What's the damage?'

'Twenty pounds, for a spray with lilies, carnations and white roses. Twenty-five if you'd like a bit more than that.'

'Twenty's fine.' He produced a crumpled note from his pocket. 'Sorry to make life difficult for you, being so late. I'll let you get on, then.' He turned to go, ignoring the others.

'See you later?' he said to Corinne.

'Not if I see you first,' she snapped.

The man laughed self-consciously, and they all watched him leave. 'He's my ex-brother-in-law, actually,' said Corinne. 'He was married to my sister twenty years ago, for a year or two. I'd better get out of your way now. Thanks for taking Bonnie on. She won't let you down.'

Simmy thought of the sodden scrap that had arrived for work that morning, and grimaced slightly. None of her doubts as to the wisdom of employing the girl had been allayed. And she was now falling seriously behind with the funeral flowers. When she saw that it was past two o'clock, she yelped. 'Gosh – I do have to get cracking,' she said. 'I've got ever such a lot still to do.'

'Bye then,' waved Corinne, as if they were already firm friends.

Bonnie and Simmy gave identical exhalations of relief at the sudden emptiness and quiet of the shop. 'At last!' sighed the girl. 'I thought she was going to stay all day.'

Simmy could think of nothing diplomatic to say, so she merely nodded and went into the back room. The new order was an irritation, and she resolved to make the quickest and simplest sheaf she could. Briefly, she put her head out into the shop. 'Can you write that card for the new order?' she asked. 'I noted the wording.'

'Okay. Is there a special pen or something?'

'No. Use whatever you can find.' Somewhere at the back of her mind, she lodged the thought that the acquisition of a particularly nice italic pen for such messages might be a good idea.

Doggedly she constructed two more tributes, forcing herself to take all necessary care to follow the instructions in the original orders. One was from two people called Graham and Trish, and the other from a woman Simmy remembered. She had come into the shop the week before and written the card herself. 'For dear Barb. You will be terribly missed by us all. Lots of love, Vicky.' The sincerity was palpable, and Simmy had made an extra effort to keep the card safe until the bouquet was done. Now, she lingered over the flowers, selecting a subtle range of yellows as requested, standing back as far as the tiny space allowed, to admire the effect.

Three o'clock came and went, with scarcely a sound from the shop. What was Bonnie doing, she wondered? Playing on a mobile phone, probably. And despite Corinne's assurances, once again Simmy worried about the girl's meagre level of sustenance. She never seemed to eat or drink unless Simmy initiated something. Simmy herself had missed lunch and now found herself ravenous.

She made two mugs of tea and ate a biscuit before going out into the shop. 'Time for tea,' she said, as undramatically as she could. 'Everything quiet out here?'

She stopped and looked around. Something was different. Where there had been displays of mixed flowers in buckets of water, and a few of Ninian's vases, haphazardly lining the way from door to till, there was now a kind of organised avenue, drawing the eye inexorably into the shop. The colours were ranged from dark near the door to light near the till, giving an astonishing effect of a pathway that one felt compelled to follow. Or so Simmy gradually understood, standing as she was at the wrong end. Unthinkingly, she moved to the door and turned to look back. Not only had the colours been magically rearranged, but the heights flowed smoothly, from tallest at the door to shorter further in. 'But . . . How?' she stammered. 'I mean – tall *and* dark? Where are the tall light things?' It was a trick, surely.

'I had to cut a few stalks,' Bonnie admitted. 'But there are still plenty of short dark and tall light, over there.' She pointed at a triangular cluster of blooms in a corner of the shop where there had previously been a somewhat jumbled assemblage of greetings cards, ribbons, dried flowers and pots. They had been streamlined in a way that Simmy knew she could never in a thousand years have managed.

'It's magic,' Simmy gasped. 'Sheer unmitigated magic.'

Bonnie laughed. 'It was easy. I wasn't sure what I was supposed to do when there weren't any customers. I'll have a go at the window next, if you like. I should probably have done that first, but I thought I should ask you if it was okay.'

'It's more than okay. You've made it look so *enchanting*.'

'Flowers *are* enchanting. Honestly, it was only a matter of moving them around a bit. I had a picture in my head before I started and just fitted it all in – sort of thing.' She tailed off, flushing slightly. 'It might make it a bit difficult for people to get to the cards, though. I might have to do that section again.'

Simmy hadn't moved from her spot just inside the door. Deep reds, purples, blues mutated via pink and orange to yellow and white in a uniquely compelling fashion, on both sides. 'I never realised such a thing was possible. And yet it really is quite simple, as you say. I feel pretty stupid not to have thought of something like this for myself.'

Bonnie shrugged. 'Nobody does, as far as I can see. It's probably just me. I am a bit mad, you know.' And to Simmy's relief, she picked up her mug and took a large gulp of tea.

The *ping* of the doorbell sounded right above her head and she jumped out of the way as Ben Harkness came in. He had his usual schoolbag over one shoulder and looked weary. He stopped just behind Simmy and blinked. She had time to note that the magical new avenue only left enough space for people to progress in single file. That could perhaps present difficulties, she thought with a little stab of anxiety. Wasn't there some health and safety edict about that sort of thing?

'Hi!' she said. 'Just in time for tea. Although you said you weren't coming again till Saturday.'

He ignored her. 'What happened in here? Why's everything so different? It looks like . . . like . . .' he floundered. 'Like something from New York's East Side. Only different,' he added helplessly.

'Bonnie did it. She's got a magic talent, evidently.'

He removed his bag and set it down cautiously. 'Too many books,' he complained. 'I'll get scoliosis at this rate.'

Simmy ignored him in return and went to make more tea. When she came back, he was leaning over the table on which sat the till and computer, looking at something on the screen. Bonnie was sitting beside him. They flinched guiltily as Simmy approached.

'What?' she demanded. 'I've only been gone two minutes and you're up to something.'

'No, we're not. We just thought it would be interesting to know how many orders for flowers there've been, for the Hodge woman's funeral.' Ben spoke much too carelessly to be convincing.

'For heaven's sake, why?'

'No reason.'

'Come on, Ben. You wanted to see exactly who'd sent them, didn't you? For some sinister reason of your own.' The sort of terrible thought that only arose when Ben was around hit her. 'You're not trying to make a connection between her and that murder, are you?'

'Of course not. That would be idiotic.' He gazed in a parody of innocence at the ceiling.

'Although she did have a very precious dog. And she did live at Troutbeck Bridge. And she did know everybody,' listed Bonnie. 'So there could be *some* sort of connection.'

Simmy had a number of simultaneous thoughts about murder and Troutbeck and dogs and her father. She remembered again his odd inconclusive testimony as to what he had overheard at the pub. For no reason she could identify, a feeling of dread washed over her. She very much wished Russell had never gone to the Gents when he did, never taken any notice of words exchanged behind a wall and certainly never reported it to the police. But it was too late, as Ben would doubtless point out.

'You're teasing me, both of you,' she complained. 'We still know absolutely nothing about the man who died or his criminal associates. If he had any, that is,' she finished clumsily.

'I know quite a bit about him, actually,' said Ben carelessly.

'So do I,' added Bonnie, with a look of surprise. 'I thought everybody did.'

'Not me,' grated Simmy. 'I've got better things to worry about.'

'You know his name,' Ben reminded her. 'And the car he drove. Moxo will have told you at least that much.'

'And his throat was slashed, yes,' sighed Simmy. 'Such a horrible thing to do to a person. The wretched woman who found him was completely traumatised, apparently.'

Ben's eyes widened. 'I didn't hear that bit. Doesn't that mean somebody out there was covered in blood?'

Simmy winced. 'Probably. I don't know.'

'Go on. What else?'

'The man lived in a small cottage somewhere near Grasmere. He has a son who's mostly with his mum in Scotland, who was staying with him when all this happened.'

'How old is he?'

She tried to remember. 'Thirteen, I think. He's called Tim.'

'Why wasn't he at school?'

'I have no idea. Maybe they added an extra day or two onto the Bank Holiday.'

'Maybe he's training up to be a dognapper as well,' said Bonnie with a sneer that startled Simmy.

'I thought we'd established that he definitely wasn't into stealing dogs,' said Ben. 'Has that changed now?'

'Bonnie couldn't find him in the police picture gallery, and people insist he was perfectly law-abiding.' Simmy felt tired of it all, and the repetitive explanations. 'But we wondered why they wanted her to go and do it now, when it was ages ago her dogs were almost abducted. We presumed it meant the police think there could be a connection, even if they can't prove it.'

'That's exactly right,' put in Bonnie. 'That's my impression, anyway.'

'Police picture gallery?' Ben's interest became intense.

Bonnie took over from Simmy. 'I had to go and look at mugshots of dognappers this morning. It was all pretty silly, actually, because even if I'd recognised somebody, that wouldn't prove anything about the murder, would it? I thought at first they were just following up these thefts of dogs, and trying to pin down the movements of a suspect, or something. Then I realised they wouldn't have

Moxon on that, when there was a murder investigation going on. So I guessed they thought if I could identify their dead man as the same one who tried to nick our best bitch, they'd have something to go on. But I couldn't.' She shrugged regretfully. 'I told them I didn't recognise anybody.'

Ben screwed up his face in deep concentration. 'Aren't you jumping to too many conclusions? Did Moxon actually *talk* to you?'

Bonnie shook her head. 'No, I just sort of thought it through. I might have got the whole thing completely wrong. I expect I have. I'm no good at this sort of thing. It upsets me a bit, actually.'

'And me,' said Simmy. 'It's all so horrible. That poor boy, without his father . . .'

'Yeah, but we owe it to him and the chap's friends to see if we can help catch his killer, right?' Ben objected. 'Bonnie, you're wrong, you know.'

'I thought I was,' she said humbly.

'No, no. I mean – you're wrong to think you're no good at it. You're brilliant.' He spoke as if Bonnie had successfully completed an assignment set by him personally. 'Welcome to the gang!'

'Gang?'

'He's joking,' said Simmy firmly.

'Me, Melanie and Simmy have solved a few murders since the end of last year, as it happens. You'll have heard a bit about it, I expect. In the news. The wedding at Storrs, for a start – and the man shot in Bowness? Simmy and I were *right there* when it happened.'

'We didn't solve anything,' said Simmy crossly. 'We mostly just got in the way.'

'And I'm going to be a forensic archaeologist,' Ben went on, undaunted.

'I know,' said Bonnie. 'Everybody knows.'

'Well, I've got work to do,' said Simmy, feeling as if she'd said the same thing a hundred times that day. 'Four more funeral tributes to make, before I can go home.' She looked at her watch. 'Which won't be until six at the earliest, thanks to you two.' The way Bonnie reacted to this suggested that she regarded it as unfair. Simmy, however, remembered the disrupted morning all too clearly. Then she looked again at the transformed shop and reproached herself. 'But you've more than made up for it,' she said warmly. 'You've performed miracles in here.'

'It's a bit short of space, though,' said Ben with true tactlessness. 'And people will be scared to buy anything, for fear of spoiling the effect.'

'No they won't,' flashed Simmy. 'Wait until the next customer comes along and see what they say.'

Bonnie showed no sign of taking the criticism to heart and merely smiled indiscriminately. 'I never thought it would be so quiet in a shop,' she said. 'Hardly anybody comes in, do they?'

Quiet! thought Simmy desperately. 'Most of the work comes through email or phone orders,' she said tightly. 'Windermere's not exactly heaving with passing trade, even in high season. Everyone's keen to get out onto the fells and lakes. The business relies a lot more on weddings and funerals than actual flesh-and-blood customers,' she concluded, with the aim of dropping a heavy hint.

'Which leaves me and Mel – me and *you* now,' Ben told Bonnie, 'to disentangle the latest crime.' He turned his back on Simmy and she took herself off to the back room with a bagful of mixed feelings.

It was good to have so much to do, she reminded herself. It was normal and straightforward, and would bring comfort to people. As the available space reduced to almost nothing, she delicately piled one sheaf of flowers on top of another, moving the wreaths to a more vertical position. Every item was the product of her own skilful fingers, not a petal out of place, and the scent of lilies and freesias filled the air. The very transience of flowers made them all the more precious. The symbolism associated with a funeral was said to focus on this brief existence, a human life no more permanent than a bloom. This idea had been new to Simmy when she heard it the previous year; she had always thought it was more that the scent of flowers masked that of decaying flesh. And it didn't work for weddings. They were meant to be anything but transient. She smiled to herself at the contradiction. It reflected the multitude of interpretations she had come across for the language of flowers. She had briefly considered making this a central element to the business, with labels and leaflets and posters on the subject, until she bought two books, which gave alarmingly different meanings to most of the flowers she intended to stock.

These drifting thoughts saw her through two more tributes, and took the time to just before five. Feeling tired and extremely hungry, she opened the door and called, 'Go home!' to Bonnie. There was no sign of Ben.

'Okay,' said the girl. 'Same time tomorrow?'

'Thanks. I'll be delivering all this to the undertaker until about half past nine, so don't get here before then. You won't be able to get in. And if it's raining, wear a mac, with a hood. And find an umbrella.'

'You must be hungry,' said the girl, ignoring these instructions. 'You never had lunch.'

'Nor did you.'

'Yeah, I did. I had two muesli bars. You didn't see.'

'Well, I am, actually. But I can wait another hour. I'll be home by then. It's been a good day, hasn't it? You've done all this wonderful work. I'll be sure to pay you a bit extra on Saturday. You've earned it.'

Bonnie shrugged, as if money mattered nothing to her. The initial questions concerning her background had only partially been answered by Melanie's account, Simmy realised. There were contradictions to be reconciled, in the personalities of both Corinne and Bonnie. The careless confidence shown by both women sat oddly with the stories of neglect, abuse and general dysfunction.

She supposed, in the end, she would have to ask Ben Harkness to help with it all.

Chapter Thirteen

Thursday finished with a hot bath and a lavish application of hand cream. Her fingers were tired and sore after so much tweaking and tying, weaving and wrapping. Her thoughts remained obsessively on the following day's funeral and the importance of getting everything right.

The phone rang just as she was drying herself. It was downstairs, so she bundled herself into the towel and went to answer it, completely at a loss as to who the caller might be. It was ten o'clock – at least it wasn't going to be someone selling double glazing.

'P'simmon!' Her mother's voice was oddly strangled. 'You've got to come. It's your father.'

Ice swept through her entire system. Fear such as she had never known gripped her and rendered her beyond speech or movement.

'Are you there? Say something.' Angie paused. 'He's not *dead* or anything.'

Simmy took a delayed breath. 'What, then?' she managed.

'He's had a terrible threatening letter. About that business on Monday when he was with you. Telling him they'll burn the house down if he gives evidence. He's gone into some sort of trance. I can't deal with him on my own. You've got to come.'

'Trance?' She chose this strange word to query, when actually it was the thought of the house being set alight that filled her mind. How could anybody defend against such an act? It would be so easy for a determined arsonist to carry out the threat. No wonder her father was so appalled. 'Can't he speak?'

'Apparently not. He just sits in the kitchen staring at the Rayburn. Even the dog's worried about him.'

'How long? I mean – when did he first read the letter?'

'Oh, I don't know. After supper. He went a ghastly pale-green colour, first. I thought he was going to be sick. Then he just slumped in the chair and pushed the letter at me. It *is* awful. But it's so unlike him to go to pieces like this. I really don't know what to do.'

'It's not a stroke is it? Does his face look lopsided?'

'No, no. At least, I don't think so. Should I call a doctor, then? They'll cart him off to hospital, and stick needles into him. He'd never get back to normal after that. Oh, God.' The helpless panic was so out of character for her mother that Simmy actually felt the earth wobble under her feet. The whole world had become unstable, all due to a malicious letter.

'I'll come. Fifteen minutes. Don't do anything until I get there.'

She threw on random clothes, and was in the car and

flying down to Windermere in less than five minutes. She pulled up outside Beck View in another five. Then her mother took an impossibly long time to open the door when she rang the bell. Dimly, Simmy noted that an additional bolt had to be released, with Angie fumbling clumsily at it. The door had tinted glass panels, through which her mother's figure could be seen. Which a criminal could smash and pour petrol through, just as he could through any of the ground floor windows, if sufficiently determined.

Her father did not look up when she went into the kitchen. Instead, Bertie yapped, in a clear display of distress. An open letter lay on the table near Russell's clasped hands. Simmy patted the dog distractedly, associating him with the ill-omened experiences on the Bank Holiday, and wishing none of it had happened. She picked up the sheet of paper and read:

We know you told the cops about what you saw in Troutbeck and you're in big trouble, mate. You and that daughter of yours in the pretty cottage. If you let them use you in a legal case, we'll come and burn your house down, with your wife and your dog in it.

'That is quite nasty, Dad,' she said, and laid a gentle hand on her father's shoulder. 'I can see why you'd be upset. How was it delivered? When?'

'Must have been by hand,' supplied Angie. 'It was just sort of *there*, on the doormat, at about seven o'clock.'

Simmy addressed her father, leaning over him. 'Dad? Come on. What's got into you? It isn't as bad as all that. It's only a letter.'

'That's what I said,' muttered Angie behind her.

Simmy squeezed the bony joint under her hand, thinking how terribly old her father looked. New lines had appeared around his mouth and his hair looked whiter than it had a few days before. 'Come on,' she repeated. 'Say something.'

'How . . . ?' he mumbled, and then made a huge visible effort. 'How can people be so *evil*?'

'Oh, Dad.' She had no idea what to say. 'I don't know,' she admitted. The tears running down her face were mostly from a release of tension, as she understood that he was not in a coma or close to death.

'It's only a letter,' repeated Angie loudly, embarrassed by the crying, as always. 'Just words on paper. It's ridiculous to behave as if you've been shot or bashed with a crowbar. It's bravado, that's all. And extremely stupid, because it makes it much more likely they'll be caught.' She took two or three strides across the room, firing angry words as she went.

Simmy mopped her face on a handy tea towel and tried to think. Only then did the police come to mind. 'Mum's right,' she said. 'Don't touch the letter again. There might be fingerprints on it. Call Moxon and tell him about it.'

'Now?' Angie said. 'Surely not? It'll wait until morning. They won't start checking for fingerprints at eleven o'clock at night.'

'I could deny I heard anything,' said Russell in a small breathy voice. 'Like they want.'

Simmy and her mother simultaneously protested. 'No, you can't let them intimidate you like that,' said Angie. 'You know you can't.'

'It's too late, anyway,' said Simmy.

'These people are idiots. Complete fools.' Angie was letting panic mutate into outrage, which Simmy found reassuring.

'Hang on – how do they *know* about you overhearing them on Monday, anyway?' Simmy said. 'That's very peculiar, when you think about it.'

'A spy in the police ranks,' said Angie melodramatically. 'Which gives them – the police – yet another way to catch the killers. They'll be able to check who knew about it, and who they might have told.'

Simmy gave her a confused look. 'I'm not sure I follow that. Most likely, it's just that some careless detective constable made it obvious when asking routine questions. Although . . .' She tried hard to think clearly. 'That really only works if it was the beardy man being questioned. He knows we both saw him. He knows I live in a cottage in Troutbeck, and I suppose it wouldn't be difficult to find out who my father is. Anybody else would need more to go on.'

'What *exactly* did you see, anyway?' demanded Angie. 'It didn't sound like much to me.'

'It *wasn't* much. Nothing that could lead to anyone being charged with murder, that's for sure. This is just blind panic, which is going to make the police's job a lot easier.'

'I want protection,' said Russell. 'It must be a whole gang of them. They won't rest till they get me.'

'For heaven's sake!' snapped Angie. 'This isn't *The Sopranos*, you idiot. What's the matter with you?'

'Easy, Mum,' said Simmy. 'It's just the shock of it, that's all.' Even as she spoke, she knew it was more than that. Her father had changed, overnight, into a frightened, intimidated citizen. And she was far from sure that her own explanation for who had sent the letter and why was the truth of it. There was the unidentified car passenger to be reckoned with. The letter referred to *what you saw*, and his face could well be the crucial detail meant by this.

And who might have read Russell's witness statement since he made it on Tuesday? Or simply heard the salient points of it? That was what Angie had been trying to say, she realised. How many people knew enough to realise that Russell could be a threat? Taken to the extreme, it would include Ben and Melanie, and probably their families. Ben's brother had a friend – Scott – who worked in the mortuary. He picked up a lot of stuff that was supposed to be confidential. But, she argued with herself, not details of witness statements, surely? Only the actual police would know about that.

But Simmy herself knew the whole story, and she had talked freely in front of not just Ben and Melanie, but little Bonnie Lawson too.

Her blood turned cold again. Had she somehow caused this drastic trauma to her father? 'I hope it isn't my fault,' she said faintly. 'I have been a bit of a blabbermouth.'

'It doesn't matter,' said Russell, equally faintly. 'Stop talking. Please. Go home, Sim, so I can lock the doors properly.'

He had been nervous already, she remembered. He had taken to checking locks and bolts before any of this had happened. Presumably by accident, the writer of the letter had tapped into a pre-existing fear and made it unbearably much worse. It was cruelty, nothing less. In a stupid effort to arrest a process that was beyond that possibility, they had brought real suffering to a decent and innocent man. *Old man*, whispered a voice. Never before had she thought of him in such a way. It was enraging that some strange criminal should have forced her to think it now.

She looked at her mother, and saw a mirroring wrath in her eyes. 'We have to do whatever we can to catch these people,' she said. 'They're foul monsters, hurting ordinary people.'

'Scum,' nodded Angie.

'No,' muttered Russell. 'They're just rats in a corner.'

'You said they were evil just now,' Angie reminded him.

'And it might just be one person,' Simmy realised. 'I'll get Ben to work on it tomorrow. Once I've delivered the funeral flowers,' she added, with a sense of obligations multiplying.

'Oh, God – the funeral!' said Angie. 'I don't suppose I can go now. What with all this.'

'You must,' urged Simmy. 'Dad can go with you.'

Russell shook his head. 'I don't want to. She meant very little to me.'

Simmy sensed an ongoing disagreement on this subject, and speculated briefly that this might be a relatively safe, even therapeutic, topic to switch to. 'Everyone seems to have liked her,' she offered.

'It's a community thing,' said Angie. 'That's why I'm going. One of the most energetic, right-minded, hands-on people the town has seen for ages has died. The least we can all do is give her a good send-off.'

'Don't worry. If the number of flowers is anything to go by, she's going to be well celebrated.'

'She's still dead, though, isn't she?' said Russell irritably. 'Nothing's going to change that. And she won't know who sent flowers. It's all just a hollow sham.'

'It's also a splendid way of showing we won't easily forget her,' added Angie, as if her husband hadn't spoken. 'Plus it'll make everything easier for Valerie. She's in an awkward situation, not having any proper role, other than best friend.'

'Except everyone thinks they were lesbians,' said Russell, with something of his old manner. 'Forty years ago, the two of them would have been ostracised.'

Simmy thought of a female couple she had encountered at Christmas, and shivered slightly. 'People are just people,' she said obscurely. 'Nice or nasty, whatever sort of relationships they might be in.'

'Go home,' her father ordered. 'It's late.'

'And I have promises to keep,' quoted Simmy, hoping to raise a smile. She and her father had been wont to quote Robert Frost to each other in former times. The effort failed, and she heaved a profound sigh. 'Sorry, Dad. You've had an awful shock. Go to bed and try not to think about it. We'll think what to do, tomorrow. I'll come in after work, okay?'

He nodded and the sadness was a cloud over the whole room.

Chapter Fourteen

She slept very badly; the main cause being a furious determination to locate and avenge herself on whoever had upset her parents so horribly. But she was at a total loss as to how that might be achieved. A man in a red car had died. A second man, in the same car, had perhaps killed him after being seen by Simmy and her father. Someone had let this fact become known to the murderer, who was now taking desperate measures to save his own skin. He couldn't know how fleeting the glimpse had been, how inadequate the description Simmy could give. But that was hardly relevant now. The man had made his appalling threat, thereby incriminating himself, and revealing his handwriting and probably fingerprints. And that made him an idiot. The police would assuredly catch him.

Or so she trusted. In her half-awake state, she imagined him staring them down, defying them to match him up with the homicide, laughing in their faces. When she did drift off into a shallow sleep, her mind presented images of a strangled terrier and a firebomb falling catastrophically through the roof of Beck View, consuming her parents in a ball of flame. Threaded through these calamities were funeral flowers in soft mournful colours, and the men at the undertaker's criticising her efforts before hoisting a coffin high onto their shoulders.

She woke in a breathless panic, having missed the dawn chorus that normally roused her in May. She kept her windows open especially to catch the musical awakening. But she had only fallen properly asleep half an hour before first light, and was now gaspingly aware that it was after eight o'clock.

For the second time in twelve hours, she tumbled into clothes and out into her car in an impossibly short time. Only in the final half-mile did she collect her thoughts, and remind herself that there was plenty of time to fulfil her obligations to Barbara Hodge and her funeral. The deadline for the flowers was ten-thirty. Even with two journeys, that would be easily accomplished. If she was late opening the shop, that would hardly be a disaster. Then she remembered Bonnie, who might be left standing on the doorstep, if her arrival failed to coincide with Simmy being there.

At least it wasn't raining. Thin cloud was sitting just above the tops of the fells, giving ground for hope that the sun might break through before long. Bonnie would have to make the best of it – although having her inside the shop and dealing with customers was clearly the preferable option. As she collected the van from its own lock-up garage and drove it to the back of the shop, she wondered what was the best thing to do. If she'd spent a few minutes explaining the security system to Bonnie, everything would be easier. The girl could have let herself in and opened up the shop. As it was, Simmy didn't even have her mobile number, so couldn't call and explain the procedure.

It was ten to nine already. Perhaps the sensible option was to wait another ten minutes and simply let the girl in and leave her in charge, as originally planned. Then she remembered she'd told Bonnie not to turn up until nine-thirty, and everything suddenly felt much easier. The first delivery of flowers would already have been made by then.

She carefully loaded the main tributes onto the wooden shelves inside the van, and stepped back to check them for balance. There must be no risk of them sliding to the floor in transit. The sense of an imminent event of great significance was getting stronger. It was unnervingly akin to the feelings on the morning of a wedding – people to be assembled, ceremonies to be observed, food to be provided. Flowers, music, clothes all crucially important. Simmy had personal experience of both, and while the emotions had been very different, the tension was familiar.

She went through into the shop from the back, and peered out into the street, wondering whether Bonnie might turn up early, either deliberately or by mistake. She unlocked the door and stepped onto the pavement. Very few people were out and about. Tourists tended not to spend much time in Windermere anyway, other than at the several popular eateries in the evenings. Everyone else was either at work, or not yet ready to leave the house. So the fact of two men walking shoulder-to-shoulder towards her was impossible to miss.

There was something unavoidably threatening about them, even though she fought this foolish response. Long hair, scruffy clothes, an earring and a shaggy dog all shouted *gypsies*. Even Simmy, born long after the time when large caravans of travelling folk criss-crossed the land, knew a gypsy when she saw one. And even Simmy, whose mother was romantically in favour of the free lifestyle and cavalier attitude to petty laws, felt an instinctive urge to avoid them.

Gypsies famously stole dogs, didn't they? She reviewed the old stories, from carelessly rude times, in which gypsies were clever and reckless and inscrutable. They might even set fire to the homes of people who annoyed them. But then the men came within a yard or two of Simmy and one of them smiled broadly at her, and the other nodded, and even the dog raised its head and wagged its straggly tail at her. They were handsomely swarthy, with a glimmer of wry humour in their eyes. 'Morning,' said the smiling one. 'Better today.'

Simmy said nothing, but gave a return smile and glanced at the sky to show she understood his meaning. Her mother would have been ashamed of her, she thought. Such prejudice, such unfounded fear! But the visceral associations were inescapable. They included an image of the man with a beard in Troutbeck, who could also be a gypsy. And hadn't Travis McNaughton sounded rather like one, too? If not part of a Romany family, then likely to be connected in some way. The stereotypes refused to dissolve completely, rather to her regret. She still imagined men who lived by their wits, on the edge of society, ducking and diving and taking little notice of the law. Carrying heavy lumps of something in a black sack, and staring straight into the eyes of a nervous female who lived alone.

But not killing each other. That definitely did not enter the automatic list of characteristics of travellers.

Drunkenness, loss of control, reckless violence – those were not how people thought of them. In the stereotypes that now occurred to Simmy, there was a dominant matriarch in a gorgeously decorated caravan, making sure the menfolk behaved according to a long-established code.

On the other hand, if they *did* get homicidal, they would probably use sharp knives as the weapon of choice, just as McNaughton's killer had done.

At nine, still thinking that Bonnie might arrive early, she left the front of the shop unlocked, but the Closed sign still in place. The girl might have the sense to try the handle and find it open. She could then stand guard until Simmy returned from the undertaker. The risk was minimal, after all. Her father's new-found paranoia about intruders could not be permitted to affect Simmy's own attitude. Realistically, she was running virtually no risk at all. Even if someone did find the door giving under their hand, and went into an empty shop, what would they do? Steal a red rose or a begonia? As they left with their booty, they would be observed by people in the street and in neighbouring shops. Or might some madman take it into his head to wreak havoc, overturning Bonnie's lovely displays and breaking Ninian's pots? Anybody crazy enough for that might equally well decide to smash through a locked door in the first place. There was some money in the till, but it was protected by a key, which remained in Simmy's pocket.

She drove the van gently out into the street behind the main centre of Windermere and headed for the undertaker. It was a short distance. When she arrived, another florist, from Bowness, was just leaving. The two vans passed with cheery waves from both drivers. Simmy had never for a moment imagined herself to be the only business supplying tributes for the greatly missed Barbara.

In the flower bay, the great majority of the shelves had been allocated to this enormous funeral. At the far end, low down, she saw a label that read 'Mr James Invermore, 3 p.m.'. On the shelf sat one modest sheaf of flowers. Poor man – probably an elderly widower, dying in a nursing home, friendless and forgotten. Overshadowed completely by Miss Hodge's wreaths and cushions and sprays, and yet Simmy knew his funeral would be conducted with absolute care and respect.

She unloaded her precious cargo and settled it all onto the shelves. Nobody came to admire them, which was only to be expected. The woman from the office would doubtless come out at some point with a notepad and write down the names of all the people who'd sent flowers. That was usual for a burial, where there was no part of the proceedings set aside for the family to peruse all the cards, as they did after a cremation. And it meant Simmy should bustle back to collect the second load. Time was rushing by, and such a small task as listing the flowers was not meant to happen too late, for fear of getting forgotten.

Back at the shop, Bonnie had still not arrived. This caused Simmy a surge of unreasonable irritation that startled her. A final straw, she supposed. A sense of misplaced trust that was all the more infuriating because she knew it wasn't fair. Even though it was only nine thirty-five, customers were liable to start showing up and she didn't want to lose any business. She had been a fool to tell the girl to delay her arrival, probably making it sound as if she could leave it as late as she liked.

She had spoken thoughtlessly, assuming Bonnie understood the nuances around a large and stressful event such as this funeral. Now the dilemma about locking or unlocking the door became more acute. It would be ten or more before she got back again. Crossly, she decided to lock it, as much to teach Bonnie a lesson as any other motive.

There was barely enough space for the final flowers on the undertaker's shelves. One sheaf had to be lightly laid on top of another, which was very far from ideal. When Bruce cleared his throat behind her, she jumped guiltily and started to defend herself.

'No problem,' he smiled. 'Nothing's going according to the rules today, as it is.'

There would have to be a second hearse, he told her, specifically for the flowers. Simmy had heard of such a thing, but never witnessed it. There would have to be two more men than usual in the team, solely dedicated to coping with flowers. It made Simmy feel important to know this and she said something to that effect.

'Poor old Mr Invermore's getting a bit neglected,' said Bruce. 'He was a nice old chap, too. Friend of my dad's, for a bit.'

'I noticed,' Simmy nodded. 'Makes you think, doesn't it.'

Bruce cocked his handsome head. 'Does it?'

'Well . . . I mean, the difference in the two funerals. It's all a bit lopsided, it seems to me.'

'It's just the way it goes. You get somebody whose name's known all over town, and this is what happens. Like that McNaughton chap, getting himself murdered. There'll be media people, snoopers, detectives – all sorts, when we come to do him.'

'Not many of them sending flowers, though,' said Simmy, once more eyeing the overflowing racks dedicated to Miss Hodge.

'Likely not. Although I remember, twenty years ago, when I was new here, there was a murder, not so different from this one, and they caught the killer through the flowers.'

'You're joking!'

'True as I'm standing here. Felt remorseful, they said. Sent a massive great wreath saying "I'm so sorry" and some bright cop thought it a bit odd, and bingo!'

'But how? I mean – it's not such an unusual thing to say.' But even as she spoke, she realised it was. People said 'With all my sympathy' or 'Thinking of you in your loss'. Their own sorrow was seldom, if ever, mentioned. 'Gosh!' she added faintly. The idea that the police might have yet more reason to investigate her role in violent deaths was highly unwelcome.

'Lucky Miss Hodge died naturally, with all this lot,' he quipped. 'Poor Janice is going to have a real job making a list of them all. You've done well out of her, looks like. That cushion from the girlfriend's quite something. We've all been out here for a look already.'

'Thanks. I've got to get back. I hope it all goes to plan. I'll hear all about it from my mum.'

'It will,' he said, with perfect confidence. None of his funerals ever went off plan, was the implication.

Mention of her mother sent Simmy's thoughts back to the previous evening. Now that her obligations to the funeral were all satisfied, she was almost painfully free to attend to other matters. Her father stood firmly at the top of the list, followed by Bonnie, and then the next day's wedding. Associated with her father, of course, was the fact of a recent murder close to her home. A murder that had to be quickly solved, with the perpetrator imprisoned and punished with all diligence. Nothing less could be tolerated.

She felt a powerful need to talk to Ben, but he had classes on Friday mornings, and was unlikely to turn up before mid afternoon, if at all. The timetable was considerably relaxed in the run-up to exams, and his movements a lot less predictable as a result.

As she went to open the front door, she was faced with two figures – one human and one canine.

'Sorry,' said Bonnie breathlessly. 'I had to bring Spike with me. I'll explain. He won't be any trouble.'

Spike was beautiful – even Simmy could see that. She realised that she had subconsciously expected something rather like the gypsy dog she had seen earlier that morning. Instead, he was sleek, gleaming and immaculate. Long, soft, white hair rippled from his back to fall in fringes along his sides. His tail was erect and plumy. His long nose had an aristocratic tilt to it, and his jaws were relaxed and friendly. He was of a manageable size, too – hardly taller than Bonnie's knee.

'Gosh!' said Simmy. 'That's quite a dog.'

'He's lucky he turned out so well, being such an odd mixture. He's famous, you know, for being so clever and wonderful.' Bonnie dropped an unselfconscious kiss on the top of the dog's head. 'He'll sit quietly at the back, and nobody'll know he's even there.'

There was no good reason to object. Dogs were not banned from florist shops. There was space behind the till where he could lie. If anybody made a fuss, he could be banished to the cool room for a while. 'Okay,' she agreed. 'But why are you so late?'

'Oh, sorry. I am, aren't I? It's Corinne, basically. She went out early and never came back. I needed her to sort something out, so I waited. Then she phoned and said she's off for the weekend. Just like that. I *never* leave Spike on his own all day. Not after . . . well, not with all this dog stealing going on. He's *famous*. Worth money. Ransom, and all that,' she finished vaguely.

'I don't blame you for being nervous,' Simmy conceded. 'Does Corinne often go off like this?'

Bonnie shrugged. 'Sometimes. She's complicated. Knows loads of people. She sings at gigs when she can. Mostly summer festivals and stuff. She says there's one down in Lincoln this weekend and they offered her five hundred quid to do a few songs.'

The story struck Simmy as barely credible. 'She's not meant to leave you on your own, is she?'

'I'm seventeen,' said Bonnie with dignity. 'But mostly I go with her. She wants me to represent her at the funeral. And then I'm working tomorrow, aren't I? So that's two reasons why I can't go.'

With an effort, Simmy told herself it wasn't her problem, so long as Bonnie performed her shop duties, such as they were. With the rest of the day liable to be positively tranquil compared to the past two days, there was little need to worry. 'It would be helpful if you came in tomorrow – just for the morning. I'll have to go and do the displays for the wedding. I'll be gone from about ten.'

'No problem,' said the girl. 'If Melanie's okay with it. Didn't she say she'd be in tomorrow?'

'So she did. I forgot. Well, it can be quite busy on a Saturday. She'll find plenty for you to do. There's a whole lot to learn about stock rotation, and how different sorts of flowers need to be kept. But if you can't make it, don't worry.'

'No problem,' said the girl again.

'I really want to pop out to see my parents sometime today,' Simmy went on. 'My mother's going to the funeral this afternoon, but I'm not sure about my dad.' Then she had a thought. 'Didn't you say Corinne was going? Has that changed now?'

'I actually said *I* was going, as well. I did want to, but if it's a hassle for you, I don't mind skipping it. Nobody's going to notice whether I'm there or not. I'm not sure I can go like this, anyway.' She looked down at herself, dressed in blue cotton trousers and a grey top.

'I think you'd just pass. And it's not far away, after all. It's fine if you disappear for an hour, for the service.'

'But what about Spike?'

Simmy felt defeated by Bonnie's constant difficulties. She gave the impression of a small harmless creature caught in a giant maze, where every turn led to a dead end. Her good intentions came to nothing, because people changed their minds or let her down or refused to allow her do something. She might as well have carried a large placard saying 'Please rescue me' – which was what Melanie had tried to do, of course. Even a simple act of persuading her to eat a biscuit felt like a life-saving feat. Enabling her to attend the funeral of a woman who had been kind to her felt like an automatic obligation.

'I expect he'll stay with me, won't he?' she answered Bonnie's question. 'He seems to be incredibly well behaved.' Already the handsome dog was stretched inconspicuously along the back wall of the shop, his head on his paws, eyes almost closed.

'No, I don't mean then. I mean, is it okay if he stays here this morning? I can take him to the funeral.'

'What?'

'Oh, haven't you heard? Barbara left instructions that dogs will be welcome. Her Roddy's bound to be there, and a few others, I expect. Barbara loved dogs. And she'd have known Valerie wouldn't want to leave Roddy at the house. Not after what happened. She's paranoid about losing him again, same as I am with Spike. He's always been like their child, hers and Barb's.'

Simmy shook her head. 'I've never heard of dogs at a funeral, but I suppose it wouldn't be the first time.' *Why not?* she thought with resignation. People probably took horses and hamsters as well, for all she knew. Her earlier irritation came back, and a sense of being badly overloaded, just as she'd expected everything to feel a lot lighter, with the funeral flowers all delivered. 'It would be the easiest solution. Now – sorry, but I've got a lot to think about, after yesterday, with worries of my own. It's fine if you want to go to the funeral. I can manage quite well without you this afternoon. And tomorrow – well, don't bring Spike in, okay? Come if you can. Otherwise, we'll have another think, next week. Sorry, but that's how I feel.'

The girl's large blue eyes fixed on Simmy's face, and filled with tears. 'I'm sorry,' she murmured. Then, in a louder outburst, 'I know I'm a nuisance. I *am* trying, honestly. Corinne *knows* how important this job is. It could lead to a whole lot of new things for me, if it goes well. But she doesn't think. She just selfishly goes off, and leaves me to sort everything out.'

'Yes, I see that. I'm not blaming you at all. But I can't just take on the role of your guardian. I'm not authorised, or qualified. I hardly know you. Maybe any other week, it would have been different. But coming at the same time as that murder, and the funeral, and my dad, and everything . . . well, it's all too much.'

Bonnie blinked. 'What's happened to your dad?' she asked.

Normally, Simmy would have let caution prevail. But she was affected by Bonnie's despair, and her own sense of guilty inadequacy. 'He had a letter last night. Threatening to burn the house down if he testified against the man we saw on Monday. Probably the man who killed Travis McNaughton. He's extremely upset about it. I'm really worried about him. He was a complete wreck last night. I need to go and see how he is today.'

'Burn the house down?' Bonnie seemed to instinctively float to her dog's side, where she sank down with an arm along his back. 'I bet I know who that would be, then.'

Chapter Fifteen

'What?' demanded Simmy, towering over her. 'What do you mean?'

'Oh, God – I shouldn't have said that. But we had something like it happen, a year or two ago. I mean – not really the same at all. Nobody was *killed* or anything. And it's idiotic to think he'd do it again. But . . .' She shivered, and the dog turned to nuzzle her face, his concern palpable.

'What?' Simmy fought an urge to shake the girl. 'Who are you talking about?'

Bonnie whimpered and the dog made a low rumble. 'I never should have said anything. It was completely stupid. Corinne would kill me if she knew. It was just one of those horrible neighbour disputes that got out of hand.' She looked up. 'I'm really sorry. It was a bad time. You reminded me, and it made me go all weak. I'm sorry.'

An ill-timed customer forced Simmy's attention away before she could demand any further detail. Bonnie got to her feet with an embarrassed awkwardness.

The woman stood just inside the door, gazing at the new

display in wonderment. Simmy realised this was the first person to see it, other than Ben, and wished she was in a better mood to accept any accolades. 'Hello,' she said.

It was a regular Friday customer, with preferences that Simmy had come to know. She wanted colourful arrangements for her hallway and living room, to celebrate the weekend with her husband who worked away from home during the week. A generous budget and a degree of knowledge made her a pleasure to serve.

'What happened? It's all different.'

'I've got a new assistant. She's very clever at design and that sort of thing.' She waved an introductory arm at Bonnie, who was standing limply beside the till.

'It's like a pathway to heaven,' said the woman romantically. 'Although it's going to make choosing something even more difficult than usual.'

'Help yourself,' said Simmy, who felt a need for a minute or two of deep breathing before she could effectively assist.

'I hate to spoil the display.'

This had been a worry from the start, and Simmy sighed. 'That's what it's for,' she said. 'We'll refill any gaps.'

Slowly, the woman selected a dozen or so of rich red and purple blooms, and Simmy added fronds of greenery and deftly wrapped them. 'It's lovely,' said the customer to Bonnie, before she left.

The hiatus had effectively defused the high drama of a few minutes before, and Simmy now faced the girl with complete calm. 'I assume my father took the letter to the police this morning. They'll examine it for any traces of the person who sent it. If you have a name to give them, they can make comparisons, and probably rule him out right away, if it's not the right man. That means you have a plain duty to tell them the name. Do you see?'

Bonnie shook her head. 'You make it sound so simple, when it's not.'

'Okay. So tell me the whole story. Was there a letter? A fire? Was anybody hurt? Did you go to the police?'

'No letter. No fire. It was never as bad as that. The bloke next door to us, Mr Browning, got in a state about the noise the dogs made sometimes, and complained to the police about them. They came round and said we were within our rights and the noise was not excessive. But he didn't leave it at that. He made threats, and one of them was that he'd come round one night and burn down the kennels. It was scary, but he never did anything. Nobody was hurt, but it was really nasty for a while. He moved away, soon after, and we downsized the dogs.'

Simmy recalled her mother's description of the set-up. 'My mum said you had about fifty dogs in the back garden, when she went to look at a puppy, only a few months ago.'

'We never had that many. I told you, we had to get rid of most of them.' Her face darkened. 'We still miss them horribly. If you're not a doggy person' – she gave Simmy a knowing look – 'you can't really understand. They're so amazing, you know. Sensitive and loyal and forgiving. And people let them down and hurt them and they can't possibly work out why. It makes you feel sick all the time, knowing there are dogs being horribly treated, all over the world.'

Simmy looked at Spike. 'You're right – I don't really get it. They're just animals, after all. They don't *think* like we do. People have turned them into toys for their own entertainment.'

'Some people have,' Bonnie agreed. 'You should hear Corinne on that subject.'

Simmy gave up, conscious of being on shaky ground. It wasn't her problem, anyway. But there were still pertinent details that she needed to clarify. 'What was that story about one of your dogs almost being nabbed? I didn't get the whole thing straight in my mind. I'm not just being nosy, either. With my father so upset, I want to be sure we're not missing any chance of helping catch the man who . . . who's such a menace.'

The girl sighed and looked away. 'It wasn't anything much. It was just before Easter. I caught somebody climbing over the fence, looking as if he meant to nick one of our dogs. Millie and Spike were in the garden, so I presumed he was after them. Millie's a great yapper, and was never going to be an easy catch. I was in the house and heard her, so I dashed outside and screamed at him. He ran away. That's it.'

'Was that after the authorities had closed you down for breeding puppies?'

'It was in the middle of it all. We were trying to get good homes for the last two bitches. Corinne was in an awful state about it. I guess everybody knew we'd been accused of bad practice. They called us a puppy farm, which was stupid. We were never that.'

Simmy waved impatiently. 'The man,' she insisted. 'Who do you think he was?'

'Well, not your murderer, that's for sure. Nothing like

him. That's assuming he's the other man you saw in the car.'

'How do you know what he looked like?' Simmy felt a cold shiver at the girl's comprehensive knowledge of something that surely ought by rights to be confidential between her and the police.

'Oh – it was on the news. The police are looking for a man in his forties with short dark hair. Wanted for questioning, or something. Anyway, the man who went after the dogs was younger than that and fairer.' She grimaced. 'It's all dreadfully complicated, isn't it?'

Simmy remembered Ben's admiration of the girl's abilities, and suspected a false modesty was at work. The more she saw of Bonnie, the deeper her character appeared to be.

'Was it really on the news? Did they say the man had been seen in a car with Travis McNaughton?' She could not imagine that so much would be revealed to the world at large.

'Not that part, no. But I just thought it must be him. It's obvious, isn't it?' Again the innocent gaze raised niggling worries.

'I don't know,' said Simmy. 'Police procedure is a complete mystery to me. It does sound as if questioning you this morning was a complete waste of time, and the last I heard, I'm meant to be trying to pick the man out, as well. Or *two* men in my case, I suppose. I'm hoping they've given up on the whole idea. Moxon never said anything about it yesterday.'

'Have you told him about the threatening letter?'

'My parents probably have by now. Let's hope there are

fingerprints all over it and they catch the wretched man right away.'

'Yeah,' said Bonnie without enthusiasm.

Simmy could see that a change of subject would be a good idea. 'So what's Corinne doing with her time, now she's not breeding dogs? Singing and giving obedience classes – is that right?'

'More or less. There's still some fallout from the dog business. People keep turning up and telling her she should have fought it, and let them take her to court. And we probably could have fought the injunction and all that. But we'd had enough. The dogs weren't properly house-trained or socialised. You can't breed them on an industrial scale and produce animals that fit into a family. They did bark a lot, and smell. So we packed it in. The bloke who tried to steal them was just another annoyance.'

Simmy had an idea. 'Do you think it was the same man who took Barbara Hodge's dog for ransom?'

Bonnie looked fixedly at the floor for a long moment, leaving Simmy unable to read her thoughts. 'Probably part of the same gang,' she mumbled. 'We're not meant to talk about that, actually. Barbara and Valerie don't want people to know they paid the ransom. They're embarrassed about it.'

Simmy heaved another sigh of profound frustration and sent out a strong mental summons to Ben and his logical approach. Bonnie, despite her frank disclosures, seemed to wreathe everything in mist. There was nothing in her account that could be grasped and used to explain the immediate issues before them. She tried again to get it straight. 'It matters, doesn't it – because the police must have thought it could be the same man who murdered somebody on Tuesday in Troutbeck.' Her voice had grown louder, reflecting the earlier desire to treat Bonnie with violence. 'And perhaps it was him who threatened my father and almost gave him a stroke.'

'Yeah,' muttered Bonnie. 'Maybe.'

'So – could it have been this Mr Browning or not?'

'Not. Forget I ever said that, will you? He's not living here any more. And he's old and pathetic. Why would he kill anyone? It was just the coincidence of the fire threat. And it could be that loads of people say that kind of thing.'

Simmy had no answer to that. She looked at her watch. 'I'm having coffee,' she said, with another surge of annoyance at this reminder of Bonnie's frailties. 'What about you?'

'I've got a drink with me, thanks. Chocolate milk, actually.'

The front door pinged as Simmy was going into the back room. She glanced round, in the faint hope that it might be Ben. But it was someone much older and hairier. Before she could get a proper look, the recumbent Spike was up and snarling, flying down the floral avenue to launch what looked like a savage attack on an innocent customer.

Before Simmy or Bonnie could move or speak, the man had swiped the dog harmlessly aside. A fluffy crossbreed like Spike was no Rottweiler or pit bull. Its jaws were narrow and comparatively weak. 'Stop it, will you,' the man shouted. 'What's the matter with you?'

'Murray,' said Bonnie tonelessly. 'He still doesn't like

you.' Spike slunk back to his patch at a silent gesture from his young mistress.

'Why's he here?' demanded the man.

'Never mind that. What do you want?'

'I'm looking for Corinne. Thought you'd tell me where I might find her.'

Simmy wished she could leave them to get on with it. After all, the man had been a customer, sending funeral flowers for Miss Hodge. Despite his appearance, he was a known quantity and nothing to worry about. She tried to suppress an unworthy but undeniable perception of Bonnie as being connected to an array of undesirable individuals. She was clearly familiar with a whole underclass of whom Simmy had so far been entirely unaware. Surely even Melanie, with her unreliable family, didn't mix with such as this man?

'She's going to that Lincoln thing. Music festival. She's got a gig there. Last-minute decision as usual.' Bonnie turned to Simmy apologetically. 'Sorry about this.' She looked sternly at her dog. 'Spike's not always such a great judge of character.'

'Lincoln? Bloody hell! Don't tell me she's gone without a phone.'

'Have you tried it?'

'What d'you think? Turned off.'

'She'll be sleeping in a tent somewhere without the charger, so won't bother to take it. Is it important?'

'It won't have to be, will it?' He gave Simmy a nod that she supposed was intended to be friendly. 'Sorry to cause ructions. Not that it was my fault.' He straightened two or three pots of flowers that Spike had dislodged in his flying assault. 'You ought not to let her bring the dog to work. It's unprofessional.'

'Shut up,' said Bonnie. 'And stop stalking Corinne. She's never going to take up with you, and you know it.'

'Stalking!' He spat the word back at her. 'Give over! I was trying to do her a favour, if you must know. It's no skin off my nose if she can't be arsed to take a phone with her.' His brow creased. 'She won't be there yet, though, will she? What time did she go?'

'Don't ask me. She was still in the house when I left to come here. She'll be driving, maybe. That's why she's not answering the phone.'

Simmy opened her mouth to query Bonnie's words, which were entirely at odds with what the girl had told her. Then she closed it again and waited.

Murray became thoughtful. 'Okay, then. Tell her I was looking for her, next time you see her – okay?'

'If I remember,' said Bonnie rudely.

'You're as bad as her, you know that,' he threw at her, and slammed out of the shop.

'Who is he, exactly?' asked Simmy.

'I told you. Murray. He's just a bloke that's known our family for ever. He's harmless, even if Spike doesn't think so. You bad dog!' she crooned, without a hint of anger.

'You lied to him, when you said Corinne was at home this morning,' Simmy pointed out.

Bonnie showed no unease at being caught out. 'So what? I don't want to make things easy for him, do I? Corinne hasn't got time for him these days.'

Simmy gave up. 'So are you going to the funeral or not? It's not long now, is it?'

'I suppose I should. I'll be sorry later, otherwise.' She spoke languidly, as if it hardly mattered. Simmy's feeling intensified that Bonnie was little more than a patch of insubstantial mist. It was like trying to tell a cloud what to do. The girl just drifted along in her own sweet way and left everyone else to make the best of it.

'After that, you might as well go home,' she said, more angrily than she meant. 'I can manage for the rest of the day. You need to find someone to mind Spike before you come here again. Sorry – but that's the way it is.'

'I know. You said that before.'

'Sorry. I'm in a foul mood today. Listen – if you go home now, you can change into something more suitable for a funeral. I'm not blaming you, exactly, but now it's gone quiet, and we've said everything we need to. Thanks for making the effort, when things sound so complicated at home.' Simmy clamped her mouth shut, determined not to sound apologetic. Hadn't she been a soul of patience and generosity?

'They *are* complicated,' Bonnie agreed. 'Which is why I was hoping you'd let me use the flat upstairs.'

'It's not a flat, and I'm not getting into that now. Just go, there's a good girl. I can't cope with any more today.'

'Okay, then. What time tomorrow?'

'You won't bring the dog, will you?'

'Not if it's just for the morning. I'll do ten till one, shall I? Would that be enough?'

'I expect so. Ten it is, then. Bye.' She was strongly

tempted to physically march the girl and her pet out into the street, but she restrained herself. A little voice kept reminding her that Melanie had recommended Bonnie, and that would never have happened if there'd been any reason to worry about it.

'Oh – and don't worry about your dad,' Bonnie threw back at the final second. 'He'll be fine.'

The effect of this final assurance was, perversely, to make Simmy worry quite a lot.

Chapter Sixteen

It was twenty to twelve, too late to catch her parents before the funeral at twelve-thirty. At least, her mother would either have already left, or be too busy with final flourishes to engage in conversation. There was no certainty about Russell. He had never intended to go to the crowded church and say prayers for a woman he barely knew. The suggestion that he should had come as a solution to his trauma of the day before. It would be a way of keeping him at Angie's side, and possibly distracting him from his own troubles.

But if he remained at home, then a little chat with Simmy would surely be beneficial. Using her mobile, she called the Beck View number. The bed-and-breakfast business demanded that such calls never went unanswered, if at all possible.

The recorded message cut in after five or six peals. *We're sorry there's nobody here to speak to you at the moment. Please leave your name, number, etc and we will phone you back*. The deliberately simple wording always gave Simmy a small pleasure. She left no reply, and finished the call hoping that both parents had gone to help send Barbara Hodge to her rest. That would be good news. And yet her anxiety level remained painfully high.

Her father's agitation made it impossible to guess his frame of mind at any given moment. If he was still terrified of an arson attack wasn't it unlikely he would leave the house vulnerable? Had the police somehow reassured him? Had her mother exerted all her considerable force and brooked no argument about going to the funeral?

Or was Russell Straw crouched crazily in the hallway with a bucket of water, afraid to answer the phone in case it was another threat? Somehow this last idea felt most persuasive and Simmy grew almost crazy herself as she let it flourish.

It was ridiculous, she told herself, to feel lonely or isolated either in Windermere or Troutbeck with people in and out of the shop and passing just outside. Even alone in her cottage she was aware of pedestrians and cars passing every few minutes. She might be undersupplied with intimate friends, but she was surrounded by community, comfortable in the society of a wide range of people.

But now she felt very much alone and cut off. Melanie was abandoning her. She had wantonly sent Bonnie away. Ninian was habitually elusive, and Ben had exams. Hanging over her was a powerful obligation to confront the horrible facts of a violent killing, which she could not avoid. Now her father needed her and she had nobody to turn to. She should close the shop and go over to Beck View and ensure that all was well. There was no good reason not to, and yet she dithered. She wanted more information, moral support, advice. She wanted to be assured that she wasn't being stupid.

She realised that there was one person who might resolve some of these troubles, or at least listen and advise. A person who was also certain to be busy and burdened by the evil that men do, and who was not in the best of health. A person who was fond of Simmy and fascinated by her, and would very probably be at her side within minutes of a call.

All of which comprised more than enough reason to swallow down any reservations, and key in the number of DI Moxon's personal phone.

But Moxon didn't answer his phone. *Obviously*, thought Simmy crossly, *he was at the damned funeral as well as everybody else*. He had put his murder investigation on hold and gone to pay his last respects to a pillar of the community. Simmy was the only person left in the whole Southern Lakes who remained at her post, then. It was a wonder she couldn't hear the sonorous tones of 'Abide with Me' wafting over the deserted town – the church was probably close enough for that, if she opened the shop door and listened hard. But then she gave herself a shake, and registered that there was still traffic outside, and oblivious shoppers strolling along the pavements.

As if to prove the point, one of these shoppers paused, frowned and made a sharp turn into Persimmon Petals, as Simmy watched.

'I wasn't sure you'd be open,' said the young woman. 'What with that huge funeral going on. I mean – flowers and stuff.' She looked round vaguely, before focusing on

Bonnie's display and smiling broadly. 'Hey! This is cool! Never seen anything like it.'

Simmy nodded. 'It was new yesterday. What can I do for you?'

The customer snorted gently at this clichéd question. 'I dunno, really. Thought my gran might like some flowers, when I go over to hers tonight. She's cooking,' she explained. 'Just a small thing for the table, I thought.'

Simmy suggested freesias, or yellow daisies. 'Something simple with short stems,' she added, thinking on her feet.

'Right. Yellow's good. Or orange.' She stared at the colours all around her. 'You choose, okay.'

The transaction was soon completed, with Simmy issuing instructions for keeping the flowers fresh until the evening, which she felt sure would be ignored. It was not unusual to encounter people who failed to grasp that flowers were living entities, requiring water and light to survive. Once or twice, she had lost patience and snapped, 'They are *real*, you know.' And there had been an occasion when she heard herself saying, 'Haven't you ever heard of photosynthesis?' only to receive a blank stare of utter incomprehension.

The customer made her reconsider about closing the shop. She made coffee and replaced the flowers that had been taken from the darker end of the row, and found it was almost one o'clock. Church bells were ringing across the town, audible even inside the shop. *Like a wedding*, Simmy thought, unable to recall the usual practice for a funeral. Perhaps Miss Hodge had made a special request for peals as the coffin was taken outside for burial. The woman had apparently made quite a lot of special requests for her last day in the world, determined to disappear with all guns blazing, so to speak.

Then it occurred to her that she could just pop over to the church and try to find her parents. If her father had in fact gone with his wife, he would be eager to get home again as soon as the service was over. They wouldn't go to the buffet that followed in a pub near the church. Protocol might be fuzzy where such things were concerned, but Angie would feel that she came sufficiently low in the pecking order for such an intrusion to be unwarranted. The church part was the main thing, after all.

Quickly, Simmy pulled on her jacket and left the shop through its street door, locking it behind her. The church was barely five minutes' walk away, but there were various routes to it, with a network of small streets to choose from. It would be all too easy to miss Angie and Russell, once they started on their way home.

She took the most direct course, and very soon found herself on the edge of a milling crowd of people, dressed in dark colours. No nonsense about bright reds and yellows for this lady, she noted. There had been a spate of requests that the celebratory aspect be dominant, over the past year – a habit that Angie especially deplored. 'It's just another form of denial,' she said robustly. 'Give me the good old Victorian approach, with black shrouds everywhere and a year of mourning.' Russell had been ordered to stay at home and be miserable for *at least* a year, if she died before him.

The atmosphere was very sombre, possibly even more so than Angie might have wished. In fact, as Simmy looked around her, the pale faces and whispered voices struck her as decidedly abnormal. Even at her own baby daughter's funeral, there had been a lightening of mood once the main event was over.

'Did something happen?' she asked a woman she knew by sight. 'I've just got here, looking for my parents.'

'Valerie collapsed, right there at the front of the church. We all thought she was dead for a few minutes. It was dreadful.' The woman shuddered. 'I've never seen such grief.'

Simmy was lost for words. She could hardly demand a detailed account from somebody she barely knew. It made it even more urgent that she find her mother, who would be able to supply a full description of whatever had happened. She looked around, hoping to see one or other of her parents in the ocean of faces. 'Gosh!' she said weakly. 'Poor woman.'

'It sounds mad, but honestly, it was exactly as if she'd seen a ghost. She was just getting into the eulogy, looking at everybody – you know, the way people do when they make a speech. Then she went white, and tried to speak, and just – passed out. There's a man over there who swears she must have seen Barbara, looking up at her. Daft, of course.'

Oh well, thought Simmy, *looks as if I'll get all the details, whether I want them or not.*

'So then what? Did they carry on with the service?'

'Sort of. There were two doctors – at least – in the congregation, and they revived her. She insisted everything carry on, and just sat in a huddle in a front pew, while we tried to sing the next hymn. The vicar did his bit, and then they rang the bells, and we all filed out. They're doing the interment now. I saw Valerie propped up between two men. I think they're cousins or something. It'll soon be finished. The whole thing was a lot shorter than it was supposed to be. Now nobody knows what's happening.'

The milling about continued, with people craning their necks to see if anyone was issuing guidance somewhere. The undertaker's team, led by Bruce, was standing stiffly beside the empty hearse, watching impassively. The whole road was blocked by the assembled mourners, making it impossible for them to drive away with dignity. Simmy remembered that poor old Mr Invermore wasn't until three o'clock. They had a little time to spare.

Simmy worked her way eastwards, thinking that would be the direction taken by her parents and she might head them off. People had begun peeling away, with frustrated expressions. They all wanted to talk about the drama, to know whether the post-funeral spread was still going to happen, and whether they should go to it. Simmy heard snatches of conversation, much of it critical of Valerie. 'She ought to know how to hold herself together better than that.' 'She should never have taken it upon herself to do a eulogy, if she wasn't up to it.' 'Do we really know who she is, anyway?' 'Why doesn't somebody tell us what to do now?' There was a general sense of having been let down, and cheated of an experience they'd looked forward to. It was shocking for a funeral to deviate from the normal pattern, and somehow blasphemous. There was unease and a desire to lay blame. 'If she was going to 'throw a fit, she should have kept it for the graveside,' said one woman, quite loudly.

'It was like that bit in *Macbeth*,' came a familiar voice. 'Where he sees the ghost of Duncan. I thought she looked paralysed by guilt.'

'Ben?' Simmy grabbed a shoulder. 'What are you doing here?'

The boy shook her off. 'I thought it would be an experience,' he muttered.

'And what's all this showing off about *Macbeth*?' she went on, feeling increasingly like his irate mother. 'You can't talk like that, you idiot.'

He scowled at her. 'I can do what I like. It's true, anyway. She looked as if she was expecting to be struck dead. And then she sort of *was*.' His excitement was irrepressible. 'It was awesome! I guess she thinks she let the Hodge lady down somehow. Imagining retribution from beyond the grave. It was like a *movie*, Sim.'

'And you're behaving like an eight-year-old. Come with me, before somebody hits you.'

'Why would they hit me?' He gave her a bewildered look. 'I haven't done anything.'

'You're being insensitive.' She pulled him along, trying not to draw further attention from the milling crowd. 'Come with me,' she said again.

He resisted for a few seconds and then did as instructed, still talking. 'Melanie's going to be furious about missing it. She's the only person not here. I saw your mum, in the church.'

'Did you? Was she on her own?'

'What? There were about a million people in there.'

'I mean, was my dad with her?'

'Not that I could see. Ah – there she is, look.' He pointed with a triumphant air. 'You can let go of me now,' he added.

Simmy's blood turned to ice. Her heart pounded sickeningly and her knees went weak, before she could work out what was happening. Angie was dressed in a dark suit, with a pale blouse under it. Her face was serious, and her hair flattened down much more than usual. Ben, unaware of any problem, called to her, 'Hi, Mrs Straw. We weren't sure you were at the funeral. We've been looking for you.'

Funeral! Simmy thought shakily. The last time she had seen her mother in those clothes was at the pathetic little ceremony that had marked the disposal of her own stillborn baby. The associations had been powerful enough to render her completely helpless, until she identified them. Before anybody could notice her state, she took a deep breath. Her heart rate subsided, but there was still a cold churning sensation in her middle.

But Angie had seen her daughter's pale face and shaking hands. 'Oh, P'Simmon! It's brought it all back, hasn't it. I should have known.'

'It's that suit,' Simmy said faintly.

Angie looked down at herself. 'Of course it is.' She rubbed her forehead. 'And now I understand why your father looked exactly the same as you're looking now. It never even crossed my mind. What a monster I am sometimes.'

'Dad? Didn't he go with you? Where is he?' She looked past her mother to the street outside, expecting to see him.

'He couldn't face it. I left him changing duvet covers. You know how long that always takes him.'

'He didn't answer the phone.'

'When?'

'Ages ago. Just before twelve. I assumed you'd both gone to the funeral.'

'He'd have been upstairs, and not heard it.' Angie showed no sign of worry, but Simmy was not reassured.

'He *always* answers the phone,' she said.

'Did you leave a message?'

'No.'

'I told him not to answer the phone. If the person who wrote that letter tries to call, I don't know what he'd do. He's behaving so oddly, I was almost scared to leave him.'

'Did you speak to the police?'

Angie nodded. 'They said they'd send someone round, but nobody had been by the time I left. Rather a poor service, if you ask me. People always seem to forget that the police are meant to be public servants, with an obligation to respond when asked. They forget it themselves. That's another reason I left your father at home – so he can show them the letter.'

'Will he let them in? What if they send someone in plain clothes?'

Angie rolled her eyes. 'That's their problem. I should have known better than to come here. I just had it fixed in my head that I ought to. It was a fiasco. There's nothing more terrible than an undignified funeral.'

'Where's Valerie now?'

'Who knows? It was awfully strange, though. I was

sitting near the back – lucky to get a place, actually. Valerie seemed to be looking right at me when she went into her fit, or whatever it was. Then the woman next to me said, "Why's she looking at me like that?" and I realised quite a few of us all had the same impression. There was a man behind us, with a boy. The lad asked the same thing. At least he said, "Dad, she's looking at you" in a loud whisper. We were all packed in so tight, it was impossible to be sure.'

'People are saying she saw Barbara's ghost.'

'Just like *Macbeth*,' came a muttered voice close by.

'Ben! Are you still here?' Simmy felt encumbered, not just by the boy, and her mother, but the worry over Russell and astonishment over the collapse of the funeral.

'You told me to come with you. Hi, Mrs Straw,' he added again.

'You were at the funeral? Shouldn't you be at school?'

'Revision,' he said patiently. 'They give us free time. Has anything happened?' he asked Simmy directly. 'What's this about a letter?'

Simmy swallowed back the urge to snap at him again. 'I'll tell you later. Can you come in at teatime? Mel might be there with any luck. I can't remember exactly what she said she was doing.' She had a thought. 'Have you seen Bonnie? She was going to come to the funeral, possibly bringing her dog. She thought Valerie would have hers here, as well.'

'Dogs!' scoffed the boy. 'Why's everybody going on about dogs all the time?'

'Are they?'

'Oh, yeah – I forgot to say. Just before she fainted, or

whatever it was, Valerie was talking about the retriever she and the Hodge lady had, telling all about how they found him together in a puppy farm, and took him home and what a bond he was, and a blessing and I don't know what. She was just getting started on the story of how they almost lost him, when she went into meltdown.'

'The man behind me coughed,' Angie remembered. 'Sort of a choking fit. That was when she looked our way.'

Simmy watched Ben's face as it did its familiar deep thought trick. 'Funny,' he said. 'Is he still here? Can you see him anywhere?'

'You're joking!' Angie protested impatiently.

'What did he look like?'

'I have no idea. He was *behind* me. I never even glimpsed him. I just saw the boy with him, as we left the church. He was just ahead of me, and kept staring all round.'

'So what did *he* look like? He must have been just about the only kid in the place.'

'About thirteen. Smart clothes. Big ears.' She stopped herself. 'What does it matter, anyway? I can't hang about here. I need to get home.'

'I'm coming with you,' said Simmy.

'What about me?' Ben whined.

'You can go and have a free sandwich at the funeral thing. Then come and see me in the shop later on. It's closed now. Melanie might be coming in at some point. I've got wedding flowers to do.' Again she felt overwhelmed, her stomach churning from the pressure of it all.

'There's Bonnie,' said the boy suddenly. 'She's with Valerie. I wonder where the dog got to.'

'What?' Simmy and Angie both tried to follow the direction of his gaze. 'Where?'

Instantly, Simmy saw a group of women, moving slowly through the crowd, which parted for them like magic. Valerie was in the middle, much larger than her acolytes. Bonnie was walking sideways, talking, dodging people who were in her path, her hand on Valerie Rossiter's forearm. She was like a small tug directing a slow, clumsy container ship. Two older women were flanking Valerie, something anxious and uncertain in their manner suggesting they had found themselves in a role they never expected. Simmy didn't know either of them, but her mother did.

'Anita,' she called. 'Are you all right? Can we do anything?'

A faded-looking woman in a wide-brimmed hat scanned the faces of the scattering crowd for whoever had spoken. 'Here,' said Angie, stepping forward. 'It's me. Remember me? Beck View, two doors away from you.'

'Oh – Mrs Straw, yes.' Relief was visible in the drop of her shoulders and jaw. 'We were just trying to help . . . there didn't seem to be anybody else. This is Susan. She's my sister-in-law.' The other woman looked equally bemused and embarrassed. They were attracting stares on all sides. 'And this is . . .' Anita indicated Bonnie.

'We know Bonnie,' said Simmy.

Her voice seemed to awaken something in Valerie, who gave her a direct look. 'The florist,' she said, with a little nod. 'Honestly, this is all so humiliating. I feel a complete fool for causing such chaos. At a *funeral*, for heaven's sake. I'm never going to live it down.'

Her tone was breathless and her skin was mottled. She looked as if she would fall again if left unsupported. Simmy's mind was wrestling with a swirl of impressions. Where were the people who *should* be helping Valerie? *Who* were they? Was it possible she had nobody close, now that Barbara was dead? And what was *Bonnie* doing? And, after all this, did Valerie actually *need* someone to look after her? On the face of it, she was perfectly capable of getting along by herself.

'What's meant to happen now?' she asked. 'Isn't there some sort of lunch? Everybody's waiting to know what they should do. Look at them!'

Valerie put a hand to her chest, and took a few deep breaths. 'Yes, everyone's been asking the same thing. I'll be better in a minute. It was all so . . . I'm such a wimp. I just need somebody with a loud voice to tell them all to get back to the plan.'

'A lot of them have gone already,' said Angie. 'They must have thought it was cancelled.'

'Didn't the vicar say anything?' Simmy asked. In her limited experience, the whole business was generally orchestrated by the officiating clergyman.

'No, but it's on the service sheets. It tells them where to go afterwards.'

'They're like sheep,' said Bonnie scathingly. 'Any little change to what they expect, and they just stand about waiting for instructions. Honestly, it's ridiculous.'

'Too right,' said Ben, with matching contempt. 'I could try and mobilise them, if you like.'

'No, no. Let me,' said Angie with a sweep of her arm.

'They'll be standing around here till midnight, otherwise.' She raised the same arm above her head, and waved it. 'Everybody!' she bellowed, at impressive volume. 'Will you all please go to the Elleray for lunch!' She flourished her uplifted arm in the direction of the pub. 'Please move along!'

Simmy sidled away, acutely embarrassed. Her mother's voice carried amazingly, impossible to ignore. People actually began to move in the designated direction, murmuring amongst themselves and casting admiring eyes at Angie.

'Thanks,' said Valerie. 'I suppose I should be leading the way. God, I hate this.'

Simmy could see Ben bursting to ask questions, and hoped he would restrain himself. Bonnie was ahead of him. 'You'll be fine,' she told the woman. 'It'll soon be over.'

The incongruity of a slight young girl consoling a large middle-aged woman silenced even Ben. Anita and Susan fell away, still manifesting an impression of people drawn into something against their will and feeling very awkward about it. Valerie took another deep breath and began walking determinedly down the street unescorted. She looked lonely, defiant and fragile. Simmy waited a moment and then asked, 'Hasn't she got any friends?'

Angie was the only one left within earshot. 'Seems not. She was so bound up with Barbara that nobody else ever seems to have got near her.'

'You'd think Barbara's friends would have rallied round her, then.'

'She wouldn't let them. Said it was all down to her to make sure Barbara's wishes were carried out. I heard them talking earlier on, in the pew in front of me. I heard quite a lot of things, actually,' she added thoughtfully.

Simmy looked around for Bonnie, and saw her walking with Ben, at the rear of the procession of mourners. 'Are you two going to the pub?' she called after them.

Bonnie turned round. 'Why not?' she said, with a little wave. Ben avoided Simmy's eye and kept walking.

'Where's Spike?' Simmy called after them.

'Tied to the church railings,' Bonnie shouted back. 'I'm getting him now.'

'I have to get home,' said Angie. 'I meant to be there by now.'

Simmy glanced at her watch. It was only twenty past one. It had felt far more than twenty minutes since she'd closed the shop and set out for the church. If they were quick, she could check on her father and get back to work not long after two.

'Come on, then,' she said.

They walked briskly southwards, and reached Beck View in under ten minutes. Angie seemed reluctant to talk, and Simmy was content to spend the time trying to order her thoughts. A strong vein of pity for Valerie Rossiter was running through her, along with an exasperation directed at Ben and Bonnie. They had each been lacking in appropriate feeling, treating the interrupted funeral as more of a joke or puzzle than the gut-wringing disaster that it truly was. Barbara Hodge had become lost in the drama – her name scarcely mentioned in Simmy's hearing. Valerie had looked dreadful. At least Bonnie had shown sympathy and concern, she admitted. It was Ben and his melodramatic remarks about Macbeth that had most annoyed her. He could be such a thoughtless show-off sometimes.

Would Valerie make another speech over the lunch, she wondered? It would, after all, be her last chance to eulogise her dead friend.

Angie had to ring the bell of her own front door, because Russell had bolted it from the inside, and she had no way to open it.

Nobody came.

'Damn it,' snarled Simmy's mother. 'What's he playing at?'

'Can we go round the back?'

'He'll have locked that as well, but I think I've got a key to it somewhere. He might even have left one under the flowerpot, as usual.' She rummaged in her bag. 'Honestly, this is getting beyond a joke.'

She located the key in her bag and managed to gain entry through the scullery behind the kitchen.

A search of the house quickly revealed that Russell Straw was not at home.

Chapter Seventeen

'But where can he have gone?' Simmy asked, yet again. 'What about the police station?'

'How did he lock the door?' asked Angie slowly. 'It was bolted from the inside.'

'The back wasn't. He went out through there, surely?'

'Hmm. Could be – but he never does that. And where's Bertie?' The women blinked at each other at having failed to notice until now the animal's absence. 'Why would he take the dog with him?'

Simmy had nothing to suggest. Her mind was empty, like the rooms in the house. A week earlier, she'd have felt no anxiety whatever at a sudden whimsical disappearance on the part of her father. Since then, he had manifested alarming changes in personality and capacity, which gave rise to images of a shambling old man with his dog, wandering through Rayrigg Woods unsure of his whereabouts. But she swept such fears aside as being impossibly exaggerated, and at least ten years premature. 'I don't know,' she said.

'We'll have to call the police. That's the only thing I can think of.'

'Are we sure he hasn't left a note?'

They went into the kitchen and stared around, then did the same in the living room and the main bedroom. 'What about the guest rooms?' said Simmy. 'Have you any people in this week?'

'It's May. Of course we have. We're full. He was changing duvet covers. I could have a look to see if he finished them.' Before Simmy could speak, Angie had run upstairs, and was back again in two minutes. 'He's only done one, and that looks as if he just dropped it on the floor. He must have come down for some reason, and never gone back to finish the job.'

'What time did you go out?'

'About twenty to twelve. I wanted to get a seat in the church. As it was I almost didn't manage it.'

'I phoned not long after that. He didn't answer. Does that mean he left a few minutes after you?'

'I told you – I thought he'd do best to ignore it. I said to him – just leave it if it rings.'

'I'm not sure he would, though, when it came to it.'

'Well, at least we can assume he hasn't been kidnapped,' said Angie with a little laugh.

'Can we? What makes you so sure?'

'Who in the world would snatch a demented old fart like him – *and* his dog? That's a ludicrous idea.'

'He's not demented, Mum. He's just upset by that threatening letter. Where did you put it, anyway? The police still haven't seen it – is that right?'

210

'I told you – I phoned them. I did mean to take it down to show them, but the guests took ages over breakfast, and after that I was rushing to do the rooms, and then it was the funeral. Russ had it in his pocket, last I noticed. He was much better this morning, actually. Up until about eleven, at least. He seemed to slump a bit after that.'

'Then what happened?'

'I'm not sure. I left him in here' – they were back in the kitchen – 'with the local paper, once he'd convinced me he had no intention of coming with me to the church. I grabbed myself a mug of coffee and he was just staring into space. I tried talking to him, but it was hopeless.'

Simmy could all too well imagine her mother's impatience, and selfish need to stick to her own timetable. Angie could be very single-minded at times. 'He *must* have gone to the police, then. That's the only explanation.'

'Except it's taking rather a long time, don't you think? Two hours or so, probably.'

Simmy looked again at her watch. It was five to two. 'We'll have to phone them and ask if they've seen him.'

'What about the shop? You shouldn't miss any more customers. It's Friday – that's usually busy, isn't it?'

Simmy rubbed her brow. 'And I've got a whole lot of wedding flowers to do for tomorrow,' she said distractedly.

'I'll go down to the police and let you know what I find. It doesn't take both of us.'

'I can't just go back to work as if nothing had happened. The shop can wait.'

'Didn't you say Melanie's coming in? Has she got a key?'

'Are you trying to get rid of me?' Her attempt at a light

note fell very flat. 'I'm sorry, Mum, but I can't think of anything but Dad.'

'He'll be perfectly all right. You're as bad as him, worrying about nothing.'

'That letter wasn't nothing. The murder wasn't nothing, either. There are seriously bad people out there and we've fallen foul of them, Dad and me. I can't understand why you're not worried.'

'Lack of imagination, probably. I simply can't visualise him and his dog being bundled into a van and kept hostage for totally incomprehensible reasons. It wouldn't make the least bit of sense.'

'But these things happen,' Simmy almost shouted. 'I know for a certain fact that they do. Look at all that business in Coniston, only a few months ago.'

Angie moaned gently. 'You're not helping. Just leave me to find him. Please. I do understand how you feel, but I promise you he'll be all right. Have faith, woman. This is your very sensible father we're talking about.'

Simmy moaned in turn. 'There must be a clue here somewhere. The door – he bolted it from the inside, went out at the back and locked that after himself. So he can't have been dragged away. He took the dog, so the house was unprotected. What does that tell us?'

'That there's not very much to worry about,' said Angie brightly. 'When you put it like that, it's obviously something perfectly straightforward.'

'No, Mum. It could easily mean he's gone back to Troutbeck, trying to find the people who wrote the letter. He thinks they're evil, remember?'

'Was the car there?' Angie said, suddenly running to the front room window and peering out. 'I never even noticed.'

The car was generally parked in the short driveway, off the street. But it was also often left further away, so as to provide space for the B&B guests. It was a complicated dance that they performed every day, according to who was due to arrive and what promises had been given. Some guests insisted on the closest possible access for their vehicle, expecting to drive to within inches of the front door.

'Can't see it,' said Angie. 'And the gate's closed.' The gate separated the driveway from the street, and entailed further complications. Russell's job was to open it for visitors, and close it when everything was settled for the night. During the day, it was almost always open.

'It's all so unnervingly *neat*,' Simmy complained. 'It feels as if he's been planning this – as if he's left home.' Her heart swelled and thumped at the idea of her father as a missing person, never to be seen again.

'Don't say that,' begged Angie.

'Could somebody have phoned him? Told him to meet them somewhere?'

'Like who?'

'I have no idea. Where's the mobile? Is there any chance he's got it with him? We could just call him, if so, and settle it all in a moment.'

Angie gave her a withering look. 'He never takes it with him. Last time I used it, the battery was almost dead. I very much doubt whether either of us has bothered to charge it since then. The thing's a complete waste of time. And who would know its number, anyway?'

Simmy grabbed the house phone and keyed in 1471. *You were called today at eleven forty-one. The caller withheld their number.* She held the handset tightly, forcing herself to think lucidly.

'Eleven forty-one,' she repeated. 'Number withheld. That must have been only a minute or two after you left. It's not the call I made, because I didn't withhold the number. Someone might have been watching the house, waiting for you to go. Then they called him and persuaded him to go off with them.'

'In our car?'

'Apparently.'

'No – I think the car might be out in the street. I can't remember where we left it last night.' Angie frowned. 'Let me think. There was a family with a toddler. Yes – they parked in the drive. They had a huge amount of luggage to unload. So ours might easily be out there somewhere. Let's go and look.'

Simmy closed her eyes against the wave of dread that was building inside her. 'We've got to find him, Mum. This isn't funny.'

Angie was wrestling with the stiff bolt on the front door, and then found it was locked as well, and the key removed. 'We'd all be dead if there was a fire, the way he hides the key. It's completely idiotic. Where the hell is it?'

'Doesn't he usually hang it on that hook?' Simmy pointed to a small board on the wall, supplied with three metal hooks, all empty.

Her mother was fruitlessly pulling at the door and continuing her rant. 'God! I hate this obsession with locking everything. It gives me claustrophobia. We're never going to get out.' Her voice was rising in the first sign of dawning panic since they'd got into the house.

'We'll go out through the back,' said Simmy calmly. 'He might have got the key in his pocket, for all we know. And we probably should make sure he hasn't got the mobile. He might have charged it and taken it, after all.'

'Nothing would surprise me,' said Angie through gritted teeth.

But the mobile was in its place on top of the microwave oven, and the car was quickly spotted, thirty yards away from the house. Neither discovery was remotely reassuring.

'We have to go to the police,' Simmy insisted. 'It's only five minutes' walk.'

'Let me go by myself. It'll be quicker if there's just one of us trying to explain. You need to get back to the shop. I suppose you've got it all locked up, the same as the house.'

'The shop can wait.'

But it couldn't, really. Not only would she lose customers, but Ben and possibly Bonnie and even Melanie might all be expecting her to update them on recent events. She had left her phone and wallet in the back room. She was hungry, thirsty and scared. The prospect of being surrounded by the youngsters, who might make tactless remarks and be painfully excited, but would also be interested and eager to help, gave her mixed feelings. There would be a welcome warmth to them – even Bonnie had a knack of offering a gentle inoffensive reassurance, in her own way.

Her mother had no real need of her. All Simmy was doing was adding to the stress by showing how worried she was. If Moxon was available, he would make sure everything possible was done, and then he would very probably contact Simmy with an update.

'We're such a useless family when it comes to phones,' she burst out. 'Normal people would be texting and calling every couple of minutes, so everybody knew exactly what was going on. We've got to pull ourselves together, after this. We need a mobile each, and an agreement to keep in touch.'

'Nonsense,' said Angie. 'What earthly good would that do? It just creates the illusion that you're not all on your own.'

'Illusion?'

'Yes. A phone can't save you, when it comes to the crunch.'

Again, Simmy closed her eyes. The world had turned cold and unfeeling, with her mother the worst offender. 'All right. You go to the police and I'll go to the shop. But I'm not staying there long. When – if – Melanie arrives, I'm leaving her in charge, and coming back here. Okay? And phone me in the shop if anything happens. I mean *anything*.'

'Of course. But if I'm not back before you, you won't be able to get in.'

Simmy raised an eyebrow. 'I will – you forgot to lock the back door.'

'To hell with it. It can stay open.' This was meant as a parting shot, and Angie began to walk determinedly down the hill towards Bowness. Simmy opened her mouth to protest, her father's recent anxieties too acute to ignore in such a way. But then she gave herself a shake. Until a few weeks ago, nobody had locked the Beck View doors until last thing at night. Despite the fearful anonymous threat to burn the place down, she could see little sense in relying on keys.

'Right, then,' she muttered, more to herself than her mother. 'Let's see what Ben has to say.'

She hurried into the centre of Windermere and opened up her neglected shop. It was half past two, and the streets were far from thronged with shoppers. There was, after all, not a lot to buy in this modest little town. It was hard enough to track down anything to eat, let alone anything else. A big tourist shop took a prominent position on the main road down to the lakeside, and others offered maps, clothes and lingerie. Only with more diligent exploring did a few others come to light.

Restlessly, she checked her computer for new orders, and then went into the back room to assess the amount of work required for the wedding next day. The shelves looked bare now the stacks of funeral tributes had all disappeared. Stocks of fresh blooms for wedding favours were worryingly low. It might be a small affair, but the order included a handsome table display, and a bouquet for the bride, as well as sprays for the mothers and sisters. No particular colour scheme, and a request to keep the prices low, gave her much more freedom than usual.

All she could think about was her father. If he was in danger, if something appalling happened to him, nothing in the world would ever seem bright or hopeful again. The fear was paralysing, and was growing worse. Picking at various flowers, squashing them together and then dropping them, she knew she would never be able to concentrate on the job in hand. A wire pricked her thumb, and she sucked it absent-mindedly. Somewhere not far away a dog was yapping. Faint voices drifted in from the street.

And then the two youngsters she had come to regard almost as family came bursting in, laughing and talking as if nothing was wrong. The sudden appearance of them both was almost overwhelming after the anguished solitude and quiet. 'Hey!' said Melanie carelessly. 'All right?'

Before Simmy could respond, Ben asked, 'Where's Bonnie?' and Melanie stared at the rearranged flowers with open-mouthed admiration.

'You saw her last,' said Simmy.

'She said she'd come back here. I thought she'd be first. Mel called me and asked me to wait for her at the church.'

The complex logistics of the mobile phone generation went over Simmy's head. Their exact movements were none of her business anyway.

'What's the matter?' asked Melanie, finally noticing Simmy's face. 'Did something happen?'

'My dad's gone missing.' It seemed starkly foolish, an echo from a melodrama that bore no relation to the people in the actual world who she knew and loved.

'No! When? How?'

'Must have been soon after my mother left for the funeral. The dog's gone as well.'

'What makes you think he's not just gone for a walk?' asked Ben.

Simmy frowned for a moment. Had she and her mother even considered such a bland possibility? She knew they hadn't, and wondered why. 'He's been gone too long,' she said. 'And . . . it would be weird to go right in the middle of the day.' She floundered, thinking that with Russell's strange moods, there was every chance he had decided to stride off along the lake shore, or even through Heathwaite to the slopes of Brant Fell. Anything was possible.

'Bet you that's what he's done. After your epic hike on Monday, he'll be all fired up to do it again. Can't you phone him?'

Melanie snorted. 'The whole family's useless with phones,' she reminded him.

It was magical the way Simmy felt so much better after a few words with the youngsters. They made everything seem so normal and manageable. But better was still not okay. 'My mum's gone to tell the police about Dad. He's been so . . . peculiar lately, we're both scared he's in trouble of some sort. And I haven't told you the full story about the horrible anonymous letter, saying they'd burn the house down. That really upset him. He went almost catatonic with the shock.'

Ben's jaw went slack. 'You took it to the police right away, I hope.'

'Well, no. It was late last night before I saw it. And we were so worried about Dad—' She stopped herself. 'Why am I defending myself?'

'So tell us what it said,' Ben suggested. Simmy did her best to repeat the wording, after which Ben just nodded with a display of satisfaction. 'Stupid thing to do,' he judged.

'Come on – get the kettle on, and we'll talk it all through,' said Melanie briskly. 'And you can do the flowers for tomorrow's wedding at the same time.'

Simmy gave her a searching look. 'I thought you didn't want any more to do with crimes and detective work.'

'I don't. But every time I come near you, that's what I get. I s'pose I don't have much choice about it.'

Simmy laughed and felt better all over again.

'But where's Bonnie?' said Ben again, looking at the door like a dog waiting for an overdue master.

Chapter Eighteen

Ten minutes later, they were arranged in a huddle at the back of the shop and Simmy was elaborating on the tribulations that had overcome her father. 'He was practically catatonic with shock,' she said again. 'I've never seen him like that before. Nowhere near it. We thought he'd had a stroke or something.'

'Rotten thing to do,' muttered Ben. 'Have you told old Moxo about it now?'

'My mother phoned to report it this morning, and the police said they'd send somebody to have a look, but they didn't get around to it before the funeral, according to my mother. She didn't seem very bothered about it. I suppose things didn't seem so bad in the light of day. And my mother's been busy.'

He frowned. 'All morning?'

'Yes, all morning. They're running a business, you know. There's a lot to do. I didn't have much time myself till nearly midday, or I would have called to chivvy them. I was too distracted with Bonnie and her dratted dog.'

'Spike?' said Melanie. 'She didn't bring him here, did she?'

'She did. And he nearly bit a man. I sent them both home. Corinne's gone to a music festival in Lincoln and left her all on her own.'

Ben sighed. 'I was hoping we could concentrate on the murder,' he said, with a hint of regret. 'I've found out a few things. But now there's this business with your dad.' He brightened. 'I suppose there must be a direct connection, if he *has* been abducted. It's a pretty daft thing to do, from the killer's point of view. Makes it a lot more likely he'll get caught. Even dafter than sending a threatening letter,' he added.

Simmy was sporadically fashioning the wedding bouquet, with Melanie handing her the flowers one at a time. Considering how distracted she was, it was coming along rather nicely. 'What things have you found out?' she encouraged Ben.

He raised his eyebrows at her and glanced at Melanie. 'The man who died. Travis McNaughton. We knew already that he lived in Grasmere, no proper job. His sister's got more about her on Google than he has. She's a professional dancer – modern ballet. Sasha McNaughton. He probably doesn't see her much these days – they don't seem to have much in common. But she's likely to show up now he's been murdered. Otherwise, we're just left with the impression that he was a likeable chap who never did anybody any harm.'

'He helped Mrs Elderflower with her garden,' Simmy remembered.

'Who?'

'The woman who found his body. She was picking elderflowers.'

'Has that got anything to do with anything?' Melanie demanded.

'Might have. Who knows?'

'There are two main questions,' Ben summarised. 'Where's the other man who was with him in the car? And were they stealing dogs?'

'And where's my father got to?' Simmy reminded him. 'Just for the moment, that's the only one I really care about.'

'Right,' Ben agreed briskly. 'But we can't answer that one by deduction. The others we might. And it'll take your mind off him,' he added kindly. 'So bear with me, if you can. Now, according to Scott, it looks as if there was just the one attacker. The farm doesn't have anyone living there and no dogs there now. But all kinds of things are possible that I can't find out. Like – maybe they were using one of the buildings to keep kidnapped dogs in, and moved them all when McNaughton died.'

'None of this is helpful,' Simmy complained. 'We're going over old ground.'

'You know something?' Ben said slowly. 'We can't be sure the dead man was the one you saw driving the Renault. You haven't had to identify him, have you? They've just assumed it is, because he's the registered owner. Maybe the two men you saw had nicked the car, and they're both killers.'

'Or maybe they've got nothing to do with it at all,' said Melanie.

'They have, though,' said Simmy, 'because they've

threatened to burn my parents' house down if my father gives evidence against them. As I ought not to have to remind you.'

'*Somebody* has,' Ben corrected her. 'You don't know who.'

'I wish I'd been at the funeral,' said Melanie, in a sudden change of subject. 'Did you and Bonnie go to the wake?' she asked Ben.

'It's not a wake,' said the boy automatically. 'That's *before* the burial or whatever.'

'What is it, then?' asked Melanie.

'I don't think it's got a name. Which is weird, I know.'

'Anyway,' Simmy clung to the thread of their original conversation, 'I think my father was not entirely sure he should go anywhere near the police, in case the house really was set alight. And then Bonnie told me she knew of a man who'd threatened her and Corinne with the same thing. Although . . .' she shook her head at the sudden thought, hoping to dislodge it, 'I wonder if she just said that to distract me. I was in the middle of sending her home, and she didn't seem too keen to go. It worked, if so. She stayed at least another hour after that.' She gave Melanie an accusing look. 'That girl's nothing but trouble so far.'

'Stick with it,' Melanie said. 'You'll appreciate her in the long run, just wait and see.'

'Who did Bonnie say threatened her?' asked Ben.

'A neighbour who didn't like their dogs. Mr Browning. He's not there now. I can't see how it could possibly be him doing it again.'

The name evidently meant nothing to Ben or Melanie.

'Have you spoken to Joe?' Simmy asked the girl.

Throughout the past year or so, Melanie had been fed snippets of information about police investigations by Constable Joe Wheeler, with whom she was in a tepid relationship. The existence of at least two other aspirants to her affections made Joe's position precarious; a situation he tried to improve by means of his inside knowledge. Combined with material from Ben's brother's mate in the mortuary, the flow of data had sometimes proved more than enough to maintain speculation that had occasionally proved significant.

'No. I don't see Joe any more, as you well know.'

'Pity.'

'Why did Bonnie go to the funeral?' Ben wondered.

'She was representing Corinne, who's gone off suddenly to Lincoln. Didn't she tell you? I saw you going off together. And what happened with Spike?'

'We went to the pub and stayed about ten minutes. We weren't really meant to be there.' He jerked his shoulders as if shaking off an uncomfortable memory. 'Spike *was* tied up to some railings when Bonnie went to help Valerie. We collected him before going to the pub. It was all a bit of a muddle.' He sighed. 'That woman's a real basket case, if you want my opinion.'

'Which woman? Valerie?'

Ben nodded. 'Her dog was tied up as well. Somebody took it out when she collapsed, and kept it out of the way. It's a big yellow thing, very protective.'

Simmy thought back to the mêlée she had blundered into, and how there had been no dogs in evidence. 'That must have complicated things,' she said.

'Yeah. Especially as Spike and the other dog don't get along. There was quite a bit of snarling.' He shuddered. 'I don't get it, the way people are with their dogs. It's unhealthy.'

'No getting away from them, when it came to Barbara Hodge,' said Melanie. 'She was still ranting about all this kidnapping the day she died, apparently. She put it in the directions for her funeral – dogs welcome. Everyone's been talking about it. You must have heard.'

Simmy shook her head. 'I had no idea until Bonnie said something this morning about it.'

'You ought to stay in the loop, Sim. This is a small town. It's not difficult.' Melanie was reproving.

'It's easy for you,' Simmy defended. 'You're related to half of them, for a start.'

'Control beyond the grave,' said Ben sonorously.

'What?' Simmy turned irritably to him. 'What are you talking about?'

'The Hodge woman. She had months and months to put everything in order, and she made good use of the time. It was all quite public. Nearly everyone got a personal letter from her – including my dad. As it happens, that's sort of why I was there. Representing him.'

'He's a teacher, isn't he? How did she come across him, when she hasn't got any kids?'

'She went to an adult class he was running, years ago. I don't remember what it was, now. She knew *everybody* – that's the point.'

'Except me,' said Simmy.

'Okay.' Ben squared his shoulders. 'Back to basics. Tell me *exactly* what your dad overheard on Monday. It comes

226

down to that, doesn't it? And what did you both see?'

'I don't know *exactly*. He did tell me word for word at the time, but I can't remember every detail now. Something about getting a job done on Tuesday while the old bloke was out, or away, or words to that effect. Dad thought it sounded like a plan for a burglary, because they said Tim could be the lookout. He was quite excited about it. I thought he was jumping to conclusions, and it could all be perfectly innocent. Then we saw two men in a red car driving away, towards Kirkstone.'

'Flimsy,' Ben judged. 'Even if you both testified to all that, it wouldn't be nearly enough to convict anybody of murder. Did he *see* them when they were speaking?'

Simmy shook her head. 'They were on the other side of a wall.'

'So a defence team could easily argue that it was two totally different men.'

Ben's skill was always breathtaking. His mind ran twice as fast as other people's and he instinctively looked for other angles. 'He's pretty sure they are the same,' she said, already much less sure herself. 'He saw a shadow of a cap with a peak, although I'm pretty sure neither of them had a hat when I saw them in the car. But we both thought they must be the same people, and he'd just taken his hat off before driving away.'

'It's not remotely useful as proof, though. The defence could use it as an argument on their side.'

'Well, I think it would be a huge coincidence if they were two completely different men.'

'Maybe,' he conceded. 'But the man who's trying to stop

your dad testifying must think you saw or heard something more incriminating. Writing that threatening letter was stupid. Panicky. And if he's that much of a fool, there isn't much to worry about, is there?'

'Even stupid people can burn a house down,' said Melanie. 'Or at least make quite a mess.'

'It's a stupid crime altogether. Fire gets out of control, people die, and it's impossible to cover all your tracks.' Ben was dismissive. Apparently arson provided few forensic challenges for the professionals.

'Meanwhile, my dad's been in a state because of it,' Simmy insisted. 'And now we can't find him . . .' Anguish flooded through her all over again. 'Where is he? What's happened to him?'

Neither youngster replied, and in the silence, Simmy heard the yapping dog again. 'Where's that coming from?' she asked. 'It sounds as if it's somewhere high up.'

'What?' Melanie blinked. 'What are you talking about?'

'That dog. I heard it before you got here. It's close by.'

'Outside somewhere,' said Melanie vaguely. 'Tied up outside a shop.'

Ben went through to the back of the shop, making a big show of listening. The yapping had stopped, so he went to the street door and looked out. 'Can't see a dog,' he reported, and then went very still. 'But I can see something interesting. Come and look.'

Simmy and Melanie joined him. 'What?' asked Simmy.

'That car.' He pointed diagonally across the street to a red car parked in a spot where parking was not allowed. 'It'll get a ticket if it's not careful.'

Simmy was slow to grasp the significance. 'So?'

'Look at it. It's red, right. What make is it?'

'I don't know, Ben. I can't see the logo thing.'

'It's a Renault Laguna,' said Melanie carelessly. 'One of my cousins has got one.'

'And what car did you see in Troutbeck on Monday?' Ben went on.

'Stop it!' Simmy ordered. 'You sound like a prosecution lawyer, with your daft questions. So it's the same sort of car as we saw. There must be hundreds of them. Why is it so interesting?'

The boy's hands were curled into fists, which he shook at her in exasperation. 'It's very likely to be the same car. There aren't hundreds of them at all. There might be five in a radius of twenty miles, at most. What was the registration number of the one you saw?'

'I can't remember. There was 09 in it, I think.'

'Well, I'm going out for a look. If it's the same one, don't you think it might have something to do with your dad's disappearance?'

'They wouldn't leave it there, standing out like a beacon,' said Melanie. 'It'll be booked any minute now, and that'll get it logged in the system.'

Ben went out and across the street to where the rear number plate was visible. He came back at a trot. 'VJ09CKB,' he reported with a smug grin.

'So what?' Simmy asked again, less confidently. It had struck her, in the past few seconds, that a phone call from her mother was due, if not overdue. The fact of her silence was suddenly ominous. It meant, at the very least, that her father had not shown up. 'I need to get back to Beck View,' she decided. 'I want to know what the police said to my mother.'

'Hang on,' Ben said. 'One thing at a time. Someone's bound to come back to the car soon. They wouldn't leave it there for very long, would they?'

'That's what I said,' Melanie reminded him.

'I know that man.' Simmy was watching a figure walking towards the car. 'But the car isn't his.'

'In which case, he's stealing it, look.'

The man had flicked something in his hand and the car had blinked its orange sidelights at him. It was the bearded character Simmy had already seen three times. 'Borrowing, more like. He knows – knew – Travis . . . whatever-his-name-is. He's the one who stopped to talk to me on Tuesday evening, when I was in my garden. Did I tell you about that?' She shook her head, completely unable to remember what she had said to who and when.

'Looks like a gypsy to me,' said Melanie.

'They *all* look like gypsies,' said Simmy impatiently. 'What are we going to do, then? He'll be gone in a minute.'

The man was already in the car, glancing in his mirror and starting the engine.

'Nothing we can do,' said Ben. 'Except make a proper note of the number.'

'Hang on! He's getting out again,' said Melanie.

As they watched, the man caught sight of them, and gave them a hostile stare. Then his gaze rose upwards to something above their heads. The yapping dog started up again, and Simmy instantly understood, at last, where it was coming from. 'There are people in the rooms upstairs!' she gasped. 'Right over our heads.'

'What?' The others both looked at her as if she'd gone mad. 'How can there be?' asked Ben. 'How would they get in?'

'Ask him,' said Melanie, as the man with the beard pushed the shop door open.

Chapter Nineteen

'It's you,' said the man. 'The woman from Troutbeck.'

'This is my shop,' said Simmy, feeling a powerful urge to explain even the most irrelevant detail.

'You've got somebody upstairs that I've been looking for.'

'Who? How did they get in?'

'Better come and see.' And he marched through to the back room, after a cursory glance around the shop for a non-existent staircase. The back door was locked, but the key sat conveniently in its hole, ready to be turned. Simmy, Ben and Melanie followed like ducklings as he pushed out into the tiny backyard and up the metal fire escape that was the only access to the upper rooms. Again, he shouldered open a door, and was quickly inside the first room. With his three followers behind him, the room was overflowing with people. And dogs.

'Dad!' Simmy threw herself at her father, where he sat on an upturned wooden crate, with Bertie between his knees. 'What's going on?'

'He's all right,' came a woman's voice. 'We're just

making sure he's not going to get us into any trouble.'

The room was dark, the window small and dirty. Simmy had a moment to wonder how the bearded man ever managed to see through it and recognise anybody. 'Corinne,' she said. 'I thought you were in Lincoln.'

'She changed her mind,' came a second smaller voice.

'Christ, Bonnie. What are *you* doing here?' snapped Melanie.

'You *are* in trouble now, though,' said Ben in a calm and reasonable tone. 'We've caught you.'

'Dad? Are you all right?'

'I am,' he said with the sort of careful diction that suggested drunkenness. 'I am absolutely all right. This lady is Corinne, as you appear to know already. She has been explaining to me that my testimony to the police is based on a profound misunderstanding. I think your friend might be able to clarify things, if you ask him.' He winked at the man with the beard, as if they were well-established mates.

'Vic. My name's Vic,' said the man. 'You and your dad have been causing me and my pals quite a bit of bother.'

'But why are you *here*?' Simmy was directing her question at Bonnie, as the most inexplicable person present.

The girl gave a disarming little smile. 'Sorry,' she said. 'I know you told me not to use these rooms. But it's so handy, you see. And we haven't done any harm.'

'No harm?' Simmy almost screamed. 'Abducting my father and making all sorts of threats—'

'They didn't, Sim,' Russell protested. 'They just phoned me and said they wanted to have a talk, and it would be best for you if I did. I brought Bertie for protection, you see. And then he kept yapping at this fellow.' He pointed at Spike, who was quivering excitedly at Bonnie's feet. 'Apparently, he's not too good with other dogs.'

'They phoned you? Who did? When?'

'Me,' said Corinne. 'When I saw your mum going off to the funeral, I took the opportunity. Vic's been on at me to have a go, so I called him as well. But he's taken bloody ages to get here.' She gave the man a savage look.

'I couldn't find it,' he protested. 'You never said how I was meant to get round the back. I didn't even know for sure which shop it was. I've been walking up and down for half an hour or more, parked on double yellows all that time. I just caught a flash of Bonnie's hair through the window, as I was driving off.'

'How . . . ? I mean, what part of Mr Straw's testimony bothers you?' demanded Ben, clearly anxious to pin down the salient points.

'They saw me carrying a bag, at the bottom of the fell, and thought it'd got a dead dog in it. Set the cops chasing after me for one of these bloody dognappers, since the bother last year. They knew right off who I was and I've had them badgering ever since.'

'But what use would it be now to get them to change the story? The damage is done. You only had to show the cops what was really in the bag and you'd be clear.'

Vic gave the boy a long frustrated look. 'Not when there's been murder done, not half a mile away. Not with my record. They'll be taking me in any time now, all on the strength of them seeing me with a bag.'

'Record?' echoed Simmy, feeling only slightly inclined to sympathise with him.

'Bit of car theft, years ago now,' he shrugged.

Simmy addressed her father. 'Did you pick him out from police pictures, or something? What did you tell them?'

Russell nodded. 'I gave a good description, plus the fact that his trousers were covered in mud. They showed me a picture and there he was, large as life.'

'When, Dad? When did all this happen?'

'On Tuesday. I went to talk to them, remember?'

'When did they question *you*?' Simmy asked Vic.

'Wednesday, if you must know. What difference does it make?'

'After you talked to me, then. What were you doing in Troutbeck on Tuesday?'

'I'm working at the caravan park. I'm there all the time.'

'I've never seen you,' she said crossly.

Ben took over, obviously struggling to maintain any kind of logical thread. 'So were you trying to make Mr Straw change the story, or what? And what *did* you have in that bag?'

'Why does it matter to you?'

'Just tell him,' said Simmy, even more angry. 'We know they found that dead terrier up on the fells, so it obviously wasn't what we thought.' She looked around at each face in turn. 'And what does it have to do with Corinne and Bonnie?'

'And did you steal the Renault?' Melanie chipped in.

Vic put his hands over his ears, his face screwed up in a parody of someone being deafened. 'Too many

235

questions,' he protested. He looked at Melanie. 'I'm just looking after the car,' he said. 'Trav left it on the side of the road. Must have been just before he was killed. The key was in it, and I just thought it would complicate things if I left it where it was.'

Simmy's heart thumped at this confession. Here, after all, was the murderer, she concluded. 'Nobody would do that unless they wanted to hide something,' she accused. 'I bet it was covered in blood or something.'

'Where's it been since Tuesday?' asked Ben.

The man threw a glance at Corinne, as if seeking rescue. 'Help!' he begged her. 'They're all crazy.'

'Vic hasn't done anything,' she said obligingly. 'Leave him alone. He sold that car to Travis a year ago, and he's borrowed it back a few times. That's all.'

'No, no.' Ben closed his eyes. 'It's more than that.' He faced Vic. 'Did you know Travis was dead, and that you were likely to be implicated? That's why you moved the car?'

'That would mean you know who killed him,' said Simmy. 'If it wasn't you.'

'Help!' said Vic again. When nobody spoke, he went on, 'I had no idea he'd been killed. The truth of it is, he was giving me a lift. We were going down to Barrow together. He'd got a bit of gardening to do, so I said I'd walk down and catch him when he finished. So that's what I did. Saw the car, and got in to wait for him. Waited half an hour, or more, and then started to worry. By that time, there was a bit of action at Town End, and a cop car turned up. It seemed like a good idea to move the Renault. There's a bit of an issue over the tax, as it happens. I didn't want the cops to start checking it on their computers, did I? So I thought I'd just tuck it behind one of the caravans where I work, for a couple of days. Then, when I heard the news, I asked Vivian if she wanted it back, and she said I could keep it. She's got her own motor – and it's not as if they were married or anything. She doesn't automatically get all his stuff. I only offered cos it seemed the decent thing to do.'

'And you never reported any of this to the police?' asked Simmy incredulously.

'Couldn't see the point. I hadn't anything to tell them that could help catch the killer.'

'People like you steer clear of the police if they can, don't they?' said Ben. 'Was it just the untaxed car, or had you got something else to hide?'

Vic's head dropped wearily. 'The fact is, I was doing something I shouldn't, right? There's a lot of rabbits on those fells and I'd got a few snares set for them.' He sighed. 'Managed to nab a couple, and take them home with me.'

'And accidentally killed a Jack Russell as well,' accused Melanie. 'Isn't that right?'

Corinne made a soft cry. 'He won't do it again,' she said. 'It was a horrible accident.'

'It's illegal to set snares,' said Ben. 'For obvious reasons.'

'But you don't kidnap dogs and sell them to rich unscrupulous people?' said Simmy. 'Or whatever it is they do.'

'I do not,' said Vic intensely. 'I love dogs. Ask Corinne. Those dognappers are bastards. Nobody with an ounce of decency will have anything to do with them.'

Corinne leant forward earnestly. 'Right!' she confirmed.

'So Travis McNaughton wasn't stealing dogs?' asked Ben.

'Course he wasn't. He wasn't doing anything dodgy. Clean as a whistle, was Trav. Ask anybody.'

'So why was he in that yard, being chased by a killer with a knife?' Ben's stark and unemotional summary made everybody in the room wince.

'You tell me,' said Vic, with obvious sadness. 'I've been asking myself the same thing all week. Nobody had a reason to kill him, I know that for a certainty.'

'And you know Corinne?' Simmy still needed an explanation of how Bonnie and her guardian had found themselves in such a situation.

'Everybody knows Corinne,' he grinned.

'You should get your dad home,' interrupted Melanie softly. 'I'm not sure he's okay.'

Simmy's heart lurched and she rushed to Russell's side. 'Dad? It's time we went to find Mum and tell her everything's all right. She's been worried about you. And Bertie's going to want his supper soon.' Hearing herself speaking so soothingly, as if to a toddler, only terrified her further. Her father was slumped, staring at the floor. The transformation had been gradual over the past ten minutes or so, Simmy realised, only apparent in the final stages. She looked around for help, and was filled with mixed emotions as Bonnie responded most quickly. Suspicion, because there was still no explanation for her presence; gratitude, because any pair of hands was welcome; and regret, because she was not going to be of very much use.

'Here. Let me.' Vic spoke with resignation, as the only person present likely to manage to lower the elderly man down the awkward staircase. 'Corinne – you can lend a hand, can't you? You brought the poor old guy up here, after all.'

They all proceeded down, step by step, Spike leading the way, showing off his agility. Bertie remained at the top, whimpering, until Melanie scooped him up and carried him. Simmy followed her father, her whole body tight with fear that he was having heart failure or a stroke or some other life-threatening event. 'Can you drive him?' she was asking Vic. 'Your car's closest.'

'Unless it's been clamped by now,' said Ben dourly.

But there was no need for the car, because waiting inside the shop, looking as if he'd been there for some time, was Detective Inspector Moxon and a younger man who was very probably a detective constable.

Chapter Twenty

Nobody showed any deference in the presence of the police. To his credit, Moxon gave no sign of expecting any. He rallied magnificently at the sight of Simmy's obvious distress over her father. 'He needs to get to a hospital,' he snapped. 'Keith – you can take him, okay? That'll be the quickest.'

At these words, Russell's head lifted, and his eyes focused. 'Hospital?' he gasped. 'No, no. I don't need that.'

Moxon and Keith both paused. 'Sir, you're ill,' said the inspector.

'I'll be all right. It's nothing much. I just came over faint for a minute. I should go home. My wife must be worrying.'

'That's for sure,' nodded Moxon. 'I've been talking to her for the past hour, trying to assure her that you'll be all right. If we let you come to harm now, she's never going to forgive me.'

'I must phone her,' said Simmy. 'And tell her we've found him. I should have done it twenty minutes ago. Except I didn't have my phone,' she added limply. Rallying, she went on, 'And she's going to tell us to take him home, rather than hospital. He hasn't gone blue or anything, look. And it's not a stroke, if he can talk, is it?'

'There's nothing wrong with me,' said Russell. 'At least, nothing a hospital can fix. You might call it an existential crisis, I suppose.'

Simmy met Moxon's eyes, and held them for a few seconds. She read decency, amusement, weariness and melancholy in them. 'I don't suppose you're the only one,' she said, partly to her father and partly to the detective.

'Don't forget Bertie,' said Russell, as he was ushered through the shop by Keith and Melanie. Moxon followed with Vic and Corinne, which left Bonnie and Ben somehow lingering at the rear. Simmy looked back at them for a moment, and smiled. Something nice appeared to be happening amongst all the confusion.

Bonnie's lovely avenue of flowers was unequal to the passage of so many people, all heading for the front door and the street beyond. Simmy realised with a rush of regret that it was not going to work. However gorgeous it might be, it was a hazard. The shop was too small, the proportions all wrong.

Outside they made a large group on the pavement. Vic uttered a wordless groan when he spotted a large sticker on his windscreen. 'Oops!' said Melanie. 'I thought that might happen.' She addressed the detective, speaking with determination. 'That's the car belonging to Travis McNaughton. I think you've been looking for it.'

'Oh,' said Moxon, gazing at the vehicle. 'So it is.' Simmy could see him making an effort to appear nonchalant. 'Keith, you take Mr Straw and his dog down to Lake Road. Mrs Brown can go too, of course.'

Simmy hesitated. 'Actually, I think I ought to stay here. They won't need me, if Dad's really not going to hospital.'

Moxon gave a small shrug, and went on with his orders. 'The rest of you have some explaining to do. This is still a murder investigation, remember. I'm hoping' – he looked from Corinne to Melanie and then Vic – 'one or all of you might throw some light on it for me.'

'Not me,' objected Melanie. 'It's nothing to do with me. I shouldn't even *be* here.'

The man gave her a reproachful look. 'The fact is, you *are* here, and with your comprehensive knowledge of Windermere society, I'm in no doubt you'll have something to contribute. You've already drawn my attention to that car.'

'There are a lot of men,' said Simmy slowly. 'I mean – who *are* they all? Corinne seems to know some of them. There was another one in here this morning. Bonnie called him a stalker. Murray – that's his name. Looks like a bit of a gypsy.'

Corinne gave a loud snort. 'Come off it! No sense trying to finger poor old Murray as a killer. He's stoned senseless most of the time.'

At the name *Murray*, Spike began a low rumbling growl, a much bigger sound than such a small fluffy animal might be expected to make. 'Hey, boy, that's enough,' said Bonnie. 'He's not here. Don't worry.'

'I wasn't . . .' Simmy began, before realising that it had sounded very much as if she was suggesting Murray was the murderer. 'I didn't mean—' she tried again.

Moxon waved her into silence. 'This is the way of it,'

242

he said, rather obscurely. 'Names get thrown about, wild ideas mostly. But it's all part of getting the bigger picture.' He looked again at Melanie. 'Which is where Miss Todd can often be useful.'

'I've never heard of a bloke called Murray,' she muttered, unsure as to how she should react. Pride at being deemed useful or resentment at being singled out – the two were visibly in conflict.

'Were you at Miss Hodge's funeral?' Simmy asked Moxon, out of the blue. 'Did you see what happened?'

He shook his head. 'Too busy for that,' he said. 'The boss went along, as far as I know. Why – what happened, then? Were *you* there?'

'I was,' came the voice of Ben Harkness. 'It's got nothing to do with any of this, though.' He frowned at Simmy accusingly. 'Completely irrelevant,' he repeated.

'Even so,' Simmy argued. 'It's where everybody was at twelve o'clock.'

'Were you there?' asked Moxon again.

'Not the actual service. I went to look for my parents at one, and got swamped by the crowd of confused mourners.'

'Why confused?'

'Haven't you heard?' Ben was finally diverted. 'It ended in chaos, because Valerie Rossiter collapsed or fainted or something halfway through her speech.'

'Eulogy,' Simmy corrected him. 'It's called a eulogy.'

'Anyway, nobody knew what to do after that, and it all got rushed through, with a hymn and bells and stuff, while she pulled herself together. She was fine after a bit. People were miffed at first. They weren't getting their money's worth.'

'What?' Simmy snapped. 'What are you talking about?'

'Oh, I don't know,' he shrugged. 'They felt short-changed, even if it does make good gossip. People always say, don't they, a funeral's for the people left behind, not the one who's died. And that's obvious, isn't it? I mean – I can see there's some satisfaction in thinking about your own funeral and how everyone's going to say nice things about you, and be terribly sorry you've gone. But at the actual *time*, it can't really be for the dead person, can it? Because they're dead,' he finished with stark simplicity. 'So when you think about it, it's just as well in this case. I don't imagine the Hodge lady would have been very impressed. There was a whole page more stuff to come that never happened.'

'Was somebody else meant to talk about her, then?'

'No. But there was something about blessing the dogs. I counted six altogether. That never happened.'

Moxon cleared his throat and rolled his eyes. 'That woman was obsessed with dogs,' he said. 'But I really don't think this is the moment to be going over all that. Haven't we got more pressing business?' He examined the faces of Corinne and Vic with a close inspection.

'You're right,' said Ben, as if he were the senior investigating officer himself. 'We need to focus on what Vic told us just now. Travis McNaughton had nothing to do with dognapping. This man can tell you all about the car and what he did with it. You can get DNA samples, which will identify the man who was in it on Monday. That's who you need to go after. He's the one.'

'Okay, son.' Moxon's restraint was palpable. 'Let's take

it a step at a time, shall we? And preferably not standing out here in the street.'

'Where, then?' said Simmy. 'There's no room in the shop for all of you.'

'I have no intention of conducting interviews in a flower shop. In fact, there's no need for you to be involved at all. If the rest of you,' he swept Bonnie, Corinne, Vic, Melanie and Ben with a comprehensive scrutiny, 'would all make your way to the station, I'd be very happy to talk to you. Although,' he paused, 'Mr Harkness, I dare say we can manage without you, at this point. Unless you have an actual testimony for me, I think you can be excused.'

Ben was speechless with indignation. Melanie gave him a little consolatory pat, and Bonnie smiled up at him with a special secret little smile that everybody noticed. Spike moved to him and gave him a nudge, for good measure. 'I'm right, you know,' the boy said loudly. 'You'll see.'

'I'm not saying otherwise. Your point about the car is a very good one. I'm calling now to ensure it's taken right away for examination. Mr . . . ?' he looked at Vic. 'Remind me.'

'Corless,' said the man, with an unhappy shake of his head. 'I need those wheels. How'm I meant to get back to Troutbeck? I was only going to be out for an hour or two. They'll be wondering about me.'

Moxon pressed on. 'Mr Corless, as I was saying, can explain everything we need to know, I'm sure.' He blinked a few times, as his thoughts began to fall into place. 'This is the car that McNaughton was driving on Tuesday? Is that what you're telling me?'

'*Yes!*' Ben almost shouted. 'It's vitally important evidence.'

'All right, lad. I'm with you. No need to shout. So you' – again he addressed Vic – 'you know who the other man was, then? The one in the passenger seat on Monday afternoon?'

'Obviously I do,' sighed Vic. 'It was Zippy Newsome.' He waited for a reaction. 'You know Zippy? Blind from birth, sharp as a razor – but not much use with one, when it comes to slaughtering his best mate.' He glared at Ben. 'Which puts the kybosh on your clever little theory, doesn't it, boy?'

Melanie spoke up. 'Zippy Newsome? I know him. Why hasn't somebody already figured out that it was him, then?' She looked from Moxon to Vic. 'Didn't you tell them when they questioned you on Wednesday?'

Vic smiled unpleasantly. 'They never asked me,' he said. 'They were just two uniformed plods, not working the murder case. All they were interested in was whether I'd been stealing dogs. Nothing about a car, or anything like that. I reckoned that since it was Monday they were asking about, I didn't need to fill them in about Tuesday. I'd got the motor back by then, anyhow.'

'Obstructing the course of justice, illegal parking . . . what else?' asked Moxon furiously.

'Setting snares for unwary rabbits, and catching dogs instead,' said Ben.

'Enough!' roared Moxon. A few passers-by had been loitering a little way along the pavement, intrigued by the intense conversation going on.

'But if the man was blind, why didn't the boy, Tim, tell you that?' she wondered.

'He wouldn't have known,' said Vic. 'Clever bloke, Zip. That's why they call him that. He seems pretty normal at first glance. And I doubt the boy got much time with him, anyhow.'

'But he and Travis were planning to do something furtive on Tuesday,' Ben continued, oblivious to the angry detective. 'How was that going to work, if he's blind?'

'Don't know nothing about that,' snapped Vic. 'All I know is that Zippy's no fool. He works in France half the time, doing something with wine. Tasting it and that. He's sharp, like I said.'

Simmy noted that Bonnie and Corinne had gone back into the shop at some point in the proceedings. She went in after them, thinking that Ben and Moxon were never going to establish a viable relationship. The boy was too young, too clever and much too outspoken. And if she'd followed the logic as she believed she had, then his assumptions were well off the mark. Her own assumptions had turned to dust at the same time. For no good reason, she had been imagining the killer as the other man in the red car on Monday. Quite why that should be, she could not now explain.

Corinne was on her mobile, while Bonnie leant against the back wall with Spike at her feet. 'Don't give me that, Frank,' Corinne was saying. 'I never said I'd go for sure. And anyway, it's not too late. I can try and make it tomorrow. That's time enough.'

Simmy felt a flash of anger. *Who's Frank?* she wanted to

know. And what made Corinne think it would be all right to just go off the next day as if nothing had happened? This woman had lured her father away from home and incarcerated him in a dusty attic for reasons that remained impenetrable. 'Only if the police will let you,' she said loudly, ignoring the protocol that gave precedence to a phone conversation over one with a person in the flesh.

Corinne made the classic face that indicated what a strain it was to speak to two people at once. 'Pardon?' she said. Then, 'Wait a minute, Frank.' She looked at Simmy. 'What did you say?'

'Aren't you forgetting that the police are going to want to talk to you?' New thoughts were arising as she spoke. 'For all I know, it was you who sent that threatening letter. You wanted to get Vic in the clear. You knew he'd been setting those snares and you didn't want me or my dad to say any more to incriminate him.'

'Shut up,' said Corinne, without rancour. 'You don't know what you're talking about.' She returned to the phone, rudely turning her back on Simmy.

'Sorry,' said Bonnie. 'She's never been much good at the social graces.'

'You're always saying "sorry"!' Simmy turned her frustration on the girl. 'What good does "sorry" do? Everything's in chaos, and some of it's your fault. The least you could do is explain what's going on.'

'We explained already. There isn't anything else. Your dad's okay. And it wasn't Corinne who sent the letter. Of course it wasn't. She doesn't do stuff like that. All she cares about is the dogs. She'd never have let Vic set snares, if she'd known about it. She won't worry if he's in trouble over it. Serves him right.'

Corinne's phone call was concluded, and she faced Simmy again. 'Did I hear Bonnie setting you straight?'

'She says you didn't send the letter.'

'Too right. First I've heard of it was today. What did it say, anyhow?'

'It threatened to burn my parents' house down if my father testified to what he saw on Monday in Troutbeck. Very nasty. It had a terrible effect on him.'

'And he saw Vic with those rabbits in a bag. He'll have sent the letter, then. I thought there must be something else.' She sighed. 'I always forget what a complete fool Vic can be.'

'So, it wasn't anything to do with the men in the car. The letter was all about Vic,' said Simmy slowly.

She was trying to think. It wasn't easy, with Ben and Moxon and Vic still outside, and her father on his way home, and the shop turning into a sort of meeting place for all these people. Melanie would be wanting to talk to her – she could feel it as a sort of pressure. She gave up. 'Can you both go, please?' she said. 'And take that dog out of my shop.'

Bonnie looked as if she'd been slapped. Corinne put a sheltering arm around her shoulders. 'No need to be like that,' she told Simmy.

'I think there's every need. You don't seem to understand what you've done. It's completely outrageous . . .' she spluttered in speechless indignation, to be saved by Moxon coming into the shop.

'If you two ladies would come with me,' he began without preamble, 'we can leave Mrs Brown in peace. I think she's had enough disruption for one afternoon.'

Simmy threw him a grateful look. 'I was just asking them to go,' she said.

'Are you arresting us?' Corinne blustered.

'Of course not. You can drop the melodrama. We need to ask you some questions – which must be obvious, even to you.' He regarded her with an unsettlingly placid gaze, which plainly conveyed his lack of surprise or concern at anything she might say.

'And me?' said Bonnie. 'Again?'

He narrowed his eyes. 'Possibly not you,' he conceded. 'For now, anyway.'

They left in a group, to join Vic who was waiting like a patient horse on the pavement. Simmy wondered how Moxon would get them all down to the police station, half a mile away, and visualised a sort of small crocodile walking purposefully along, and attracting interested glances as they went.

Ben and Melanie came in, half a minute later, and suddenly everything felt familiar and normal again. 'I'll make us some tea,' said Simmy.

By a small miracle – or so it felt – a customer came in moments later. Melanie stepped forward and helped with a choice of flowers for the weekend. Ben made himself useful straightening the two lines of pots and pails that comprised Bonnie's arrangement.

'Don't talk,' Simmy pleaded, when she came back with three mugs of tea. 'At least, nothing that's going to hurt my brain.'

'Fat chance,' said Melanie cheerfully. 'He's bursting with it. Look at him!'

It was true that Ben was in a state of great excitement. His eyes sparkled and he couldn't keep still. 'That was so . . . *epic*!' he marvelled. 'All those people, right in the middle of things. Poor old Moxo didn't know where to turn.' He laughed. 'He's not the brightest of blokes, is he? I thought he'd never get to grips with it all.'

'And you did, I suppose,' said Simmy. 'Honestly, Ben, you make me feel exhausted just to look at you. Besides, it really isn't that exciting. Think of my poor father. And bloody Bonnie,' she added furiously. 'That girl . . .'

Both youngsters looked at her in astonishment. 'What did Bonnie do?' asked Melanie, at the same time as Ben demanded, 'What do you mean?'

'She's always *there*. She's like some supernatural creature, popping up and causing trouble. She was even at the funeral, at Valerie Rossiter's side. That was weird enough. Then she's upstairs tormenting my dad. She always looks as if she knows what's going to happen next.' She shook her head in confusion. 'How *dare* she take them upstairs, like that? I *told* her I wouldn't allow it. And nobody seems to see it but me,' she finished helplessly. 'Look at you, both of you, all ready to jump to her defence.'

She remembered how, only half an hour before, she'd thought it sweet that Ben and Bonnie were getting along so well together. Now she felt as if the boy was in grave danger. 'And she's such an innocent little thing, I know. That's what people think. That's what *I* thought. But now I see it in a different way. I think she's malicious. And I don't like that dog, either,' she finished with a flourish. The bile was pouring out of her, and she felt better for it.

'Blimey, Sim,' said Melanie. 'She's really rattled your cage, hasn't she?'

'Whatever that means,' snapped Simmy.

'It's only that she's clever,' said Ben quietly. 'That's all it is, you know. Clever people are annoying, for some reason. It's not her fault.'

'Like you annoy Moxon,' nodded Melanie. 'Let me say now, Ben, that you're not to marry Bonnie. Two clever people together is a waste. You should spread the genes around a bit, and both marry thickoes. Besides, you'd be sure to annoy each other a million times more than other people.'

Ben flushed a deep red and scowled.

'Stop it,' said Simmy, like a mother. She looked at her watch. 'Nearly four! Why's business so slow today? Fridays are normally quite busy.'

'Duh! Think about it,' said Melanie, with a roll of her good eye. 'What has everybody in the whole town been doing this afternoon?'

'Oh, yes. Silly me. The funeral. I might as well shut up shop for the day, then, don't you think?'

'Up to you. The after-the-funeral business will have finished by now, so people might decide to do some shopping next. Is there something else you'd rather be doing? Have you got everything sorted for tomorrow's wedding?'

Simmy hardly knew where to start. She wanted to be with her father, most of all. She also wanted to sit down with DI Nolan Moxon and try to discover just where she and Russell stood regarding their observations in Troutbeck. But he would be much too busy to go along with any such exercise. She also felt a lingering concern for Vic Corless, who might yet prove to be a murderer, but who had kind, sad eyes and a basic good nature, if she was any judge. He wasn't very bright, and that was working to his disadvantage. It seemed a shame.

'I feel a bit sorry for that man Vic,' she said, ducking Melanie's questions.

'Whatever for?'

'I keep remembering how he fell over in the mud, and how he came to talk to me the next day. I thought he was being threatening, but now I wonder if I got it wrong. He might have just wanted to talk about his friend getting killed.'

'I'm not sure we've heard the whole story. What time was it when you talked to him?'

'Oh, Ben,' she sighed. 'Something like seven, I suppose. It was evening, and I was in the garden. Everything was lovely and peaceful. And then he came and told me there'd been a murder, down by Town End. He's just explained all that to us. There's nothing more to say about it.'

'We can't be sure. Do you know him?' Ben asked Melanie.

'I know the name. Never actually met him before. He's got a brother they call Hank. I did see him a few times when I was about nine. He had a bit of a thing with my mum's young sister, for a while. Had a kiddie with her – called it Madison, for some reason. He'll be nine or ten by now. Lives with Vic's mum most of the time.'

Simmy felt hopelessly beleaguered by the complexities of local relationships. 'So he's the father of your cousin. Good God, Mel! Is there *anybody* round here you're not related to?'

'Course there is. And I'm not actually *related* to Vic, am I? It's no big deal.'

'She is pretty much linked to almost everybody, all the same,' said Ben. 'Don't forget Bonnie's best friends with Chloe. That's why Mel brought her along as her replacement.'

'I realise that,' said Simmy, with a sense of actually understanding very little of the connections and currents existing just below the surface. Windermere was small enough for everybody to know everybody, particularly those families who'd been there for generations. Remove the incomers and the visitors and you were left with a close-knit community with centuries of shared history. 'It's the reason I keep trying to give Bonnie the benefit of the doubt. But after today, I'm not managing too well. I never know what she'll do next.'

'Like bringing you face to face with Murray-the-stalker,' laughed Melanie. 'I bet that's the first and last time he's ever going to step inside a flower shop. Did he knock anything over?'

'The dog did, when it flew at him.'

'Wow – did it bite him?'

'No. He wasn't even scared of it. And nothing actually tipped over. I was exaggerating.'

Ben was ignoring much of this exchange, staring hard at a bucket of lilies, plainly lost in thought. 'We need to get back to basics. I can't get some of it straight at all – especially who knew what and when.'

'Stop it,' said Simmy again. 'I've had enough. I'm giving it ten more minutes, and then I'm closing up and finishing the wedding flowers in peace. You two can go.'

'You forgot something,' said Melanie. 'I've only just thought of it.'

'What?'

'You're meant to deliver flowers to an address in Bowness. Didn't they ask for Friday afternoon?'

Simmy stared in horror. Never once had she forgotten an order so completely. 'I haven't even chosen the flowers for it.'

'Won't take long. It's still the afternoon. You won't be very late.' Melanie was briskly reassuring, but showed no sign of lending a hand. 'Shut the shop and do it now,' she advised. 'We're going.'

They went and eight minutes later Simmy was trotting out to her van with a handsome sheaf of spring flowers for a Miss Lucy Lacey on Longtail Hill. 'Lucy Lacey,' Simmy muttered. 'Must remember to tell Dad that one.'

The delivery took half an hour, from leaving the shop to parking the van back in its customary spot. The drive had cleared Simmy's head, and she felt reprieved from having to worry any more about murder or arson or convoluted theories. The wedding flowers were all completed over the next hour. It was to be a simple country ceremony, requiring nothing gaudy or complicated, which Simmy found very appealing.

It was a bright evening, and the prospect of simply

going home as usual wasn't very enticing. So she opted to do something she had done a few times before, and pay a quiet visit to the grave which would be piled high with floral tributes, many of them created by her. It was always satisfying to see the results of her labours, and it might give her a moment to say her own few words to the deceased.

She walked up to St Mary's and let herself into the graveyard. Only when she had rounded the corner, past the big dark church, did she see Valerie Rossiter kneeling by the fresh grave with a large yellow dog at her side.

Chapter Twenty-One

Simmy had every intention of creeping away without disturbing the grieving woman. But the dog heard her and stood up, his tail slowly wagging. Valerie looked round and saw her. 'Hello,' she said flatly.

'I'm terribly sorry. I really don't want to disturb you. How awful of me.'

'It's all right. It's sweet of you to come. I decided I had to retrieve this, after all.' She held out her hand, the palm flat. In the middle of it sat the little porcelain flower. 'After all – what would become of it otherwise?'

'I'm glad you did. You're feeling better, then?'

'Pardon?' The expression on her face was of sheer disbelief. '*Better*?'

Simmy shook her head. 'Sorry. That was stupid question.'

'Oh – you mean because of my ridiculous fainting fit at the funeral. Well, yes, I suppose I can walk and talk again now. I don't know what came over me.' She was still kneeling on the grass, and put a hand on the dog's stalwart back. 'I suppose I've been rather short of sleep for a long time now. I'm planning to spend a week in bed, starting from tomorrow.'

'Good idea.'

'You know – I've just had enough of all those *people*. It's a huge shock to the system for a recluse like me. I thought I was tougher than this,' she finished miserably.

This time, Simmy thought of Ninian on his little fell, ignoring the phone and forgetting his friends.

'I should go,' she said.

'You don't have to. You've been great, you know. I'm always going to associate you with flowers and nice smells. Roddy likes you too.'

Simmy looked past the woman, wondering who she meant until the dog wagged again at his name. She felt hot and embarrassed at the words of approval.

'Oh dear,' said Valerie. 'I'm sorry to discomfit you. You just seemed so kind and understanding when I came about the flowers. And then again today, after the funeral, there you were, all calm and collected. I suppose you just felt like a port in a storm, or something.'

Simmy looked at her more closely. She hadn't changed, and the funeral clothes were now oddly dark and sinister. Black trousers and a tailored jacket, with a dark green shirt underneath had been perfect for the occasion, but now the jacket was losing its shape, the trousers scattered with dog hairs. 'Well . . . I'm glad about that.'

Valerie finally got to her feet. She looked uncomfortable and warm. As if to confirm this impression, she began to fumble uninhibitedly at her chest, tweaking an invisible undergarment impatiently. 'This bloody bra!' she

258

complained. 'How do women wear them all day, every day? This is the first time I've put one on for a good ten years. It's too small for me. I can hardly breathe. It was probably that which made me faint.'

Simmy wished her mother were there, as an ally for Valerie. She too found bras intolerable.

'Maybe you could slip into the church and take it off,' she suggested, with a little laugh.

'No, no,' said Valerie with a small bitter laugh. 'I'll be all right. I'll go home in a minute.'

'You live somewhere up past Cook's Corner, is that right?'

'Bit further than that, but we enjoy the walk.' She flushed slightly, and Simmy wondered whether she was reproaching herself for using the word 'enjoy'. She remembered in her own case that any hint of lightness or optimism brought waves of guilt with them, in the first days after losing baby Edith.

She instinctively sought to reduce the pain by keeping the conversation going, focusing on mundane details. 'Have you got people staying?'

'Actually, no.' Valerie laughed again, more sadly than before. 'And that's even worse. I'm a mess, as you can tell. They did try to warn me. There was a lovely Macmillan nurse who told me I should make plans for when all the caring stopped. I did most of it, you know. Lifting Barb in and out of bed, taking her to the loo, pushing the wheelchair. Just being with her all day. It's like losing half of my body with her gone.'

The silence was palpable, and she sighed. 'Sorry. That

sounds like self-pity, doesn't it? The great British taboo. And it's not even entirely true. I should be thinking about getting my life back. All I've done for ten years is try to keep another woman happy. I've almost forgotten I'm a separate person.' She sighed deeply. 'Maybe I'm not, after all this time.'

'Of course you are. But it'll take a while before you believe it.'

'You sound as if you know what you're talking about.'

'Sort of. I lost a baby.' The words never came easily. She never knew how to arrange her face as she said them. 'She was stillborn.'

'You poor thing.' The words were uttered with evident sincerity, and Simmy warmed to the woman as a result. 'I've never been pregnant. It's always struck me as terribly *dangerous*.'

'It was for me, I suppose. I never thought of it like that.'

'I grew up in Poland, you know. Even in the sixties, everything felt precarious. Life was cheap.' She paused. 'No, that's not right. But life had to be *earned*. We all knew we were survivors, and that meant we had to justify ourselves. It was a huge relief to come here when I was twenty.'

'Your English is perfect.'

'Thank you. I don't feel foreign any more. Barbara helped with that.' Her face changed as she spoke, turning grey and pouchy. 'God help me, whatever am I going to do now?'

'Take it a day at a time,' said Simmy. It was a platitude, but she knew it carried its own small wisdom. 'Be nice to yourself.'

Valerie gave a brief rueful smile. 'Easy to say.'

Simmy looked at her watch, letting the woman see what she was doing. 'I'm sorry, but I should be going now. I really am sorry I disturbed you.'

'You didn't. It was just what I needed – a little chat with somebody so well balanced and understanding.' She bent down to grasp the dog's lead, her features still tragic. 'Thanks for listening.'

They parted company with Simmy thinking how likeable the woman was, and how it might even be possible in the future to approach her again with a view to forging a friendship.

She should be finishing off the bouquets and table pieces for the wedding next day, but she felt too weary. She could find time next morning, if she got up half an hour early. The simple ceremony planned for the next day was a relief after the complicated funeral. The couple were realistic in their expenditure, and probably in their expectations. The sort of wedding, she fantasised, that she would have herself if there was ever to be a second time around. A few well-chosen guests, everything over with by suppertime, and on with the much more important business of living with another person.

She sighed. It felt so unlikely as to be the wildest of dreams. Even if matters progressed with Ninian, they were highly unlikely to lead to marriage. What would they do for money? How would he incorporate a wife into his ascetic lifestyle? And why, for heaven's sake, was she thinking about marrying anybody anyway?

She made her way on foot down a small street towards Lake Road and her parents' house. She hadn't consciously intended to go back there, but when she caught herself heading that way, she realised she was still worried about her father. Presumably she would have been told if he had been taken to hospital after all, but there was still a worry over his health. Besides, her car was somewhere near Beck View. For the moment, she couldn't recall exactly where she'd left it so many hours before. Juggling the florist's van and her own car regularly meant that neither vehicle was quite where she wanted it to be.

The front door was locked again when she tried the handle, so she rang the bell. Her mother appeared quickly, looking unflurried.

'Is everything all right?' Simmy asked.

'Absolutely fine. Don't worry about us. Get home and have a quiet evening. That's what we're going to do.'

'Aren't there any guests?'

'Yes, but we've told them not to bother us unless the house is on fire. They thought we were joking,' she added darkly. Simmy understood that matters were not entirely calm, after all. Her mother was doing her best to ensure that Russell had no further disturbances that day, including further discussions about murder with his daughter.

'Okay,' she agreed. 'I might call in tomorrow, after I close up. You can give me some lunch.'

Angie sighed. 'If we must,' she said, with characteristic lack of hospitality. Simmy sometimes wondered just how it had ever come about that this woman not only ran a bed-and-breakfast service, but that she had made such a massive success of it. When it came to visits from friends and family, she could often be decidedly unwelcoming.

'Where did I leave my car, I wonder?' she mumbled as she turned away. Her mother either didn't hear her, or saw no reason to reveal her ignorance of the answer. Instead she closed the door with a snap.

Her vehicle was not visible in the road running past the house, and Simmy racked her brains as to where she'd parked earlier that day. She'd left it in some small street without any conscious thought, being so completely occupied by the funeral to come. It must be in one of the streets on either side of the library, she supposed, and set out to track it down, feeling a familiar panic that she might never find it. She even had dreams now and then, where she combed the streets, with their tree names, vainly searching for her car.

She had begun to wonder whether it could possibly have been stolen, when a man called her from behind. Surely it couldn't be, she thought. Was he *never* going to leave her alone? She turned impatiently at the unmistakeable, 'Mrs Brown. Hold on a minute.'

It was Detective Inspector Moxon, of course. He looked heavy and weary and at least as surprised to see her as she was to see him. 'Sorry,' he said. 'I wasn't sure it was you at first.'

'I can't find my car,' she complained. 'I left it here somewhere.'

'It's over there, look. Right behind mine.' He pointed a few yards ahead. 'I recognised it.'

She didn't pause to ask how in the world he knew her vehicle. It was months since he'd last seen it, as far as she was aware. But he answered anyway. 'The broken wing mirror. Someone's done a good job with the duct tape.'

'My dad,' she nodded, with a pang. Would Russell ever again be competent to fix such problems? The very question brought a lump to her throat.

'I've just popped out for a bit of shopping,' he explained, waving a white plastic bag in the air. 'I'm taking the evening off.'

'Good for you. Thanks for pointing out the car. It's daft of me to lose it.'

'Come in for a minute,' he invited, astonishingly. 'This is where I live.' He tilted his head at the house adjacent to them. 'Have a cup of tea or something.'

'What?' The rudeness was unavoidable. Since when did senior police detectives invite women they'd been questioning on criminal matters in for tea? Although, she supposed, she wasn't actually *accused* of anything criminal. She wasn't even much of a witness. If any testimony was still regarded as meaningful, it was that of her father.

'It's all right. My wife's at home. You'll be perfectly safe.' He smiled ruefully and all her assumptions about him fell to dust.

Chapter Twenty-Two

She followed him into the house in a daze. How had she failed to be aware that he lived so close to her parents? Hadn't he told her, months ago, that he lived in Bowness? Perhaps, at a stretch, this could just qualify as being on the boundary between the two towns, but she suspected that he had at the time simply wanted to deflect any personal questions. How had she persuaded herself that he was single, probably divorced, and quietly but desperately in love with her? Embarrassment began to flood through her. The house was handsome but an ordinary semi-detached. The front garden was a plain display of pruned rose bushes, tulips and a healthy looking clematis twining between the struts of a trellis. Built of stone, most likely in the nineteenth century, it was well maintained. Simmy supposed a detective inspector's income was reasonably good. If Moxon was too busy to paint his own woodwork, he could pay someone else to do it.

'Sue?' he called gently. 'We've got a visitor.'

The woman who appeared from a back room was in her

mid forties, with faded fair hair and a modest amount of spare flesh around her middle. 'Hello,' she said easily.

'This is Mrs Persimmon Brown. She runs the florist shop in town. We've had a few encounters over the past months.'

'Of course.' She chuckled, as if he'd made a particularly good joke. 'I've been hoping to meet you. I suppose I could simply have come in to buy some flowers, but somehow I didn't think of it.'

'Oh?' said Simmy faintly.

'Of course,' said the woman again. 'You saved my husband's life. I should have made a proper effort to thank you.'

'I didn't,' said Simmy forcefully. 'Is that what he told you?'

'You certainly helped,' said Moxon. 'You can't deny it.'

'Never mind. We're embarrassing her,' said Mrs Moxon. 'Would you like a drink? I was going to have a gin any minute now.'

'Oh! Well . . . no thanks. I'm driving.'

'Now you've found your car,' said a weirdly jocular policeman. 'She was outside our house searching for it,' he explained to his wife.

'I lose mine all the time,' smiled the woman. 'I'm always thinking about something else by the time I've parked it. Sit down, do. Should I call you Persimmon?'

'Simmy.' She sat on a squashy sofa, and was instantly joined by a tabby cat.

'Push him off if he's a bother,' said Sue. 'Tea, then? Or coffee?'

Simmy accepted coffee and stayed for twenty minutes

266

enjoying the relaxed normal banter of a comfortably married couple. It transpired that the Moxons had two sons, both away at college. They had lived in the same house for twelve years and Sue worked as a credit controller for an insurance company. Simmy was convinced that nobody in a million years would guess what DI Nolan Moxon did for a living, if they were observing the scene.

When his phone rang, he left the room with it, and Sue leant towards Simmy confidentially, mere seconds later. 'That business in Coniston saved our marriage, you know,' she whispered.

'Oh?'

'We'd been drifting apart, usual story, not paying attention. Then he nearly died and I remembered why I loved him.' She smiled sentimentally. 'He has so many virtues in a quiet way. Don't you think he's changed dramatically?'

Simmy reproached herself fiercely for taking so little notice. But she could hardly say – *yes, he's cleaner, and shaves more often*. The impression of a shabby, neglected man had taken root many months ago, and remained well rooted. But on reflection, she realised that he was no longer like that. The greasiness of his hair had gone, and his head was not so sunk between his shoulders.

Although he still gave her the same soulful looks, with the same mixture of puzzlement and concern, it still felt as if he had feelings for her beyond those of a normal police officer for a member of the public. And she could hardly give voice to *that*, either.

'I haven't really seen much of him,' she prevaricated. 'It's been a very busy week.'

Then the man himself came back into the room and the women had to pretend to be talking about the weather.

'How's your father now?' asked Moxon.

'I'm not sure. I was there just now, but my mother wouldn't let me in. Said he needed peace and quiet. It's not at all settled yet, is it? I mean – we don't know who the men were that he heard, or what they were planning. He's not going to feel safe again until you catch the person who killed Mr McNaughton.' She gave herself a small mental congratulation for finally getting the name right.

Moxon sighed. 'I've heard of red herrings, but never come across one as big and bright as this. It's like being in the middle of a very elaborate conjuring trick.'

'How do you mean?'

'The thing with Vic Corless and the snares. All along he's been obscuring the more important matter, getting in the way with his threatening letter. He's got nothing to do with McNaughton's death. The trouble is, you see, you and your father gave *two* testimonies. One about the conversation and the car, and one about a dead dog and a man with a bag. We all jumped to the conclusion that they were connected, and we were wrong.'

'Are you sure about that?'

'Reasonably, yes. There's nothing concrete to link them. We've been chasing shadows all week. And yet . . .' he tailed off with a frown.

'What?'

'I still can't shake off a feeling that there is something big that we're missing. Something that might connect to Corless after all.'

'Melanie would say it was dognappers. So would Bonnie, probably.'

'And Ben?'

'I don't know.'

'Corless isn't a dognapper. They're a gang working mostly out of Carlisle, although they've got a couple of local blokes helping them. We're close to getting them. It's been a good piece of police work, if I say so myself.'

'But everyone says the police have been dismissing it as trivial, and not doing anything to catch them.'

He tapped the side of his nose in a jokey gesture that made her smile. 'That's what we *wanted* them to think,' he said.

'So they come down to Windermere and steal dogs, and then take them back to Carlisle?'

'I can't say. It's all on hold for the time being, anyway, until we sort this murder investigation. That's why we all hoped there was a connection – would have been very convenient. Too convenient,' he admitted glumly.

'But they're going to think they've got away with it, and keep on doing it?' She thought of Spike and Roddy and all the other beloved dogs which might be vulnerable. 'It is an awful thing to do, isn't it? I've been thinking it's all a bit of a joke. But people are so fantastically attached to their dogs. Even my father's much fonder of Bertie than he admits.'

'It's a very serious crime,' he said solemnly. 'The problem is, there's a lot of money to be made by it. Certain kinds of dogs sell at a very high price. And if that isn't the plan, then they ransom them. Those are less often reported to us, because the owners are so scared the dog'll be killed. Just as if a child had been kidnapped.'

'Beastly,' said Simmy. She thought of her father's outrage at the threat to burn his house down, and his assessment of some people as totally evil. 'Don't they have *any* feelings? No conscience? What's *wrong* with them, that they can cause such suffering?'

Moxon made an open-handed gesture as if waiting to intercept a football. 'That's the question we ask every day, in my line of work. And we never come close to an answer. Are they mentally challenged, or taking revenge on the world, or just so limited they can't see the consequences of their actions? Generally we conclude it's all of the above, plus a lot more. It's not useful to speculate, in the end. All we can do is try to stop them.'

'Depressing,' she said. Then she stood up. 'I should go. Thank you for the tea. It was really nice to meet you.' She smiled at Sue, still experiencing vestiges of surprise at the woman's very existence. 'We'll probably bump into each other a lot now.'

'I might call in on you for a chat one day. After all, I know where you are.'

'Yes,' said Simmy, aware of the slight lowering these words caused. Too many people knew how to find her, and took full advantage of their knowledge.

Moxon saw her to the door, and watched her unlock the car and drive away. Glancing at his face again, she was sure she could identify the same yearning look there had always been. Something a long way from lust or even love, but definitely a bond of some kind. He liked her, and worried about her, and enjoyed being with her.

All of which inevitably made her think of Ninian Tripp, who was available and accommodating, at least some of the time. Perhaps he would be in now, preparing some sort of amorphous stew for his evening meal. Ninian cooked on a ramshackle old stove fuelled by bottled gas. He bought meat from a local farm, just as Angie Straw did, but on a much smaller scale. Friends gave him surplus vegetables. He always had a few bottles of wine stashed away, much of it home-made. Simmy imagined a hunk of slow-cooked lamb with carrots and parsnips and a drink made from fermented berries. All sheer fantasy, she reproached herself. Much more likely, he would be opening a tin of soup, or baked beans, and barely bothering to heat it up.

But she hadn't seen him for a few days, and the week was almost over. There was still no reason to hurry home, even if it was well past seven now – and every motivation to seek out a warm body and an unenquiring mind. Ninian wouldn't be interested in murder or stolen dogs or strange girls who were hard to trust.

There was no point in phoning him, so she had little option but to simply show up. The very worst-case scenario would be that she found him in bed with another woman, and while that would be hurtful and annoying, it certainly wouldn't break her heart. It was absolutely worth the risk. Besides, she was almost facing Brant Fell already. A simple right turn would take her through Lickbarrow and within half a mile she'd be there. It was a clear mild evening, the gardens blooming luminously in the slowly fading light. Despite being only yards away from Bowness and the shores of the lake, there were fields and trees, and the sudden rise of the funny little fell, all there to enjoy.

Ninian opened the door cautiously, peering around it like a man with something to hide.

'Got another woman in there?' asked Simmy gaily. 'Let me in, so I can see.'

'Actually . . .' he began, and the gaiety evaporated.

'Come on, Ninian. This is looking bad. What's the big secret?'

'Oh, nothing, really. It's not you. I just learnt a long time ago that two women together with a man is generally a recipe for discomfort. I had no idea you were going to show up,' he concluded feebly.

Simmy pushed the door open and went in, saying, 'I promise not to cause you any discomfort.' Her own insides were sufficiently turbulent for them both. It wasn't jealousy, she insisted. More a sour disappointment, and the helpless sense of being betrayed. At the very least, she felt she was due the bleak satisfaction of discovering who her rival was.

The woman sitting on Ninian's battered leather couch was less of a surprise than she should have been. *Perhaps I'm beyond surprise today*, Simmy thought. 'Hi, Corinne,' she said.

Chapter Twenty-Three

'It's not what you think,' said the purple-haired woman, with a grin. 'I've got enough men in my life as it is. I've just come here to escape for a bit.'

'Escape from what?' Simmy asked coolly.

'People,' shrugged Corinne. 'That's what I need to get away from, And all this crap that's going on.'

'Right,' said Simmy vaguely.

'I've done a stew,' said Ninian proudly. 'Isn't that lucky? I meant it to last all weekend, but I'm happy to share.'

It appeared that he was addressing Corinne as well as her, which Simmy found irksome. As an only child, she was familiar with threesomes, in which one person was always out on a limb and struggling to be included. Her parents had made it easy, but in other situations she found it unpleasant. Even with Melanie and Ben, she understood that her assistant often felt pushed out by the other two. Now there would be a tedious situation in which she and Corinne fell into inevitable female behaviour, competing for the attention of the one man in the room. Ninian himself had referred to it, almost the moment she had arrived.

'I don't know,' she said. 'I don't want to intrude.'

'Don't be daft,' said Corinne. 'We weren't doing anything. I'm just hiding away here for a bit. I won't talk, if that helps. I can read a book.' She delved into a large cotton bag and produced an electronic tablet in a red case. 'I've got about a hundred on here,' she added.

'You can understand it,' said Ninian apologetically. 'Poor old Corry's got dragged into something nasty, when she never deserved to.'

Simmy closed her eyes for a moment, trying to square these words with her own experience. 'She abducted my father,' she said flatly. 'Isn't that enough?'

'Pardon?' His lanky body went stiff with surprise. 'That can't be right.' He looked to Corinne for an explanation. 'Can it?'

'We didn't *abduct* him,' she said scornfully. 'He was happy to come with us. And it all got sorted, didn't it? That was down to me and Bonnie. He'd still be scared his house would be burnt down if it wasn't for us.'

The casual lack of concern enraged Simmy. 'You and that man Vic, more like. Bonnie can't have known what she was doing. You're an awful influence on her, it seems to me.'

'Hey!' Ninian protested. 'That's a bit rich. Corry's given that girl a home when nobody else would. She was just telling me about it when you got here.'

'How long have you two known each other?' Suspicion swirled darkly through her mind, with anybody capable of anything – even the ineffably benign Ninian.

'Couple of years,' shrugged Corinne. 'What's that got to do with anything?'

'She's been a foster mother for years,' he said. 'I expect you knew that. She was listing some of the kids she's helped. Tell her about that boy,' he urged Corinne. 'The one you looked out for when his dad was in prison.'

'Raymond,' she nodded. 'I've been a bit worried about him, to be honest. His dad's had him back for nearly a year now, and I'm hearing some dodgy stuff about them.'

Simmy wasn't at all sure she was interested. It felt like a diversion away from more sensitive topics. She contemplated Ninian speculatively. 'You weren't at the funeral, were you?' she said. 'Did you hear what happened to Valerie?'

He flushed. 'As it happens, I did go along, after all. So obviously I did see the whole awful thing. It was impossible to miss. Poor woman. She got so choked up, talking about Barbara and how she loved dogs, and the good she did, and then she just turned to stone. It was terrifying.'

'Wish I'd been there,' said Corinne. 'Sounds awesome.'

'It was pretty bad,' Ninian agreed. 'They couldn't just go on with the service, with the chief mourner laid out on the front pew, could they? It all went on hold, and then the vicar told the organist to play the last hymn, and we struggled through it, and then they carried the coffin out to the grave.' He sighed. 'After all that planning, as well. There was a good twenty minutes yet to go, according to the service sheet.'

Simmy's mental picture of what had happened was only minimally enhanced by Ninian's account. From what she had seen of Valerie, before and since, her breakdown, or whatever it was, sounded highly uncharacteristic. She recalled Ben's intemperate remarks about guilt and Macbeth. 'Ben thought she looked guilty,' she said. 'As if an avenging angel or ghost had appeared before her.'

Ninian laughed. 'That sounds like the Ben Harkness we know and love,' he said.

'I saw her at the church, just now,' Simmy said, feeling an odd sense of betrayal. 'That makes four times that I've actually spoken to her – and I think she's going to have a hard time over the coming months. I really rather like her. She's terribly lonely, poor thing. Did you know she was Polish originally?'

The others looked blank. 'I don't really know her at all,' said Ninian.

Corinne scratched her neck and said nothing. Simmy faced her. 'You did, didn't you? Bonnie said you did. And yet you never went to the funeral. All that stuff about going to Lincoln wasn't even true. Did something happen between you and Valerie?'

'Of course not. I *meant* to go to Lincoln, but then Vic called me and I got diverted. You don't have to worry about me,' she said emphatically. 'Nor Valerie, come to that. She's a good woman. She was happy with Barbara and the dog. She didn't deserve all the aggravation she's had this year.'

'With Barbara dying, you mean?'

'And before that, when Roddy was stolen. That was a dreadful thing. It got Barb so upset that her cancer flared up again and she died a lot sooner than she might have done. Those bastards who did it should be flayed alive.'

She clamped her lips together as if she'd said too much.

'But they got him back – Roddy, that is.'

'After they paid five hundred quid in ransom.' She looked at Simmy. 'And don't you go shouting your mouth off about that to the police. You and your little amateur detective friend would only have made it all worse, if they'd gone public about it.'

'What? Why would *I* have had anything to do with it? I never knew Barbara Hodge or her dog.'

'Yeah – but you've got a habit of getting involved. You should watch that – it's not a reputation everyone would want.'

Simmy was speechless. She stared at Corinne, aghast at the implications of what she had said.

Ninian tried his clumsy best to help. 'She never gets involved deliberately. You're not being fair.'

Corinne shrugged. 'Just saying how it looks. It's not meant nastily. You're being great with Bonnie,' she offered.

Simmy felt soiled and upset. Somehow she had taken a wrong turn, letting herself be drawn into an underworld populated by people who could not be trusted. People who would steal and snare and even kill. Corinne, sitting there so confident and brazen, was closely acquainted with such people – and yet it didn't seem to bother her. Simmy had never knowingly met a criminal until coming to Cumbria and setting up her floristry business. Since then, her horizons had expanded all too painfully.

'I won't get any more involved,' she said. 'Not with Vic or Murray . . . any of them. One of those friends of yours could have killed that poor innocent man in that yard, for all I know. I really don't know how you can live with yourself, if that's the case,' she finished. The rage was leaking out of her, leaving only a residue of bitterness. 'And there's my perfectly harmless father, knocked sideways by the whole business.'

'Oh, come on,' said Corinne. 'That's got nothing to do with the killing. We explained all that to you before. You're muddling everything up again. Do yourself a favour and just stick to your flowers. You're good for Bonnie. She says so herself. She likes you and your shop. And she likes Ben Harkness,' she added, with a mischievous smile at Ninian. 'Quite a little romance brewing there, I shouldn't wonder.'

'How sweet! They should be good for each other,' said Ninian blithely. At the same moment, Simmy felt a flash of concern for the boy – so clever and so vulnerable. If Bonnie broke his heart, the consequences could be shattering.

'I hope so,' she said tightly.

'Come and have some stew,' said Ninian. 'And we can talk of other things. I make pots, you know. I can tell you all about them, if you like.'

'I did know that, actually,' she said sarcastically. 'And you know I did.'

'Joking,' he sighed. 'I thought I'd remind you of the time you said you'd buy a couple. That was years ago now. Let me show you the latest ones.'

'You do that,' said Corinne, getting out of the couch. 'Come on, Simmy Brown. Enjoy yourself, for a change.'

It was nine o'clock when Simmy got back to Troutbeck, and twilight had turned the world to muted greys. Despite

Ninian's efforts to keep it cheerful, Corinne's words had rankled at all levels. There was no escape from them, whichever way she turned. She was a killjoy, a sneak, an ignorant incomer. She looked for complexity when actually all was plain and simple. She was probably regarded as a snob, as well. Not one of these epithets was true, she insisted to herself, and yet they had hurt. Surely that meant there was at least a dash of accuracy in them?

Introspection did not come to her very often. Simmy Brown habitually looked outwards, watching others and doing her best for them. Melanie, Ben and now Bonnie looked to her for good sense and predictability – and got it, she believed. DI Moxon acted as if he credited her with a good heart, too. They were all, in their different ways, concerned for her welfare. Even Ninian was solicitous of her, his lovemaking aimed at pleasing her at least as much as himself. Nobody ever hinted that they found her disagreeable or selfish or spiteful.

But she was far too serious, she knew. She didn't often laugh or let herself go. She was careful and wary, and she was implacably on the side of truth. A killjoy and a sneak, for sure. Damn it.

The evening was almost over. Tomorrow there was a nice little wedding for which she was doing the flowers. Her father was at least not in hospital, not dying, and very probably on the way to complete restoration of his usual self. There was much to be thankful for. Compared to those who knew and loved Travis McNaughton, she had absolutely nothing to complain about. He was permanently violently dead and it was a desperate and dreadful thing.

The way his demise kept fading out of focus, obscured by other events, disconnected and distracting, was shameful. If Vic Corless, and his illegal snares, was not responsible, then somebody else was.

And the only person Simmy could depend upon to agree that this was the highest priority; who would cut through the smokescreens and diversions to concentrate on what really mattered, was young Ben Harkness. If she knew Ben, he'd be back in the shop the next morning, hovering around until she closed up at lunchtime, and then bombarding her with his latest theories.

Then she remembered his new infatuation with Bonnie. Would that mean he forgot all about the police investigation into the murder? Would he arrive early next day and devote all his attention to the girl, ignoring Simmy in the process? It seemed all too likely, she decided gloomily.

Well, then, she would just let it all go as well. She'd take the flowers to the hall where the wedding reception was to be, and then deliver the bouquets and buttonholes to the house, and after that there were orders and stock, displays and future plans to think about. Summer was coming, which ironically could sometimes spell slow business for a florist. With gardens and hedges so awash with blooms, people felt less inclined to buy their own from a shop. If they wanted a table centrepiece or a colourful vase of flowers in their hall, they could go out and gather it for themselves, for free. Simmy and Melanie had discussed this at length, and concluded there was a need for lateral thinking. Hanging baskets, window boxes – the more flamboyant the better – could be part of the stock in the shop. Restaurants could be approached with ideas for summer displays, indoors and out. 'They'll pay you to do their thinking for them,' said Melanie. 'Especially if you offer to hang the baskets and position the boxes as well.' It would all involve more work and, she hoped, a steady income.

Such forward-looking thoughts served to cheer her considerably. Life would go on; she would avoid self-pity as she would a virulent virus – and she would use that phrase to tease Ben, if she remembered. Or perhaps her father, who enjoyed wordplay. Even if he never fully regained his old ways, he was always going to have fun with puns and the more arcane aspects of grammar.

She went to bed early, and dreamt confusedly about dogs at a funeral, chasing a boy with large ears and entangling their leads round Simmy's legs. One of them was Bertie, who hugged himself tightly against Russell Straw's legs and flinched at every approach. There was no barking or whimpering, just exuberant behaviour. The boy climbed into the church pulpit and threw hymn books down at the dogs. When she woke, she remembered the slapstick scene with amusement. Where had all that come from, she wondered?

Chapter Twenty-Four

She described the dream to Melanie, who turned up promptly on Saturday morning, explaining that she could only stay an hour, and would handle any new orders, as well as checking the stock for flowers that needed to be replaced.

'I have no idea who the boy was,' Simmy mused. 'I'd never seen him before. He had ears like great flat mushrooms. Nobody in real life would have ears as big as they were.'

'Something you've heard somewhere,' Melanie said idly. 'I never think dreams mean anything in particular.'

It came to Simmy then. 'My mother – she said there was a boy with big ears behind her at the funeral. She thought Valerie was looking at him and his dad when she had her meltdown thingy. I bet that was it.'

'Probably Raymond Eccles, then. Bonnie said she'd seen him.'

'Raymond . . . where have I heard that name recently? Who is he? A boy at school with Bonnie or something?'

'He's a bad lad, from a bad family. Corinne fostered him for a bit, which is how Bonnie knows him.'

'Right! She said something about him yesterday. The father's been in prison.'

Melanie was concentrating on the computer. 'He's not interesting. Can't imagine why anybody would dream about him,' she said.

Wriggly little ideas were happening in Simmy's head, ideas that threatened to become questions and then theories. They were very small and very new, and a careless word might flatten them, but they began to connect together in a picture that demanded attention. Was this how Ben's head felt all the time, she wondered, and then recalled herself wondering the same thing a few days ago. For some reason, Simmy's mind had been a lot more creative lately, tying things together and forming unsettling conclusions.

She clamped her lips together, afraid of Melanie's scorn. She needed Ben. He would listen and take her seriously. If she was leaping to foolish conclusions, he would explain her lack of logic. He would also make suggestions as to how the hypothesis might be tested – even if such suggestions might turn out to be reckless or even dangerous.

But Melanie could not be ignored. She had talents all of her own. 'Um . . . Mel. You know that Travis man who was killed . . . ?'

'Not personally, but yes. I know who you mean.'

'It's right, isn't it – he'd never been in trouble with the police. Never done anything that would make people hate him. Isn't that what everybody's saying?'

'Pretty much, yeah. Why?'

'Just wondering. It seems so horrible that he should die like that, for no reason anybody can see.'

'Since when were the reasons obvious? What about the lady in Ambleside, and the man in Coniston? Nobody could understand why they were killed, either.'

'True, I suppose.' Her questions had taken her off track. She tried to formulate another. 'How old did they say his boy is?'

'Twelve, thirteen. Something like that.'

'So Raymond Eccles is older?'

'Sixteen, I'd guess. But he's small for his age. What's all this about, Sim?'

'Nothing. Just getting the picture straight, that's all.'

Melanie looked up from the screen and gave Simmy a close scrutiny. 'What are you thinking? What's this about boys?'

'Nothing – I told you. I'm going to deliver those wedding flowers now. Can you hang on till I get back? It won't be later than ten-thirty.'

'No problem,' sighed Melanie.

The wedding was to take place in the register office at Kendal, and then back to a village hall at Ulverston. Simmy had to drive the ten miles down to the pretty hall, setting out an arrangement for each of the eight tables, as well as positioning a large display near the door to welcome the guests as they came in. 'Keep it simple,' the bride had ordered. 'I'd like it to look like an old-fashioned homespun affair, if you know what I mean. As if the local girls had gone out and gathered flowers from the hedgerows.

Forsythia, jasmine, honeysuckle – that sort of thing.' As usual, Simmy found her customer blissfully unaware of the seasons, and what might be found in a May hedgerow. All the same, it was a pleasing assignment, and she was proud of the results.

Having garnished all the tables as requested, she drove back to Craig Walk where she was to deliver posies and buttonholes as well as the bridal bouquet. It was a pleasant road, to the east of the main street through Bowness, the terraced houses made of the same dark stone as almost every other building in the town. Mrs Jennings, soon to become Mrs Moffat, opened the door, looking calm and cheerful. Simmy recalled other brides, with their hair in rollers and their eyes wild with panic, and smiled. 'You'd better have a look and make sure they're what you wanted,' she said.

The woman opened the large flat box and fingered the contents. 'They smell heavenly,' she breathed.

'That's the freesias,' said Simmy. 'I'll go and get your bouquet now.' She went back to the van for the last of its contents, and took the carefully wrapped arrangement into the house.

'Lovely,' said the bride. 'Absolutely perfect. Was everything okay at Ulverston?'

'Fine. There wasn't anybody there, but the door was unlocked.'

'The caterers will be in and out, I suppose.' A small frown of worry appeared. 'Nobody's going to go in and wreck it, are they?'

'Of course they're not,' said Simmy emphatically. 'Who would do that?'

285

'You're right. It's awful the way we're all so uptight about security, isn't it. Imagine in Hardy's day, anybody even having such an idea.'

'Hardy?'

'Thomas. I told you – I wanted to try to imitate the kind of wedding you find in his books.' She laughed. 'Although it's all fallen apart a bit, without a church service. And everybody driving from Kendal to Ulverston in cars. All the same, you must admit I've bucked the trend for fancy hotels and hours of drinking. Not to mention the disco.' She shuddered. 'I've always hated discos.'

'Didn't they dance in Hardy?' Simmy had a faint memory of a book they had to read at school. 'Something about the greenwood tree.'

'We've got a band of Morris Men coming.' The frown was back. 'I told you that as well.'

'I'm sorry,' said Simmy. 'I'm sure you did. Back when you ordered the flowers.' *Six weeks ago*, she wanted to add. 'So, good luck with it all. Have a lovely day. I've got to get back . . .'

'Thank you,' said Mrs Jennings, warmly. 'You've done a fantastic job. I'll come in and pay next week, shall I?'

'Wait till I send the bill,' laughed Simmy. 'Bye, then.'

She was back in the shop dead on half past ten, rather to her own surprise. The whole trip had taken an hour and ten minutes, which she felt was an achievement in itself on a Saturday morning. The presence of growing numbers of holidaymakers had sent her in a looping diversion through quiet streets, avoiding the busy heart of Bowness.

Melanie was impatiently waiting to leave. 'How did it go?' she asked.

'Fine. Why are you in such a rush?'

'Lots to do,' said the girl. 'I really won't be able to fit you in after this, Sim. It's all taking off with the hotel stuff. I've got a second interview in Grasmere this afternoon. They phoned yesterday. I'm all behind with everything. You'll have to make do with Bonnie. Wasn't she meant to come in today?'

The breathlessness was irritating. 'I think she was, yes. Up till one o'clock, she said. Gosh, Mel, yesterday was such a mess. I went to Ninian's after work and Corinne was there. I never knew they knew each other.'

'Why wouldn't they?' Melanie was almost out of the door, and plainly in no mood for any further chat. Simmy had a premonition of how much she would miss her, with her undisguised interest in everybody's lives and loves. Melanie had provided support, advice and good sense, more like a mother than somebody young enough to be Simmy's daughter.

'One more thing,' she said, wanting to grab the girl's arm. 'If Ben and I get any more gen on the murder, do you want to be kept informed?'

'Gen?'

'You know what I mean. Information. Ideas. Well, do you?'

'Not really.' Melanie shook her head. 'I think it's time I let all that go. It was fun for a while, working with you. And I'll call in and see you, one morning next week. But now – sorry, but I'm really going. Be nice to Bonnie. You won't regret it, I promise. She's a lot cleverer than me. She has a good heart, deep down. Don't judge her too harshly. You don't really know her yet.'

And she was gone, trotting down the street, large and determined, heading for her new life.

Two customers came in, ten minutes apart, the second one a middle-aged woman browsing unhurriedly. Simmy was jangled by Melanie's departure and its lack of ceremony, as well as restless at the implications of her involuntary theories about what had happened in Troutbeck on Tuesday. Images from the week flitted through her head, like stills from a movie, run together to form an increasingly compelling narrative. But it remained a narrative with several holes in it, and a conclusion that would shock almost anyone who heard it.

Where was Ben when she needed him? When the customer finally left with a small bunch of very undramatic carnations, Simmy was tempted to give the boy a ring. Despite his imminent exams, not to mention his family, she felt entitled to his attention. Everything was in suspense without him. She had no idea what she might do on her own, but with Ben's encouragement, anything was possible.

At last, just before eleven-thirty, the door opened and two youngsters came in. Simmy had her back to them, tidying away some tired-looking flowers which wouldn't last until Monday. 'Hi!' called Ben. 'It's us.'

He was holding hands with Bonnie and looking both proud and sheepish. 'Can't stay long. Bonnie's coming back to mine for lunch.'

Simmy took a deep breath, forcing herself to remember she was a generation older than them, and therefore simply not allowed to rely on either of them for any emotional succour. But she could reproach Bonnie for failing to abide by her promise to work all morning. 'I thought you said you'd be here at ten,' she said.

'Did I? So much happened, I wasn't sure how we'd left it.'

What was the good? She heard Melanie's parting words again, and forced herself to reserve judgement for a while. 'I was hoping you'd show up, for a number of reasons,' she said. 'I wanted to try a theory on you, if you've got time.'

'Theory? What about?' Ben looked puzzled and wary.

'Murder.'

'Golly Moses, Sim. That's not like you.'

'It is now. Actually, I was wondering if you'd come with me somewhere. But that's probably not a good idea. I guess I should just phone Moxon and tell him about it.'

'About *what*? You're not making any sense.' He glared at her, and she understood that he, like Melanie, was no longer finding the death of Travis McNaughton the most pressing subject of the moment.

'Bear with me for a minute. Let me list a few facts, okay? First – there's a man called Eccles, with a son called Raymond. Raymond's sixteen, and his dad's been in prison. I don't know what he did . . .'

'They were at the funeral,' said Bonnie. 'It was Eccles who had the coughing fit.'

'Good! Great!' Simmy almost clapped her hands with satisfaction. 'That's what I hoped to find out. You know them, then?'

'Corinne fostered Ray for a bit. He still pops in now and then to say hello.'

'And his father?'

Bonnie flushed and hesitated before answering. 'I don't know,' she mumbled. Her gaze was flickering from one display of flowers to another, suggesting rapid thoughts forming behind her eyes.

'What do you mean, you don't know? *What* don't you know?'

'Hey!' Ben protested. 'Don't yell at her.'

'It's okay,' said Bonnie, her head drooping. 'I've just had one or two scary ideas. I think I need to tell you something I did . . . I knew it would come out eventually. I *told* Corinne it never does any good to lie to the police. They always find out in the end.' The precocious wisdom behind these words made Simmy wonder yet again just what had gone so wrong in this young girl's life.

'You lied to the police?' Ben stared at his new beloved in horror.

'I won't do it again. Corinne said we should give him a chance. She's had words with him about it. He's getting his act together. I mean – he came to the funeral. That's his way of trying to be respectable and part of the community and all that stuff.'

'Who?' Ben almost shouted. 'Who's *him*?'

'The Eccles man,' said Simmy quietly. 'You saw his picture on the police computer, but didn't tell them. He was the man who tried to steal Spike and the other dog. Is that it?'

Bonnie's expression was full of shame mixed with admiration. 'How d'you work that out?'

'It's true, then?'

The girl nodded. Ben closed his mouth slowly. 'Blimey,' he said.

'And did he steal Roddy? Barbara Hodge's dog.'

'Seems like it. I mean . . .' She made a visible effort. 'Yes, he did. He gave him back, though. And Corinne made him give the money back, as well. Nobody knows about it.' She leant forward pleadingly. 'He put it right again. He's never going to do it again. When you told me and Melanie about seeing Vic on Monday, and the dead dog on the fells, I just assumed it was Barry Eccles you'd seen, and he was at it again. Especially when you said there was a boy in the red car, as well. That made me all the more sure. I phoned Corinne to tell her. She'd been doing so much to help him get clean. It felt like a kick in the teeth. I *had* to tell her.'

'But it wasn't him at all, was it?'

Bonnie shook her head like a six-year-old child caught stealing sweets.

'He's lucky,' said Simmy. 'Probably luckier than he can possibly imagine.'

'I'm not getting it,' said Ben crossly. 'Where's this going?'

'I don't think I should say any more until I've spoken to DI Moxon. I owe it to him to keep quiet for now. Thanks, Bonnie. You've filled in the picture very nicely.'

'You *can't* tell him about it,' the girl begged. 'Why would you?'

Simmy examined her face for any indication that she'd understood all the implications, but remained unsure. 'I don't think he's going to worry too much about a little oversight on your part,' she said. 'All you did was make a mistake. It's not a crime.'

'But Corinne obstructed the course of justice,' said Ben. 'She failed to report a crime.'

'True. But again, I don't think much is going to happen. There are bigger things involved.'

'Your dad?' Ben hazarded. 'Is that what you're bothered about?' He frowned. 'Can't see how that connects, all the same. Wasn't it all settled yesterday?'

'Not my dad,' said Simmy. 'Although I dare say his testimony might have some little part to play when the whole thing comes to court.' She thought about it for a moment. 'But maybe it won't. I have a feeling I'm going to be more useful than him.' She sighed. 'Poor man. It's terrible the way one little thing can make such a huge difference to a person's sense of well-being.'

Bonnie was clearly concentrating hard. 'You mean like Barbara Hodge,' she said in a small voice.

'I mean precisely that,' said Simmy.

Ben wouldn't give up. 'You've got to explain,' he insisted. 'It's not fair otherwise.'

'I get it,' said Bonnie. 'Or I think I do.' She clasped Ben's hand, and gave it a little shake. 'Don't get heavy with her, okay? It might be completely wrong. Just a lot of ideas coming together and adding up to a wild theory. And that's what caused all the trouble to start with.' She gave Simmy a tragic look. 'It was all my fault, wasn't it?'

'I think you're just one link in a chain. But she's right,' Simmy told Ben. 'We mustn't rush anything now.' She met Bonnie's eyes with her own surge of admiration. Everything she knew or suspected about the girl was swamped by a sense that here was a very special person, with talents in

292

abundance. Her understanding of human complications had doubtless been gained through hard experience, giving her a core of steel beneath the fragile exterior. At the same time, this was balanced by an alarming tendency to ignore authority, to march into situations that she couldn't control and to lie her way out of trouble if it suited her.

Melanie was wrong about Bonnie and Ben, Simmy realised. Ben was all theory and bloodless facts. He hadn't known fear or despair or loss of control in his comfortable middle-class family. Bonnie could teach him a lot that was missing from his character. And he could give her a degree of stability and confidence. Knowing it was sentimental, Simmy nonetheless felt that this was a perfect match, which she would do well to safeguard to the best of her ability. Ben would teach Bonnie to tread more carefully and think more logically. Each would help the other to grow up.

'So what happens now?' asked Ben, striving to remain cool in the face of two implacable females.

'I think I will have to go to Moxon, but first I ought to see my parents. I want to make sure they're okay. Plus, there's something I need to ask them.'

'Do you want us to mind the shop for you?' asked Bonnie. 'You could go right away then.'

Simmy looked at her, aware all over again of just how young she was. She supposed there was no official regulation setting a minimum age at which someone could be in charge of a shop, but anybody coming in and finding two seventeen-year-olds there on their own might have concerns. Especially if there was canoodling of some sort going on.

'No, no, thanks all the same,' she said. 'I can close up in an hour or so anyway. If I went now, I'd only have to come back to lock up everything and set the alarm.' Only then did she remember how Bonnie and her friends had effectively broken into the rooms upstairs, without permission. However vigorously the justifications for it might be made, this was still a strong sign that trust could yet be misplaced. 'I'll make us some coffee, and we can hang on until one o'clock.'

'This is beyond weird,' said Ben. 'You think you've worked out who killed Travis McNaughton, and Bonnie's read your thoughts by magic, but now you're in no hurry to go and tell the cops, either of you? You're happy to let them waste time and taxpayers' cash on some false trail, until you can find a minute to do your civic duty. Is that right?'

Simmy grimaced at him. 'That's the bare bones of it. But how many times have you said yourself, there's no case without hard evidence?'

'So? If you can point them to the right person, then they can *find* some evidence. They'll know where to look. They can compare what they've got with your person's fingerprints or whatever. That's the way it works.' He scowled at her. 'As you know very well.'

Simmy turned her back on him, and went to put the kettle on in the back room. She was not surprised to find her hands were shaking. The impact of her theory had been slow to come, but now that Bonnie had apparently reached the same conclusion, with very little help, the implications were forcing themselves on her. It was both more and less frightening, having a second person with the same idea. If it was true, then Bonnie could back her up, add her own details to the picture, and share her trepidation. If it was false, all the risks of slander and unforeseen consequences were doubled, and Bonnie might well spread unjustified rumours before she could be stopped.

She repeated the steps of her reasoning to herself, and formulated the central question she needed to ask her father before she could take it any further. She made herself a mug of strong coffee, and filled a chipped brown teapot for the others. They were so young, she reflected again – too young to have acquired a taste for coffee. Ben would drink it, but could never quite suppress his shudder of distaste. It made Simmy smile. Teenagers took to beer and vodka much more quickly than they developed a liking for coffee.

She carried the rattling tray back into the shop and quickly plonked it down beside the computer. Bonnie had her phone to her ear.

'Who's she calling?' she asked Ben, with a sudden apprehension.

'Corinne, I think.' His frustration was still in evidence. 'Neither of you are telling me anything.' He paused. '*Is*, I mean. Neither one of you *is* telling me.'

'Don't be pedantic,' she said, relieved that he was not so angry that he couldn't monitor his own use of syntax. 'You're just like my father.'

'We hold the survival of the language in our hands,' he claimed, with a reluctant grin.

'You mean you're holding back a natural evolutionary progress.' It was an exchange they'd had before, more than once. She was glad of the distraction, until she heard Bonnie say something that alarmed her.

'I think you should go and warn her,' came the incredible words.

Without thinking, Simmy snatched the phone away from the girl, and pressed its red button to abort the call. 'What are you doing?' she cried.

Bonnie cowered away, her expression confused and scared. 'What?' she whispered. 'What's the matter?'

'Warn who?' Simmy demanded.

'Nobody you know. There's a woman who works in the library. She found me some books about flowers that I thought would be useful for my job here with you. Corinne got a call from her just now, saying they've arrived, and would I go and collect them. Corinne's going to do it for me.'

Simmy's eyes narrowed. 'Come off it. What's that got to do with warning somebody?'

'I just meant we should warn her I might not return them very quickly. I'll want to make notes and stuff, and I might take a while. Honestly, Simmy, that's all it was. You never let me finish what I was going to say.'

'I wish I could believe you.' It was the plain truth. She wished profoundly that she could take the girl at her word. But the story felt thin and hastily invented.

'If it was what you think, I'd be an idiot to say it right here in front of you, wouldn't I? I'd know it'd make you mad.'

Ben was once again open-mouthed as he watched them. But he knew whose side he was on. 'You're being a right bitch today,' he told Simmy. 'D'you know that?'

She was instantly deflated. Perhaps Bonnie was as

innocent as she claimed, after all. Her final point was a good one, anyway. She felt strung out and barely in control. 'Sorry,' she said. 'Here.' And she gave the girl her phone back.

She poured out two mugs of tea and they all drank in silence for a minute or two. The next few hours loomed ominously, as she tried to thread her way through a legal and moral quagmire that she would far rather ignore completely. The indistinct face of Travis McNaughton hovered insistently in her mind's eye, along with everything she knew about him. By no means a saint or a pillar of the community, he had nonetheless not in any way at all deserved to die so horribly, at such an early age. The savage injustice of it was dreadful, an extreme consequence of a chain of events that had been none of his making. The collateral trauma to the woman who found him in a lake of blood was almost as shattering. The taint left on the yard and surrounding area, like a returning ghost, was imbued with shame and irrevocable tragedy.

'Right,' she said. 'You two can go now. Please don't say anything to anybody, Bonnie. I'm trusting you, okay? It's important. You can call me later today to see how it went, if you like.'

'No, I'm coming with you,' said the girl. 'You won't be able to stop me, so don't even try.'

The core of steel had never been more apparent. 'Well, all right,' said Simmy. 'But I don't like it.'

'And if she's there, I'm going to be as well,' said Ben.

Again, Simmy felt the mixture of gladness and annoyance. Moxon would perceive them as a deputation, rather than a friendly offer of help from someone already involved in his investigations. Because underlying everything else was a sense that she should in some way atone for the way she had thought and behaved towards DI Moxon, ever since first meeting him. She had misjudged him, at the very least. There had been moments when she'd felt repulsed by him, and might not have adequately concealed her reaction. And although she had done everything she could to help when he'd been hurt, she had failed to follow it up afterwards with visits or enquiries as to how he was mending.

'So let's get on with it, then,' she sighed.

'What about going to see your folks first?' asked Bonnie. 'Something you wanted to ask your dad. We can wait outside, if you're quick.'

'Better than that – go and have some lunch,' she suggested. 'I'll get something from my mum, while I'm there. If you still want to come with me, let's say we meet at the police station at two o'clock. Right?'

'They've closed the front desk, you know,' said Ben, out of the blue. 'You can't just stroll in off the street any more and expect someone to welcome you.'

'That's right,' Bonnie confirmed. 'I was there a couple of days ago, and it's all different now.'

'I'll phone him, then, and ask what he wants me to do.'

'Us,' said Ben. 'Not just you. All of us.' He gave her a long look. 'You can't shake us off, you know. We'll stay right outside the house while you talk to your father. Lunch can wait.'

Simmy did not want to speak to Moxon on the phone. She wanted to assess his responses face to face, taking the whole thing step by careful step, ready to modify or even abandon her theories, if he rejected them forcefully enough. She wanted no risk of her words being recorded, either. Making accusations of murder against a person ought not to be done lightly, especially if there was no scrap of hard evidence to support the accusation.

There was also the faint hope that the detective might miraculously have reached the same conclusion as she had; that some information had come to him from another source to lead him to the same point. By delaying as long as she could, she might be making this outcome more likely, letting herself off the painful moral hook she was on.

But she doubted there was to be any reprieve. Murder was murder. It stood huge and implacable before her, as it had done on other occasions, and there was no denying it.

As she ushered the two youngsters out onto the pavement, and set about locking the door behind herself, the reprieve she had despaired of materialised. Both her parents were walking down the street towards her. 'P'simmon!' called her mother, 'I need you to come with us. There's something we have to do.'

Chapter Twenty-Five

Yet again, Simmy found herself part of an uncomfortably large group of people blocking the pavement in the middle of Windermere. She was primarily delighted to see her father looking fit and well, his face suggesting a full understanding of and concern with the present moment. The jut of her mother's chin promised something decisive and potentially helpful.

'We were just coming to you,' Simmy said faintly. 'Has something happened?'

'We had a phone call from Corinne Whatever-her-name-is, twenty minutes ago.' Angie looked at Bonnie. 'She said it was your suggestion. All to do with that man and his boy sitting behind me at the funeral. Said we ought to go and talk to—'

Simmy cut her off quickly. 'So that story about the library books was a complete lie,' she accused the girl. 'Really, Bonnie, I can't believe a word you say, can I? You told Corinne to phone my parents, didn't you?'

'Actually, no. I didn't.' Bonnie stood her ground and spoke out clearly. 'How do you think there'd be time? It's only been ten minutes since I was talking to her. That was *after* she called your mum.'

Simmy was confounded yet again by the girl's logic. Accustomed to it from Ben, she had not yet come to expect it from Bonnie. 'So – what on earth is this all about?' She was increasingly afraid that a name would be mentioned that ought not to be, until she had shared her thoughts with the police, especially now that there were two more people to hear it. 'Mum. Do you think you and I could have a quiet word, just the two of us?'

'Whatever for? There's no time for that. Corinne wants you and your father to have a good look at the man and his boy, and see if you recognise them. She says they're in the Elleray having lunch.'

'Good Lord,' snapped Simmy. 'What does it have to do with her? And how does she know they're in the pub? Where's she?'

Russell spoke up for the first time. 'She's trying to put things right,' he said. 'She and that Vic person have had a few ideas, after hearing all about yesterday's events from Bonnie. Vic knew the murdered man, remember? And now he's worried that it wasn't him we saw on Monday after all. If he's right, it'll help the police, don't you see?'

Simmy absorbed this speech slowly. It did nothing to further encourage her as to her father's return to health. Rather, it sounded like a man desperately trying to sound rational, and failing. 'We saw him wave to the men in the car,' she reminded her father. 'Are you sure you've understood him properly?'

'So we did.' Russell frowned. 'Is that helpful?'

Simmy shook her head at him, and turned to her other parent. 'Mum? Where's Corinne now? And what on earth does she want from me? She already knows who everybody is.'

'You're being deliberately stupid,' Bonnie accused her. 'Corinne needs to be sure before she tells the police what she did. Don't you see that?'

Simmy's heart thundered at this new twist. She had not factored in any action on the part of Corinne, having filed her away with Vic Corless as being only concerned with snaring animals and driving illegal cars.

Angie pulled at her arm. 'It can't do any damage, can it? Just in case they're right, you should come. It's the least we can do, if it helps to solve a murder.'

Simmy resisted. 'It'll take ages, all the way up there and back.'

'So what's the hurry?'

'It's pointless. I already know everything I need to.' Then she had a new thought and completely changed her mind. She turned to Ben and Bonnie. 'All right, then. I'll go. Don't you two come. Wait down by the Baddeley Tower, and I'll be there in fifteen minutes. I won't let it take longer than that.' Then she gave her parents the same treatment. 'And you needn't come, either. I'll run over to the pub, put my head round the door, as if I'm looking for somebody, and be out again in no time.'

'We'll come,' said Angie, brooking no argument. 'If you want to talk to us as well, you can do it on the way.'

It was the best she could hope for, so she set off at a brisk pace towards the northern part of the town, back towards the church where the funeral had taken place. Ben and Bonnie remained where they were, murmuring questions to each other. Russell fell back as his wife and daughter headed uphill.

'It's the wrong way round,' Simmy began. 'Corinne's got everything back to front.'

'You don't seem surprised, though. Where were you going just now, with those youngsters?'

'The police station. I worked something out myself this morning, and wanted to explain it to Moxon. Bonnie thinks she knows what it is, but Ben's still in the dark. Although now you've turned up with this silly wild goose chase, he might get there as well.'

'There were two men both with boys,' panted Russell. 'And we need to know which is which.'

'Yes, Dad.' Simmy paused to enable him to catch up. 'That's right. Except I know already. The ones in the pub are called Eccles. The boy's Raymond. They're dognappers. Or the father is.'

'Oh!' Angie put a hand to her mouth. 'Then—'

Simmy watched her warily. 'Don't say it. And especially don't say anything to Corinne, if you're phoning her back, as I suppose you are. I don't trust her or Bonnie. They've every reason to dislike the man, but for some reason, they seem to be on his side.'

'Did *he* kill Mr McNaughton then?' asked Russell, still breathless. 'Are we going to call the cops and get him arrested?'

'No, Dad.' The realisation that he was nowhere near as recovered as he had first appeared hit Simmy hard. A week ago, he would have been easily keeping pace with her thinking.

The Elleray public house stood four-square in front of them, only five minutes later. The scene of other encounters on previous occasions, Simmy liked it for its lack of pretension and good plain food. It was also convenient for her current purpose, having only one large bar, with no alcoves or high-backed benches where people might hide.

But she had no need to open the door and inspect the drinkers inside. As she approached, the door opened, and two people came out. It was Mr Eccles and his son, talking comfortably together, the man laughing easily.

Simmy stepped forward, doing what she had intended to all along. 'Excuse me,' she said pleasantly. 'You're Mr Eccles, I think?'

'That's me.' He was surprised but not alarmed in any way.

'Do you mind if I have a few words with you? I'm Persimmon Brown. I know Corinne and Bonnie Lawson, her foster daughter. They mentioned you.'

'Good woman, Corinne,' he nodded. 'Ray – hold on a sec, will you?'

The boy had started drifting down the street, apparently thinking the adult conversation had nothing in it to interest him.

Simmy turned to her parents, who were simply standing there, shoulder-to-shoulder a yard or two away. 'Dad, does his voice sound familiar to you?' She waved at Eccles.

'It's not one I heard on Monday, if that's what you mean. This gentleman has an accent I believe hails from some way east of here. I'd guess North Yorkshire, perhaps.'

'Lived in Ripon till I was thirty,' smiled Eccles. 'Well done, mate.'

'Do you know anyone called Zippy Newsome?' Simmy asked him.

'I know who he is. Blind chap. Met him a couple of times, years ago now.'

'And Vic Corless?'

'Never heard of 'im.'

'Where do you live?'

'Hold on, love. This is getting heavy now. What's it about, then?'

'Sorry. Honestly, I really am sorry, but it's important. I'm not trying to get you into any trouble. Just straightening something out.'

A wariness was developing in his manner and expression. 'You're not after me on account of those dogs, are you? Has Corinne been blabbing about that? She *knows* I'm past all that now. No harm's been done. We gave him back, anyhow.'

'Roddy. The yellow retriever. The trouble is, Mr Eccles, quite a lot of harm *has* been done, as you probably know. I'm guessing that's why you went to the funeral yesterday. You wanted to make some sort of amends. You never thought Valerie would recognise you, I suppose.'

'She wouldn't 'ave, if I hadn't started coughing. Damn lungs have been playing up ever since I did time. Those cells did for me. That's why I'm not about to go back there. Not for anything.'

'But she'd seen you before?'

He sighed. 'It was dark. I gave her the dog back, one

evening, kept my face away from 'er. How'd she know it was me?'

'She must have got a better look than you realised. Were you coughing then, as well?'

'Might 'ave been.'

'And she knows you've got a son, I expect.'

'It was more likely the dog,' he said. 'It came up to me in the church and started wagging its tail. I was good to 'im, you know. We made friends together, in the week I had 'im with me.'

'A week? He was lost for a week?'

'Right. Then they paid the cash and got 'im back. No harm done.' He stubbornly repeated the words, clinging to them as his one justification.

'I forgot to tell you that part.' Angie's voice reminded Simmy that there was an audience to the cross-examination. 'At the funeral. The dog trotted down the aisle and stood wagging at this man. Valerie was watching it all. She was talking about dogs at the time, you see. Roddy was supposed to be at her side, not wandering off.'

'And I gave the money back,' persisted Eccles, more loudly. 'Corinne says there's no way it'll go to the police now. Specially after all this time, with the woman dead, an' all.'

'The woman was ill when you took her dog. The shock and worry of his disappearance made her a lot worse. It probably shortened her life, and even if it didn't, it added to the suffering. Hers and her friend's. It was a dreadful thing to do.'

Simmy wished she had spoken these words, but it was

her father who confronted the man with the consequences of his actions.

'What's it to you?' Eccles demanded defiantly.

'I think it has a lot to do with me,' said Russell slowly. 'I think you've done a great deal more damage than you realise.' He looked at Simmy. 'And my daughter knows precisely what I mean. I fancy she worked it out some time ago now.'

'I'm not taking any more of this. Come on, Ray. Time we were off.'

The boy, with his big ears and bony shoulders, stood where he was. 'You took their dog, Dad? After you'd promised us you'd stay clean? What's Linda going to say about that?'

'Linda's not going to know, is she? We're out of here next week, and that's an end of it. One little mistake's not going to wreck it all now.'

Raymond looked doubtful, but Simmy could also see hope and relief in his eyes. It was Raymond who elicited the next thing she said. 'I meant what I said at the start. There's no reason for you to get into trouble. I just hope you've had enough of a fright to convince you to live a decent life from now on.'

'Don't worry,' said the man. 'You haven't met Linda. She's taken me up as a project. Lovely woman,' he added dreamily. 'So long as this young man keeps his mouth shut, we'll be right.' He gave his son a probing look.

'Linda's okay,' he confirmed. 'Even my mum thinks so.'

Another complicated mixed-up family, Simmy assumed. 'You have no idea how lucky you are,' she told Eccles.

'But I think you'll be finding out in the next few days.'

'What?' he said, but she had turned away from him and his boy, back to her parents.

'That's it, then,' she said. 'The full story.'

Angie gave an angry laugh. 'Maybe you and your dad think so, but as far as I'm concerned, it's still a complete mystery.'

'So come with me to see DI Moxon, and it'll all become clear,' said Simmy. 'And by now I expect Ben's worked it out, as well.'

Chapter Twenty-Six

'It's all wrong, though,' said Russell for the third time. 'That poor woman! You can't just let that man go. It was all his fault.'

'It's not up to us,' said Simmy. 'The police can decide about that. And he *knows* what he's done. I don't think he'll rest easy for a long time to come. Isn't that enough of a punishment?'

They were almost at the Baddeley Tower where Ben and Bonnie could be seen waiting for them. All five would troop down to the police station, where the public could no longer just walk in and expect a friendly welcome from an officer on the front desk. They would knock or ring or do whatever it took to gain access, and hope to find Detective Inspector Moxon ready and waiting for them. Simmy had tried to phone him, ten minutes earlier, and only got his voicemail. 'We're coming to tell you something,' she told the machine. 'We'll be at the police station in a few minutes.'

'It's not fair to blame him too harshly,' Angie said. 'After all, he *was* nice to the dog. You could tell it liked him, the way it behaved yesterday.'

Simmy gave a short laugh. 'In a way, the dog got its revenge, as well. If it hadn't been for him, we might never have worked it out.' Then a cold hand clamped itself on her heart. 'But, of course, now . . .'

'That's what I've been trying to say,' put in Russell. 'What's going to become of him now?'

'Why? What do you mean?' asked Angie. 'He's got Valerie, hasn't he?'

She looked from one silent face to the other. 'Hasn't he?'

Simmy closed her eyes against the tangled morality. Whichever way she looked, there was pain and injustice and the uncompromising results of doing a wrong thing. 'I don't think he has,' she said.

'But it's all *wrong*,' said Russell for a fourth time. 'I know I can't stop you, Simmy, but really, I wish you'd just think it through first.'

'I have, Dad. A thousand times in the past couple of hours. And there's no way around it. We've been forgetting Travis McNaughton, and his son. His friends and family didn't deserve what happened to him. We can at least put that right. We have to. You know we do. There's nothing so dreadful as an innocent victim. And you know what? The final clincher is that even if she'd got the right man, *he* wouldn't have deserved it either.'

Angie put a hand on each of them. 'Wait,' she begged. 'The right man? The *wrong* man was killed? Somebody meant to kill the Eccles man, instead of Travis McNaughton? You mean . . . *Valerie*? *She* did it?' Her face went white. 'Oh

God, yes. I see it now. Why have I been so slow, when it's all been right there in front of me? Valerie Rossiter.' She took a deep breath. 'Oh, well. Everybody always said there was something *dark* about her. Even her dog doesn't really like her much. Corinne told me that months ago.'

Simmy met her father's eyes, which were twinkling with helpless amusement. 'Trust you, Ange, to put everything into perspective,' he said.

But Simmy was remembering a grief-stricken woman in a graveyard and felt immeasurably sad.

Bonnie and Ben had plainly wasted no time in reconciling facts, drawing deductions, resolving moral ambiguities and planning the golden future they envisaged for themselves – probably in roughly that order. 'We won't come with you,' said Ben. 'We get the whole thing, now. Bonnie's been explaining it all to me. She worked it out *hours* ago, you know. Can you just *imagine* the team we're going to make?' He clumsily put his arm around the girl's shoulder, and she leant her head on him.

'Hours ago?' Simmy repeated. 'Like before about half past eleven this morning?'

'Well, maybe not the *whole* thing,' she admitted. 'But when you asked about the dognapping, and whatever, everything sort of landed right side up. If you see what I mean.'

'So you're okay with me going to explain it all to the cops?'

'You do what you have to do,' said Bonnie graciously. 'It'll keep you in that detective's good books, if nothing else.'

'Come on, Bon,' urged Ben. 'Our work here is done.'

She giggled and they walked off towards Helm Road, where Ben lived with his family.

'Ben and Bon,' murmured Russell after them. 'Lord help us.'

The police station was barely two minutes' walk down the gentle hill towards Bowness. They reached it just before a car drew up at the kerb close by. A woman emerged, paid the driver and stood rigidly on the pavement.

'It's her!' said Angie. 'In a taxi!'

Valerie Rossiter ignored the threesome who were all blatantly staring at her. 'Sshh,' Simmy warned her mother. 'We can't say anything to her now.'

But Russell thought differently. 'Miss Rossiter?' he said. 'You don't know me, but I think I understand why you're here. Can I be of any assistance, do you think?'

She blinked unseeingly in his direction. 'Who are you?' she asked.

'Russell Straw. This is my daughter. And my wife. We've just been speaking to a Mr Eccles. He used to kidnap dogs, apparently.'

'And he's lucky to be alive,' breathed Valerie. 'Does he realise that?'

'I think not.'

'He soon will.' Valerie squared her shoulders. 'I've come to report myself as a murderer.'

'I can't begin to imagine how much courage that takes,' said Russell thickly. 'Let me come in with you. I have a feeling my testimony will help the police to make sense of what you have to tell them.' He turned to Simmy and Angie. 'We'll be fine now,' he said. 'You two go home and have some lunch.'

Angie lurched forward, as if to protest, but Simmy pulled her back. 'He's right,' she said. 'Like Ben put it – our work is done.'

Some hours later, they were sitting in the Beck View kitchen, with Bertie on Russell's lap, receiving a much more thorough fondling than he was accustomed to.

There were gaps in the story that only Russell could fill. How did Valerie come to mistake her victim? How did she get away after the deed was done? And what was going to happen to her?

'It was premeditated murder,' said Russell unhappily. 'She'll be in prison for years. There's no convincing mitigation. She took the knife with her, with the deliberate intention of cutting a man's throat.' He groaned. 'And that woman Corinne's far more involved than we realised. Valerie got all her information from the woman. She insists Corinne had no idea what she meant to do, but I'm doubtful.'

Simmy thought back. 'I think it's true,' she said slowly. 'Corinne was always more bothered about the snares set by Vic Corless. She never showed any sign of worrying about Travis McNaughton's death. I don't think she came close to making that connection.'

'Maybe so. The biggest question was – how did Valerie know her victim was going to be in Troutbeck that afternoon?'

'Except he wasn't,' Simmy pointed out. 'Somebody else was, who looked like him.'

'Right. She was looking for a man in a red car, with a

teenage boy, who was quite possibly still kidnapping dogs. I'm afraid you're part of this bit, love.' He sighed again. 'Valerie explained the whole thing. Remember Melanie brought Bonnie into the shop on Tuesday morning, and you talked about that dead dog we saw on Monday? And then you must have talked about two men and a boy in a red car, all mixed up with suspicions about dognapping. And then you must have said something about me going to the police about it. Well, Bonnie added all that up, and multiplied by ten before she passed it on to Corinne, who went straight to Valerie, saying it sounded as if the evil Mr Eccles was up to his tricks around Troutbeck. So Valerie went up there with her knife, saw the red car, and followed the man into that farmyard. Watched while he went for a pee behind a barn, and then walked up to him and attacked him, probably before he had any idea what was happening. I saw it. A weird old-fashioned thing, with a blade like a razor. She actually demonstrated how sharp it was on her own hand. It was incredible. She just pressed it lightly on the skin and it cut instantly. They took it off her pretty sharpish, I can tell you.'

Simmy shuddered. 'I hate knives.'

'They certainly make a good murder weapon,' said Angie, swallowing hard. 'Silent and quick. But what kind of a person can *do* that?' She put a hand to her own throat. 'It makes me feel sick.'

'Moxon walked back here with me,' said Russell. 'He thought I might pass out again, I suppose. They'd kept me waiting a bit while Valerie was taken away to be interviewed, and he felt a bit bad about that, I suspect. Anyway, he filled in a bit of background. Her father was a master butcher in Poland, apparently. She knew how to cut a throat. It's not as easy as most people think. You need to get the jugular, you see.'

'Okay, Dad. We don't need the details.'

'You want me to bury it all and never speak of it again? Do you have any idea what that might do to my emotional well-being? Do you want me to be like those World War One soldiers coming back and never mentioning the trenches?' His mock indignation made them both smile. 'That's not going to happen,' he assured them. 'I don't see why I should be the only one having bad dreams for the next six months.'

'Such dreadful luck for poor Travis McNaughton,' moaned Angie. 'Everything worked against him from the start.' Then she had a thought. 'But *were* they going to do something illegal? What was all that about a lookout and an old man being out on Tuesdays?'

'We don't know for sure, but Moxon thinks it might have something to do with elderflowers. There's a specially good field of them, apparently, with no public access. The owner's not the most welcoming of chaps, so anybody wanting to do a bit of scrumping needs to be careful. The woman who found the body said something about it, but she was going on so much about the darn flowers that nobody really listened to the details. Only now are they connecting up that particular set of dots.'

'I don't think I said anything about the old man and Tuesdays,' said Simmy uncertainly. 'When I told Bonnie and Melanie about it, I mean. So Valerie must have just gone to Troutbeck on the off chance of running into them.

For all she knew, they were in Kirkstone or Grasmere – or absolutely anywhere.'

Russell and Simmy both pondered this for a while. 'Sheer bad luck,' said Simmy at last. 'There can't be any more to it than that. And Troutbeck's a small enough place, if you're looking for someone.'

'She said she felt Barbara's spirit was guiding her,' said Russell reluctantly. 'It was all for Barbara that she did it, after all. She made Valerie promise to get revenge on the man who stole the dog. That's why she didn't report it to the police. She thought they'd just laugh it off as a victimless crime. Moxon feels bad about that.'

'Ben said she looked as if she'd seen a ghost in the church,' Simmy recalled. 'Maybe she did. Maybe Barbara was standing behind Eccles, pointing a glowing finger at him, as if to say *This is the man you were supposed to kill*.'

'Which means she got it badly wrong the first time, thinking Barbara was directing her,' said Angie dourly. 'Just shows how careful you have to be where ghosts are concerned.'

'I think she just waited near the pub in Troutbeck until she saw a red car and followed it,' said Russell. 'When she saw it stop at Town End and the man get out, she couldn't believe her luck.'

'Even though she didn't recognise him, and he didn't have his boy with him. Wouldn't a person need to be far more sure than that before cutting someone's throat?' Angie was still plainly unconvinced.

'Moxon said Travis left his boy at the pub, that afternoon. Travis was doing some work there, and Tim was going for a walk with a friend of his, before being put on a bus back to Scotland. When Travis never showed up at three o'clock as planned, he phoned his mobile and got the police. So Valerie could have seen him, and thought it more than enough to confirm his identity.'

'Well I blame that Corinne,' said Angie flatly. 'It's only credible if she filled in a whole lot more details for Valerie.'

Simmy remembered something. 'She had a phone call on Tuesday, just as she was leaving the shop. I bet that was Corinne, telling her what Bonnie had passed on.'

'The case of the Chinese Whispers,' said Russell. 'Bonnie exaggerated Simmy's account of my little testimony, and Corinne magnified it even further. Given what a state Valerie was already in, the whole thing falls into place. With the wretched Travis doing everything he could to make it easy for her, if only he'd known.'

Angie still seemed unsatisfied, rubbing her face as if presented with an impossible puzzle. Then she lifted her head. 'The man and his boy, behind me in the church,' she said. 'They were talking, before it all got started. Somebody sitting next to them was joining in, and said something about the murder in Troutbeck. I *knew* I'd heard more about it – and couldn't think where it was. Now it's all come back to me. This woman – and I have no idea who she was – was talking in that loud sort of whisper you really want to hear, because it's obviously something interesting. She said Travis McNaughton had been doing well with finding work, gardening in Troutbeck, and what a shame it was he'd died just as it was going so nicely. The man – Eccles – said he'd been finding the same thing. Hotels and guesthouses were all desperate to keep their gardens looking nice, and this time of year was great for odd-job men who knew a bit about plants and hedges and all that. So that would be another clue for Valerie, do you see?'

'Sort of,' said Simmy. 'She'd be watching out for a man working in a garden. Hadn't Travis just knocked off, after doing something for the garden at the Mortal Man?'

'Had he?' frowned Angie.

'He had,' confirmed Russell. 'Before leaving the boy there to go for his walk.'

'There we are then,' sighed Simmy unhappily. 'What a very sad story. I can't forget how much I liked Valerie. I can't believe we had such a nice little chat in the graveyard.' Then she gave a watery smile. 'But at least we can assume Corinne will take on the dog.'

For some reason, both her parents seemed to find this amusing.

The next day, less than a week after the fateful Bank Holiday Monday, Simmy was once again at the Mortal Man. Outside it was raining, so she and her companion were in the untidy wood-panelled bar, eating a ridiculously substantial roast lamb Sunday lunch.

'Better than my cooking,' said Ninian ruefully.

'I prefer your gravy,' said Simmy. 'It was noble of you to come,' she added with a smile.

'I hiked five whole miles for this,' he boasted. 'In the rain.'

'You did. And in return you can spend a long lazy afternoon in my warm, dry little cottage.'

'Only the afternoon?' He stopped chewing, a worried frown on his face. 'I thought I was staying all night.'

She smiled again. 'You're welcome, if that's what you'd like. I can drive you home in the morning.'

'Thank you. That would be lovely,' he said primly.

''Ello there,' came a voice. 'All right, then?'

It was Vic Corless, of the beard and the dog snares and the anonymous letter. He stood awkwardly, sideways on to their table. 'Thought I should say something,' he went on.

'There's nothing at all to say,' Simmy told him coldly.

'Yeah, but there is. You were a real lady, through all the trouble there's been. Corinne and Bonnie think you're their hero, for all you did. It'll be the making of Bonnie, working for you. That's all I wanted to say. Just that it's good to know you, Mrs Brown. You're one in a thousand.'

Ninian looked up at him, wide-eyed. 'What are you saying, man? She's one in ten million, at least.'

'Stop it.' Simmy was blushing. Suddenly springtime and romance and sweet-scented flowers were all she could think of.